Readers love *Second Hand* by MARIE SEXTON AND HEIDI CULLINAN

"I love when these two authors write together, they always create something so special."

—Diverse Reader

"... I have always enjoyed these two authors and could only imagine how good the story would be with both of them writing it. I was so glad my instincts were dead-on as *Second Hand* is a great book that I enjoyed immensely."

—Rainbow Reviews

"Excellent book, highly recommended."

—Joyfully Jay

"So, Heidi and Marie, just go ahead and push all my buttons, and then reach in and pull my guts out. You both seem to be good at that sort of thing. Also: Hurry the hell up with your next books, so I can fling myself on the altar of your brilliance all over again."

—Instalove

By Heidi Cullinan

With Marie Sexton: Family Man

COPPER POINT
The Doctor's Secret

TUCKER SPRINGS
By L.A. Witt: Where Nerves End
With Marie Sexton: Second Hand
Dirty Laundry

Published by Dreamspinner Press
www.dreamspinnerpress.com

DIRTY
LAUNDRY

HEIDI CULLINAN

Published by
DREAMSPINNER PRESS

5032 Capital Circle SW, Suite 2, PMB# 279,
Tallahassee, FL 32305-7886 USA
www.dreamspinnerpress.com

This is a work of fiction. Names, characters, places, and incidents either
are the product of author imagination or are used fictitiously, and any
resemblance to actual persons, living or dead, business establishments,
events, or locales is entirely coincidental.

Dirty Laundry
© 2019 Heidi Cullinan.

Cover Art
© 2019 Reese Dante.
http://www.reesedante.com
Cover content is for illustrative purposes only and any person depicted
on the cover is a model.

Mass Market Paperback ISBN: 978-1-64108-127-6
Trade Paperback ISBN: 978-1-64080-904-8
Digital ISBN: 978-1-64080-903-1
Library of Congress Control Number: 2018961345
Mass Market Paperback published July 2019
v. 1.0
First Edition published by Riptide Publishing, January 2013.

Printed in the United States of America
∞
This paper meets the requirements of
ANSI/NISO Z39.48-1992 (Permanence of Paper).

for everyone who dreams a little
harder for their happy ever after

Acknowledgments

THANK YOU to Dreamspinner Press for giving Adam and Denver a new home and for the chance to finish polishing *Dirty Laundry*. Thank you to Sasha Knight for being the only editor I could imagine coming along on this ride with me, for helping me through this story and so many others. Thank you to Jan for your help in allowing me to understand Adam in ways I wouldn't have otherwise been able to.

Thanks to my family, Dan and Anna, for their patience, love, and support, and as always thank you to my patrons for their emotional and financial dedication to my work. Thank you in particular to patrons Rosie M and Marie.

CHAPTER ONE

THAT ADAM Ellery found his true love in a dirty laundromat was pretty ironic, considering his rap sheet of neuroses.

He didn't recognize his destined partner at first. The beefy, surly-looking cowboy in a white tank top had nearly been enough to send Adam running for cover. The only reason Adam hadn't ducked out the second their eyes met was because Cowboy had been bent inside a machine when Adam entered, and by the time he'd emerged in all his bulky glory, Adam had already deposited clothing and money into a washer.

To be fair, Cowboy hadn't so much as glanced at Adam twice. Adam would know because he'd barely taken his eyes off the man. He'd had to use the smaller table to sort out his socks and underwear, which meant he had a lovely view of the choose-your-communicable-disease bathroom, but he knew where the larger man was at all times, and most importantly, he wasn't blocking Adam's way to either exit. Adam tried not to watch too overtly, because if Cowboy caught him, Adam probably would give off the wrong signals.

Because Cowboy was cut.

Not handsome. He wasn't ugly, but he wasn't magazine-slick, not even close. But muscles? Oh, yeah. Normally Adam didn't go for muscles because muscles scared him. Muscles could hurt him. Muscles had hurt him on more than one occasion. Muscles stood good odds of hurting him again. On Cowboy, however, muscles seemed acceptable, at least for simple viewing.

It wasn't that Cowboy looked ready to make trouble so much as Adam wasn't taking any chances. Adam's anxiety, always ready to tip into overdrive, had sprung into high alert once it realized the two of them were alone, and now his internal panic machine was set on *potential attack!* mode whether he wanted it there or not. It didn't matter that Cowboy hadn't done anything more interesting than shift clothes from a washer to a dryer, or read magazines other people had left strewn about the booths and tables. Anxiety didn't work that way.

Relaxing as much as he could, Adam hurried about his business, and nothing happened except he ran out of quarters and had to go around the corner to the coffee shop and get change. He also got a latte, despite knowing the caffeine would wreak havoc on his nerves. He used the toilet there too, because it was a single-stall unit and much cleaner than the one next door.

When Adam returned, Cowboy was gone, and six frat boys occupied the laundromat in his stead.

None of them were older than twenty-two, and that was probably pushing it. They acted twelve. Three of them were definitely drunk, and two were possibly high as well. They weren't as big as Cowboy, but they were bigger than Adam.

Unlike Cowboy, they noticed Adam right away, and they didn't ignore him. They leered, and their evil smiles promised nothing but trouble—for Adam.

You don't have to be such a victim. Adam could hear his ex's lecture as if Brad were standing in front of him. *If you act like a scared rabbit, they'll treat you like one. Ignore them and act like you don't give a damn about them. If you keep painting a fucking target on yourself, looking like you expect to be harassed, you will be.*

Brad had brought up Adam's cowardice and his penchant for panic in the presence of potential conflict many times, and Adam had done what he could to correct his deficiency. It just never worked. He wasn't sure if he was too old to learn, if the bullying had started when he was too young, or if he was stupid. Sometimes he thought it was because he was nothing more than a rabbit. On the male evolutionary ladder, he occupied the bottom rung, where he had to survive by constant vigilance and the ability to hop the hell out of danger at a moment's notice.

According to Brad, Adam's problem was that he was mentally ill. Technically this was true, but even Adam's mediocre therapist would argue clinical anxiety was more complex than that. Brad's insistence in making Adam's illness a blanket excuse had become a red flag of warning, which had led to their breakup and Adam moving out.

It had also indirectly landed Adam in this laundromat, his clothing held hostage by a pack of drunk frat boys.

Adam did his best to ignore these intruders the same way he had Cowboy, but this time his laundro-mat companions were entirely focused on him. The frat boys leaned on the table where Adam had left his bas-ket of folded socks and underwear, and one of the guys giggled at Adam's electric-blue hipster briefs which, like so much of him, screamed *gay*. The frat boy made eye contact with Adam, and Adam froze at the door of his dryer, trying not to look scared.

With an evil grin, the boy murmured something to the others. As his buddies turned their smirking, stoned-out gazes to Adam, the instigator pulled out the elec-tric-blue briefs and tossed them in the air. Adam would have crawled into the dryer with his damp clothes if he hadn't thought they'd turn it on and barricade him inside.

They threw around his briefs, his club shirt, and his *Ten Reasons You Shouldn't Bug an Entomologist* tee. "Look at this shit," they said, laughing.

One of them leered at Adam, dangling his under-wear just out of reach. "This yours?"

Adam knew better than to answer. They were teas-ing him, but they weren't hurting him yet, and they might not hurt him at all if he played his part in the game well. If he was lucky, he'd just lose a pair of un-derwear and a few of his favorite shirts.

He didn't want to think about being unlucky.

"You wear this freaky blue shit, huh?" They snick-ered in unison as the frat boy snapped the briefs near Adam's cheek and one of them bumped Adam's shoul-der. "What color you wearing right now?"

Adam did his best to stifle his flinch, pushed his glasses higher up his nose, and hunkered deeper over an ad circular. He was well past *potential attack!* and firmly into *attack mode engaged!* which ironically made him so much calmer. That was the thing about anxiety. It always knew an attack was coming. It was the absence of danger that made it uneasy. Once its point was proven, it tended to settle down.

Just ride it out, he told himself. *Keep calm and ride it out.*

"We're talking to you, fag," one of them said.

When Adam continued to ignore them, they took his glasses. Right off his face.

Okay, that was a little more than he could ignore. He had a backup pair at home, but he couldn't drive without them. "Please." Adam reached out to take them back, then stopped himself, knowing that would make it worse. He'd been in this position before. It was time for him to beg. It wouldn't do any good, but it was the only role he had in this play. "Please give me my glasses back."

"Show us your underwear first, freak."

The nervous flutter in the pit of Adam's stomach turned into sick fear. "Please," he whispered.

His fear only fueled them now. "Strip, faggot." Someone shoved at his shoulder again. With a sick heart, Adam realized he'd soon be removing his clothes. He only hoped this was where it ended.

"*What the fuck is going on?*"

Adam startled, but so did the frat boys. One of them swore, and all of them staggered back, parting from their circle around Adam's table, allowing him to see the newcomer.

Cowboy.

He sauntered in from the side door, ambling toward Adam with a slow, steady gait that made his hips roll enticingly in his beat-up jeans and was punctuated by the clip-clop of his equally worn cowboy boots. The closer he got, the more he slowed down, giving the frat boys plenty of time to take him in. Best yet, Cowboy didn't look pissed. He looked irritated.

When he glanced at Adam, however, that irritation melted away. "You okay, boy?"

Eyes wide, heart pounding, Adam nodded. *Holy crap.* None of Adam's fantasies had involved a muscle-bound, cowboy-hat-wearing avenging angel before, but they would now.

Initially thrown by Cowboy's entrance, the frat boys recovered. "We're just messing around, old man," one of them murmured.

Cowboy said nothing, only stared at the boys. His gaze lingered on the one holding Adam's glasses.

The one holding Adam's glasses took a step back.

One of the others, though, had apparently decided six frat boys outranked even Cowboy's muscle, because he tossed his hair out of his eyes and took up a stance. "Did we pick on your boyfriend, honey? We're sorry."

A few of the frat boys giggled. The others shrank away from Cowboy.

Something bounced against Adam's hand. When he looked down, his glasses lay beside him on the bench. With a relieved gasp, Adam swiped them and put them on. Lifting his gaze, Adam saw Cowboy now stood one beefy arm's length away from the ringleader. His expression up to that point had remained cool, but now Cowboy's face split in a nasty grin. The other frat boys shrank into the corner, whispering various panicked expletives under their breath. The ringleader tried to keep his cool, but Adam could see his facade cracking.

The laundromat went silent as Cowboy ran a thick, gnarly finger down the frat boy's chest.

"Don't be jealous. You want my cock, little boy, all you gotta do is bend over."

The frat boy sputtered, swore, and swung.

Cowboy blocked the blow, grabbing Frat Boy's nuts. "Tell your buddies to give the man his clothes back."

Frat Boy yelped in pain as Cowboy's grip tightened. "Fuck—do it," he cried, and seconds later Adam's clothes came sailing and landed on the tabletop.

Cowboy jerked his head in a curt nod. "Good boy. Now all of you apologize. And just so it's clear, you're getting this one shot to do it without your pants in a long, hot cycle in the washer and your dipshit asses waiting outside until they're done."

Adam kept rigid, head spinning, as the frat boys came up one by one and murmured terrified apologies before speeding like bullets out the door. The ringleader was last, making his apology on his knees before the table, hair held tight in Cowboy's grip. Then he was gone as well, leaving Adam frozen in place with his mouth gaping open, alone with his rescuer.

Cowboy tipped his hat, turned around, and walked away.

Adam stared after him, unsure of what he should do now.

Outside of a flicker of irritation in his jaw, Cowboy gave no clue he'd routed six men and saved Adam's pathetic hide. He simply went to his dryer, pulled over an empty cart, and began folding his clothes. He made no eye contact with Adam, not until Adam got his spinning psyche under control and was able to walk up to his rescuer, nervous hands tangling in front of his belly. As Adam shoved down the last of his panic, Cowboy stopped folding and waited for Adam to speak.

"Thank you," Adam managed at last.

Cowboy acknowledged him with a jerk of his head. "Not a problem."

He resumed folding his clothes.

Adam stood beside his cart, watching. The need to keep talking to the stranger burned inside him, but the man wasn't making it easy. When Cowboy stopped folding again and leveled that cool hazel gaze at him, Adam stuck out his hand, trying not to let it or his voice tremble. "I'm Adam Ellery."

Cowboy accepted Adam's hand, closing it in his warm, rough grip. "Denver Rogers."

Their hands lingered a moment before coming apart once more. All Adam could think of was how no one had ever rescued him before, and he wasn't sure how to respond. Offering to buy the man something to drink seemed appropriate, so he gestured toward the coffee shop. "Can I get you something? As a thank-you?"

Denver stopped folding and searched Adam's face. Eventually he shook his head.

This time Adam was glad the man had turned away, because he was blushing in mortification. Rescued and then rejected. *Well, what do you expect? He rescued you out of pity, not as a come-on.*

Adam murmured another thanks and went in search of more of his laundry, gathering up the basket the frat boys had been messing with and adding it to his stash at his table by the door. On the way past his remaining washer, he saw it had finished, so his next move was to switch it to a dryer.

Something perverse and obstinate made him use the one next to Denver. It also encouraged his mouth to flap again, much to his surprise. "Do you live around here?"

"Few streets over."

"Me too. The Park Place Apartments across the highway. I just moved in." He gestured at the laundromat. "This is my first time without facilities on-site. Well, I have them, but I found out today they're very dirty and in questionable condition. So here I am."

Denver nodded and went back to his clothes.

Adam kept talking, because he was nervous and starting to panic, and it was either talk or go fetal at this point. "I'm a grad student at Eastern Centennial. Entomology. Bugs. I want to learn more about pollinators. I started with bees, but now I'm into moths. You wouldn't believe how much the world would change without them. No food, no flowers—wow, I should really stop talking."

By the end of his babble, he was blushing scarlet, but just when he was considering climbing under one of the laundry tables, Denver glanced up with a reassuring grin. "You're fine."

"Not as fine as you," Adam said before he could stop himself. Then he melted into the wall, half falling into his dryer and knocking his glasses sideways. "Oh God." He held up a hand and shook his head as Denver regarded him with surprise. "I'm sorry. Really. I just—"

His voice died as Denver came around his dryer door and stood in front of Adam.

Denver's hard gaze made Adam want to run screaming and spread his legs at the same time. He was half in the dryer and trapped between Denver's door, his own, and Denver himself. Three million pounds of hot, beefy cowboy bore down on him, not saying anything, not glaring, just... looking. Adam stared back, unable at this point to do anything else.

The world fell away until all that was left were his small body, Denver's huge one, and the damp towels underneath his ass. Denver neither advanced nor retreated, only continued to stare at Adam. Measuring? Waiting? Adam couldn't tell. Something told Adam, though, the next move was his.

He pushed his glasses back up onto his nose.

Quit acting like you're afraid of the world all the damn time.

Adam was always afraid. Afraid of what might happen. Afraid of what had happened. Afraid of rules broken or bent sideways, of things being out of place, as if this might invite the world to fall in around his ears. Afraid of not having control. Afraid of what people knew about him just by looking at him. Afraid of what they might find out. Afraid of what they thought of him, what they might do to him. Adam was afraid of the uncertainty that went with absolutely everything about planet Earth.

However, right now with Denver in this laundromat, desire kept pace with fear. It wouldn't take but a little shove to put it in the lead.

Remembering the way Cowboy had handled the frat boys, reminding himself how Cowboy hadn't asked for anything for that service, realizing that Cowboy was waiting for Adam to give full permission even now, Adam drew a slow, deep breath. Then he let it out, shifted his weight back farther into the dryer, and pushed his knees open.

Heat sparked in the back of Denver's gaze, and his mouth quirked into a slow, crooked smile.

When Denver's big hand rested on Adam's knee, the touch went straight to his cock, and Adam's lips parted on a gasp. His other knee lifted slightly, eager for Denver's other hand as his mind spun erotic scenarios faster than the speed of light. But that hand never came. Instead Denver examined Adam critically.

"This you being grateful, or are you wanting to play?"

Play. The simple pressure of that hand on Adam's knee made him hard. He nodded. Realizing he needed to give more clarification, he whispered, "Play. Except I don't really know what you mean. It just sounds… good."

That half smile came back, making Adam want to whimper. "It means I'm going to tell you what to do and you're going to do it." The smile dipped a little. "Not because you're grateful I chased away the idiots. Not because you're afraid of me. But because it makes you hot and because I'm promising you I'll make you come so hard you won't be able to stand."

Adam was pretty sure he couldn't stand now. "Th-that sounds good to me."

Denver's smile was wide and full of promise as he nodded at Adam's dryer. "Finish loading your stuff. Then you're going to see to mine."

Adam couldn't tell if there was innuendo in that last part, but he didn't care. He was fairly certain even folding Denver's underwear would be erotic.

CHAPTER TWO

DENVER REALLY did have Adam fold his underwear, an endless supply of plain old tighty-whities. What had the back of his teeth aching was while Adam folded, Denver's hands skimmed beneath the unbuttoned waistband of his briefs, mapping the surface of his ass and hips.

Adam still couldn't get over that they were making out in the laundromat. He'd naively assumed they'd finish up their laundry and move on to one of their respective apartments to have sex. That thought in itself had sent him into a quiet panic spiral, but before he could begin psyching himself up for that battle, Denver had undone his zipper, complimented his red-and-white-striped underwear, and stuck his hands down it. Then he'd told him to start folding.

So Adam had. Now here they were.

It wasn't that being fondled was bad, but it was unnerving to have it done in public. While it was more than a little hot, it also seemed dangerous. What surprised him was that this particular kind of danger made him feel sexy. He'd never had someone hold his ass like this before. He'd never folded someone's underwear while they held his ass. So *wicked*, especially with all the windows. What if someone saw? What would they think of him?

Why was that fear so... delicious, almost as yummy as Denver's roving hands?

The only fly in the ointment was that even turned on, Adam was nervous. What if someone came in? What if they called the police? What if he was arrested and he ended up playing fold-the-underwear with someone who wasn't Denver? What if his advisor found out? Would public sex do something to his teaching assistantship? Would he be able to get a job? Would getting felt up in a laundromat inadvertently lead to him living on the streets, starving and exposed, selling his body for sex, which meant he would contract a disease and die?

"Turn your head off," Denver drawled. He sounded amused. Patient. *Kind.* "Unless I'm doing something you don't like?"

God, no. "I just—I don't want to get caught."

The hand on Adam's hip tightened. "You're already caught."

Was he ever. "I mean, I don't want to be arrested."

"Cops don't usually patrol laundromats." Denver's fingers dipped into Adam's crack as his other hand tugged the briefs farther down. "I got you. Just do as you're told and stay relaxed. I'll make sure you have a good time." He pressed against Adam's opening. "And that you don't get arrested."

Denver's words didn't do half as much for Adam as that finger did, especially once it disappeared and

came back cold and slippery with lube. Adam wondered briefly where the hell that had come from, and
then he moaned and fell forward onto the folded laundry as Denver pushed inside.

Relax. Do as you're told. The words echoed inside
Adam, loosening the chains of his mind even as they
bound his body. Adam let out a breath and spread his
legs wider on a sigh.

"That's right." Denver massaged Adam's left ass
check with one hand, pulling it aside as he fucked deeper with his other. "Don't worry about who's watching.
I'm watching, and that's all you should care about. I'm
caring about everything else for you. But I sure am
watching you, baby. I'm watching my finger go into
your ass, watching you. Are you going to open wider
for me?"

Moaning, Adam nodded and tried to spread his
legs, but the briefs kept him trapped.

"There's a good boy. Sweet and eager. You want
me to open you more? That what you want?"

Whimpering, Adam lifted his ass higher. "*Please.*"

Laughing low, Denver pushed a second finger in
alongside the first, patting Adam's ass in approval as
he flexed and took the digit eagerly. "Look at you. You
really did want it."

"I really want it." Adam felt feverish, wiggling
against Denver's fingers. It had been so long since he'd
been fucked, and it had *never* been like this. Nothing
had ever been like this.

"Honey, I'm gonna give it to you, don't worry."
He fingered Adam gently, still kneading his cheek with
his other hand. When Adam shuddered, Denver ran
his thumb along the stretched pucker of Adam's ass.
"This is just teasing you, isn't it? Want me to stuff you a

little more? You gonna take my cock next, sweet thing? You gonna moan all over my clothes while I fuck you? Right here on the table where everyone can see?"

Adam whimpered and clutched at the folded laundry, straining for the last remnants of self-control. "I'm messing up your things," he rasped, then groaned and arched his back as Denver twisted his fingers.

"Yep. You're going to make my laundry dirty, baby. You're going to come all over it."

Shutting his eyes, Adam surrendered. When Denver tugged Adam's pants to his ankles and shoved more clothes underneath Adam's ass to lift it higher, Adam didn't have a single care about who might see him behaving this way, he only made sure Denver could arrange him the way he wanted. When Denver withdrew his fingers to pull Adam open wide, Adam relaxed the muscle so Denver could gaze into him as he liked.

He was Denver's to do with what he wanted right now. He was nothing else.

"You're a good, obedient boy." Denver held Adam open a few seconds longer, then thrust his thumb inside, turning it as he pumped it in and out. "This is a fine ass you have here too. Real nice. You mind if I give it a few slaps?"

I'm going to get spanked in the laundromat. Adam's voice barely worked, and his asshole flexed in eagerness. "P-please do as you like."

"Such a good boy. You're going to get a reward later. Though maybe you're one for whom spanking is a reward?"

Adam had no idea. He'd never been spanked before.

He gasped as the first slap fell on his cheeks. They weren't awful, but they jolted him, getting his attention.

They kept coming, sharp and hard, *slap*, *slap*, *slap*. Oh, but it stung a little now, the flesh getting warm. Too warm. Adam wiggled.

"You want me to stop?" Denver's thumb grazed Adam's asshole midblow. "Or you going to let me tell you when we stop?"

The stinging was driving Adam crazy. He wanted it to end. But if he spoke up, would the spell break and he'd be nervous again? He didn't know. He didn't want to find out.

He also didn't know that he *actually* minded the way his ass was burning. He wanted to find out about that too.

Adam shook his head, then realized this answer was unclear. "I... you tell me when."

He'd spoken so softly and mostly into the under-wear that he worried Denver hadn't heard him. The next thing he knew, though, Denver had stopped spank-ing him to lean over Adam's back and tuck a rolled pair of underwear into his right hand.

"I'll tell you when, but if you change your mind, let go of those briefs. I'll stop right away. This way if you want to whisper *stop* or *no* while I spank you, you can do that too, but I won't stop. Sometimes that's fun. All depends on what game you want."

Adam's head spun with the possibilities Denver lay before him. "I've never done anything like this."

"I can tell. But you're not afraid of it at all. Turns me on."

Adam couldn't breathe.

Then, before he could even think of how to explain to Denver how wrong his perception was about him, the spanking resumed, and Adam went quiet.

Slap. Slap. Slap. Denver kept moving back and forth in rhythm, shifting where the blows fell slightly, but since he kept them raining down, it didn't take long for the same patches of skin to receive repeated strikes. Stings became burns, and Adam began to whimper as well as wiggle. His glasses shifted askew, not falling, but no longer of any use to him. Adam could imagine what he looked like: a debauched nerd. A debauched nerd spread over a pile of laundry with his pants down so he could get his ass spanked.

The mental image made him moan.

Denver's answering growl was like a panther's purr. "You giving me a line, telling me you never done anything like this before? Because you sure do like your ass spanked, don't you."

Apparently so. Adam struggled to reply to Denver's question. "I… wouldn't lie to you."

"No, I don't think you would. I also see you're still clutching that pair of underwear pretty tight. Don't feel like letting go yet?"

Adam wouldn't let a whole pack of frat boys pry that pair of briefs from his hand. "No, sir."

The spanking paused briefly as Denver pushed a finger into Adam's hole, then withdrew. "Such a well-spoken young man. I better treat you nicely. And by nicely, I mean that I'm going to spread these legs open wider and spank you a little harder."

Oh God. "Yes, sir."

When the blows resumed, Adam's thighs were open so wide he had to bend his knees and lift his feet. His hole gaped slightly, and he could feel the breeze Denver's strikes made with his big arms against Adam's trembling pucker, so intense now that Adam yelped each time. It was almost too much. Except it was only *almost*. Spanking made Adam harder than he'd ever been. Even as his overloaded nerve endings trembled, he couldn't stop pushing his ass into Denver's hands. He felt like a dirty whore begging for more.

He'd never been so content in his life.

When the spanking stopped and Adam cried out in protest, Denver laughed, a wicked sound. "You aren't what I expected at all." Before Adam could figure out how to respond, something squirted, and then Denver's fingers were at his ass again, cool and slippery. Three of them this time. They pushed inside roughly, a blunt invasion made sharper because of the spanking.

Grunting, Adam pressed his stomach into the table and bore down, relaxing to let Denver's fingers in as quickly as possible so he could do what he pleased here as well.

He was rewarded with a thrust and a guttural sound of approval from his lover. "Don't you look a picture, ass in the air in a laundromat, cherry red from a spanking while you get fingerfucked by a guy you just met. Humping his laundry." The fingers pushed deeper as Denver moved them inside Adam, making a squishing sound. Adam groaned, and Denver began to fuck in greater rhythm. "That's right. Let me hear you make noise. If you want my cock inside this ass, make noise while I finger you. Tell me how much you like this. Give me all them big college words."

The heat from the dryers was nothing compared to that coming off Adam's face. Being asked to speak had lifted him out of his sexual haze, and though part of his brain still screamed in pleasure, part of it now cata-loged all the ways this was wrong, wrong, wrong. What in the world was he thinking, letting a stranger—a big, muscle-bound stranger—fingerfuck him and spank him and tell him to make more noise, and in public? This was insane. This was crazy.

This was so freaking hot Adam was nearly melting from it. For once in his life, even his anxiety was turned on. It had been exactly as Denver promised: nothing else mattered except that he do as he was told. And he wanted to keep doing it. He wanted to do what Denver said. He wanted to tell him how much he liked this.

He wanted to go back to the sensation of not having any fear.

No fear. When was the last time he could say he felt that way? He was afraid when he was asleep—his dreams were nothing but anxiety nightmares. He was on such powerful meds he had to have sleep medication, and even with that he was still afraid. He'd lost the only boyfriend he'd ever had to fear. Until he'd moved to Tucker Springs, he'd had to see a psychologist twice a week to manage the burden of living life. Now he went every other week, and honestly, it was less than he should be going.

Right now with Denver, the only emotion Adam knew outside of being turned on beyond his wildest dreams was being so overwhelmed with relief he wanted to cry.

Denver's free hand ran down Adam's back, finding his spine through his shirt. "Let go, Adam. I told you: you're safe. Turn off your head and let go, because I've got you."

Adam drew in a slow, shaky breath. He held it for a moment.

Exhaling so hard he went boneless, Adam let go.

Everything was gone now, everything but sensation. People might have come into the laundromat; Adam wouldn't have known. All he knew was Denver and what Denver told him to do: tell Denver how good he made him feel.

"It's tight." Adam clutched his safety underwear and shut his eyes as he attempted to vocalize his feelings. "It's a tight pressure, and it hurts a little, but I like it. I like the sting on my ass where you spanked me. I'm sad that's over. I keep wishing you'd do both. Finger-fuck me and spank me at the same time."

Denver's free hand cupped Adam's left ass check. "I can do that for you."

"I don't want to tell you what to do. I like that you're telling me everything. I like not thinking. I like that everything about what you're doing to my body is what you want. If it's something that I want but you don't want it and I don't get it, that almost makes me feel more peaceful."

Something hot and wet closed over the place where Denver's hand had been. His mouth, Adam realized. "Boy, you're just trying to turn me on now, aren't you."

"I'm sorry. I'm just doing as you asked me to do. Telling you how much I like this. Am I doing it wrong?"

"No, I'd say you're doing it about right."

"Okay." Adam let out a sigh, relaxing again and riding the waves of Denver's thrusts into his body. "Should I keep letting you know how I feel?"

"Tell me how my finger feels inside your ass."

"Very tight and slightly painful, as I said. There's a lot of pressure."

"I'm thinking about pounding these fingers harder. What do you think about that?"

"Please go ahead, if you'd like that."

For some reason this made Denver swear under his breath, and Adam worried for a second, but then the thrusts were so hard and fast Adam cried out each time, keen, high-pitched gasps as tears spilled down his cheeks.

He couldn't push back any longer. He could only lie there and accept what Denver gave him and clutch tight to the rolled-up briefs. When Denver added a few sharp slaps to his left ass cheek, the noises that came from Adam's throat sounded like they belonged to an animal.

He wasn't aware of Denver's fingers leaving him, only that one moment Denver was pumping into him and the next he'd hoisted Adam away from the table to roll one nipple between his fingers, nudging his cock into Adam's gaping ass.

"Relax," Denver told him as he entered him, tugging at Adam's pebbled nipple the entire time. "Hold still. I'll fuck you good and let you come."

Nodding, Adam lifted his chest a little so Denver could get a better grip on him there, but other than that, he didn't move at all.

Adam sighed out loud, a long, staccato exclamation as his cowboy claimed him. Denver's penis was thick as a post, as beefy as the rest of him, and just as perfect. Adam focused on how that cock felt inside him, nudging against his prostate though not quite stimulating it. Whimpering, he tried to thrust back, but Denver clamped a hand on the back of his neck and held him in place, forcing Adam to take his cock at Denver's pace.

Adam liked that hand on the back of his neck almost as much as he liked the fat cock inside him and the fingers against his nipple, so much so that when Denver took the hand at his neck away, he couldn't help crying out, "Please, keep it there."

The big hand returned, thumb stroking the edge of Adam's hairline, fingernails ghosting over Adam's skin. Then the grip was back, pushing him down, pinning him to the table.

Adam relaxed and let go again.

That was all there was, Adam captive in Denver's grip as Denver plunged in and out of Adam's body. When he went deep enough to scrape Adam's prostate after all, Adam moaned and gasped, remaining absolutely still while his cowboy let go of Adam's nipple to slap at his ass some more, squeezing the reddened flesh until Adam cried out.

Adam never wanted it to end.

Denver took Adam's cock in his hand, stroking it in time to his own thrusts, urging Adam toward his release. Adam followed that electric sensation, letting Denver tip him over the edge. He shuddered and spent against the clothes beneath him, trembling in aftershocks as Denver pulled out, took off the condom, and shot all over Adam's back.

Adam lay there, ass bare and sore, glasses dangling from one ear, shirt covered in spunk, as Denver's belt buckle clinked. He didn't move even when a damp, warm washcloth—*bless you, laundry*—trailed over his backside and between his legs, cleaning him up.

"If I'd known I was giving such a sweet bottom a spanking, I'd have brought along lotion."

With effort, Adam drifted from his haze. "There's some in my bag. In the side pocket."

This time when Denver reappeared, it was to smear cool CeraVe all over Adam's stinging flesh. It felt amazingly good, and Adam couldn't help but purr.

Denver smoothed a hand up Adam's spine, massaging with a soothing, gentling touch. "I found the bottle of water you had in your bag and put it beside you on the table here. I want you to drink it once you've rested for a minute."

Adam was content to lie there being touched for as long as Denver wanted him to, but eventually the gentle caress against his skin went away, drawing him back to reality. Denver helped him sit up, easing him onto a pile of clothing as his reddened ass protested, and handed him the bottle of water.

When Adam straightened his glasses and attempted to get dressed, he faltered. That his legs didn't seem to want to bear him up didn't help, but that wasn't the problem. When Denver tugged Adam's pants back into place, the real world came back with them. It dawned on Adam what he'd done, how he had behaved. What he'd allowed a stranger do to him, how much he had exposed himself in ways that had nothing to do with being fucked in public, with how far he had strayed from safe with Denver.

How empty he'd feel if it never happened again.

"Hands up," Denver murmured, and like a child, Adam lifted his arms, letting Denver strip the semen-stained shirt off his body, pulling the neck wide to keep his glasses from getting smudged. When Denver came back with his *Top Ten* T-shirt, Adam allowed himself to be dressed.

Denver looked down at him, searching Adam's face, and Adam stared back up at him, unable to do anything but beg Denver silently not to make this the end of their encounter.

Eventually Denver nodded at the table full of mangled, semen-soaked clothes. "You messed up my laundry, boy."

The edge to Denver's tone should have tempted Adam to be afraid, but somehow it only made a thrill race down his spine. He dipped his head. "I'm sorry, sir. I'll wash them for you again if you like."

"I'm out of quarters." He caught Adam's chin.

Adam met his gaze. "Yes, sir." He wasn't even sure what he was agreeing to, he just knew he agreed with whatever Denver said.

Denver released Adam's chin and ruffled his hair. When he started to gather his semen-stained clothes into an empty basket, Adam realized his cowboy planned to leave without so much as an exchange of phone numbers.

"Wait." Adam put his hand over the top of the basket, screwing up his courage and looking Denver in the eye. "I still have quarters. I want to wash your dirty laundry for you."

Denver frowned at the dirty clothes. "I gotta get to work, so I can't stay."

Get to work? Adam glanced at the clock on the wall, which read nine thirty. "Where do you work?"

"Lights Out."

A gay bar, the one for the locals instead of the ones that were part of the college club scene. The gay bar Adam hadn't been to because he didn't do bars without the rest of the Bug Boys as backup, and since he didn't live with or hang out with them anymore, he couldn't go to a bar at all.

He ignored this problem, too eager to continue this encounter. "I can finish them for you and get them to you later. When you get off work, maybe."

Denver looked amused. "I get off at two thirty in the morning."

Something in his tone made Adam swallow his offer to hang out until then. "Oh."

His cowboy regarded him with a clear-eyed gaze that burned into the back of Adam's brain. It made Adam want to fidget and freeze all at once. Mostly he clung to his yearning, wanting more than anything to prolong this encounter, to get back to that place where he wasn't afraid, only hot and wild and free.

Denver held out his hand. "Give me your phone."

Digging into his pocket, Adam passed it over, watching as Denver punched at the screen for some time before giving it back.

"Give me a holler if you want company at the laundromat again sometime." Picking up the basket of clothes, he winked at Adam as he headed for the door.

CHAPTER THREE

DENVER ROGERS thought about the cute grad student all through his shift, and as he went to bed, and again when he passed the Park Place Apartments on his way to the grocery store.

Park Place Apartments, where Adam had said he lived.

It worried Denver, this preoccupation.

Everyone at Lights Out knew Denver's mission was to fuck his way through every twink that came to the bar, and it wasn't the first time he'd given out his cell number to someone he'd met outside of the club. However, this was the first time he'd ignored ten different texts and photos while he'd done his shift at the door, turning down several offers of bed warmers and backroom blow jobs as well.

He told himself it was because nobody had caught his eye.

Not like the cute entomologist with messy blond hair and glasses at the laundromat.

When Saturday morning rolled around and his head was still full of Adam, Denver headed for the one person he knew would give him a therapeutic dose of reality.

El Rozal sat behind his counter at Tucker Pawn, bronze arms covered in nicotine patches, a scowl on his face. When he saw Denver, he gave a curt nod and leaned down to scratch the ears of his black-and-white mop of a dog. "Hey."

"Hey yourself." Denver grinned at the patches and shook his head. "Trying again, I see."

El grunted and pushed his black hair out of his eyes. "Sorry I had to bail on you for laundry. I can't wait until Paul's done with this certification crap."

El's boyfriend was studying to be a vet tech. "When's his test?"

"Tuesday." El fumbled into his shirt pocket, realized what he was doing, and sighed. "What'll it be, Mr. Rogers? Buy, sell, or trade?"

"Buy, as in I'm buying lunch if you'll haul your ass out from behind that counter for it."

Grimacing, El glanced at the clock on the wall. "Believe me, I'd love to, but I promised Paul I'd meet him on campus with sandwiches at one."

"Oh. No problem." Denver tried for a no-worries smile, but he wasn't feeling it.

If El hadn't quit smoking, he'd have stared at Denver over the tip of the burning cherry. As it was, he simply stared, his hard, dark eyes assessing. "Business is slow, though, and it's a long time until one. What do you say to a cup of coffee and a croissant?"

This time Denver didn't have to fake the grin. "I say flip that sign and get Mojo's leash."

"You're still buying," El said, ruffling the head of the dog, which had gone wild at the word *leash*.

El preferred the local Mocha Springs Eternal coffee shop to Starbucks, which was fine with Denver, as he only ever ordered black coffee anyway, and Mocha Springs' drip coffee was exceptional. He got El his usual frothy caramel thing and brought both drinks out to the patio, where Mojo was already settling hard into her owner's lap.

"Few more weeks, it'll be too cold to sit out here," Denver observed as he arranged himself in the metal chair across from El. It groaned under his considerable size, but he knew from experience this one could take him.

"I'll be out here wrapped in scarves in December unless they let Mojo come inside." El sipped at his coffee. "So, muscle boy. It appears you have something on your mind."

Denver shifted in his seat, making the metal groan more. "Nothing really. Just had an interesting night is all."

"Last I checked, that isn't unusual for you. Unless you did three at once again?"

See, this right here was the problem. Instead of that kind of teasing getting him excited, it made him feel guilty. "No." He took a fortifying sip of coffee. "I hooked up at the laundromat."

El laughed. "Are you kidding me? For real? Jesus, after all the jokes?"

That at least made Denver smile. Ever since El had met Paul, El and Denver had been joking about how Denver's Mr. Right would walk into the Tucker Laund-O-Rama. "For real." His smile faded a little. "Just a hookup, though."

"Still, that's pretty funny. Your place or his?"

"Uh." Denver took another swig of coffee.

"Your truck? How do you even maneuver in there? You barely fit to drive."

Why wasn't this fun? Why wasn't he leering and bragging? Denver didn't understand. "Actually, it was *inside* the laundromat."

"They finally disinfected that bathroom?"

"No." Denver tugged at his hat and pulled it lower over his face. "Over a table. On my laundry, which reminds me, I'm going to have to go back this afternoon and do another load." When El stayed silent, Denver looked up at him, holding his friend's probing gaze. "It was hot as all fuck. And it shouldn't have been. He was this skinny, rabbitlike thing being bullied by drunk frat rats. Cute, but way too scared to play as hard as I do, so I didn't even have him on my radar. Then all of a sudden he was sitting in a dryer, spreading his legs, and I lost my head." Denver hunkered in his chair, which was starting to protest with serious alarm. He ignored it. "He's a grad student at East Cent. Studies pollinators or something." His cock stirred. "Damn ass you could bounce a quarter off of, and when you slap it…." He lingered in a moment of lust, body responding in a more familiar, comfortable way as he recalled what it had felt like to spank Adam. When he emerged from his haze, El still watched him, but he had a worrying, knowing smile playing around his lips. "What?" Denver demanded.

"Nothing." El sipped his drink, letting his tongue slip out to catch the foam from the rim.

"Nothing, the hell. And quit looking at me like you caught me with my pants down and my dick all shriveled."

El set his coffee aside and settled his much more manageable weight into his chair, lazily stroking his dog's head as she lolled in ecstasy. "I told you that you'd never meet Mr. Right in the bar."

Denver sat up so fast he nearly knocked his coffee over. "Get off. I fucked him over my laundry."

"Yeah. And you took me out to coffee to tell me about him. When was the last time you did that?"

Never. He'd never sought El out to tell him about a trick. He slumped, defeated. "Fuck."

El didn't laugh, and his smile gentled. "It's not the end of the world." Denver looked meaningfully at the dog, which El had acquired because of his own Mr. Right. El grinned and leaned down to nuzzle his girl. "It's not the end of the world at all."

Denver sipped his coffee as the October breeze blew around him, and he watched his best friend make out with Mojo, trying to tell himself El was wrong, that he wasn't hung up on Bug Boy, that it had just been a weird hookup, that he wasn't going to end up adopting a dog or a cat or something else insane. That he wasn't going to be the one rearranging his life for someone else.

Even if, sometimes, he wanted to.

AFTER DROPPING El at Tucker Pawn, Denver headed over to Tiny's Gym for his regular Saturday-afternoon routine, and after fifteen minutes at the free weights, he felt a lot better. When he left the gym two hours later, soaked head to toe with sweat, every muscle aching, he'd forgotten all about how hot Bug Boy had been and how badly he wanted to fuck that sweet little mouth. In any event, by the time he stood in his own shower back at his apartment, his blood was too busy repairing his abused muscles to bother with his cock, and as he made his six-egg-white omelet for dinner, he rationalized his unexpected and unwelcome crush.

He was getting caught up in everyone else's relationship drama, that was all. First Jase, then El had practically gotten married, and at this rate Seth was probably headhunting a sweetheart. Just because they all wanted to jump off a bridge didn't mean he had to also. And just because he'd hooked up in the laundromat like he and El had always joked didn't mean a damn thing either.

Of course, he couldn't help checking his phone for messages from Adam, which wasn't like him. Denver didn't chase anybody. He had a system, and it worked.

Except this time it wasn't. Usually by now he'd have at least one *thanks for the great time* text, but Adam hadn't sent anything.

Nothing. At all.

To distract himself, Denver went back to the gym on Sunday, even though he wasn't due until Monday. Deciding he could use some extra leg work, he put in another two hours and then five miles on the treadmill. He went to bed Sunday night sore as fuck, exhausted, and cranky, because he still didn't have any texts.

Denver wasn't sure what upset him more: that Adam hadn't reached out, or that Denver cared so much that he hadn't.

CHAPTER FOUR

THREE BLOCKS from the northern edge of East Centennial University and west of Frat Row was a sprawling former sorority, which was now the dominion of the Bug Boys.

Crispin House had been home to entomology students since 1998, when Sigma Delta Tau had given up the building to move into better digs. The house was now owned by a retired professor, and every new male entomology student was given the opportunity to take a room within. When there were extra rooms, they were leased on a yearly basis to other students in the biology department, but entomology students lived there for the duration of their studies or until they chose to move out. Theoretically girls were welcome to join the house too. In reality, they took one look at the place—which even when it was clean was a nest of porn, video games, lab equipment, and more porn—and politely declined.

Adam had moved into Crispin immediately upon his arrival at East Cent. He'd done his undergraduate work at Iowa State University, where he'd lived with his uncle and aunt, but on the advice of his therapist, he'd looked elsewhere for graduate school, and Crispin House was the biggest reason he'd chosen East Cent. It had seemed at the time a beautiful bridge between living with relatives and living entirely on his own.

After the breakup with Brad, Adam had moved out of Crispin House, but he'd unwittingly left a few things behind, so today he'd returned. He'd known he needed to come on the errand for a week now, but it had taken him this long to work up the courage and suss out the logistics of getting the task done.

To everyone else, it wasn't a difficult task and required no buildup at all. When he called to inform the Bug Boys he was on his way, Ollie was bewildered. "Just stop by, man. You know you're always welcome here."

That was the crux of the issue, right there. To Ollie, to the rest of the Bug Boys, to all neurotypical individuals, an invitation to visit someone's house was normal. It wasn't a source of stress, since they had been invited, and that made things okay. Nobody got worked up thinking they "didn't belong" in that house or apartment or dorm room. Thinking that way wasn't reasonable, healthy behavior, and no one expected it in others or knew how to behave when they experienced it in Adam.

Adam Ellery was brilliant. He navigated the world of academia with a grace most people couldn't dream of. But Adam had another side of him, one he preferred others didn't see, though at times like this there was little he could do to hide it. He suffered from clinical

depression and anxiety, had regular panic attacks, and
as a delectable cherry on the top of his neurotic sundae,
he also suffered from a rather sophisticated case of obsessive-compulsive disorder.

Because it was how he coped, once he was diagnosed, Adam threw himself with vigor into the study
of his diseases, particularly OCD. The latter's vaga-
ries, he discovered, were what got in the way of living
life the most. Oh, everyone made jokes about hand-
washing and cleaning things and alphabetizing the
cupboard, about being upset if a picture was cockeyed.
Simple things, funny things. In Adam's experience,
very little was laughable. He was a bit of a cleaner, yes,
but only in times of great stress, when there was no
other way to put the world to rights. Yes, he preferred
an alphabetized cupboard. Who wouldn't want to be
able to find things more easily? If that were the worst
of things, being clean and organized, everyone would
pine for some OCD.

But Adam wasn't only a cleaner and an alphabet-
izer. Many other things in his life had to be *just so* or
his brain easily convinced him the world would not
continue to turn properly on its axis. Intellectually, he
understood these odd rituals and obsessions did not
technically do anything to adjust the functioning of the
planet. In reality, functional Adam Ellery wasn't possible without a great deal of effort and therapy. He found
comfort in the knowledge he didn't have something
truly crippling, like the poor boy who couldn't reply in
conversation until he'd repeated the words spoken to
him by someone else backward in his head. He didn't
count every red car when he was driving—though he
could see the appeal, in an abstract, alarming sort of
way. He did dunk his tea bags three times, hold them

submersed for three seconds, then dunk them once more before taking them out entirely—and this all occurred exactly three minutes after he'd immersed the bag in the hot water.

There was one unique-to-Adam OCD handicap, however, that got in his way more than any other neuroses he had.

Adam didn't know how to navigate the anxiety morass that was other people's spaces.

He didn't remember when it had first manifested. His parents told stories about his distress as a young child when they visited friends or family, of how unsettled he became for reasons they couldn't understand. Hotels and their ilk weren't possible. After the third time of having to leave in the middle of the night when Adam cried so hard he threw up, or being thrown out by the management because neighboring guests couldn't sleep, they stopped staying in public houses. They bought a Winnebago and drove it whenever they went visiting overnight. They took turns going out until he was old enough to stay on his own since he'd never been able to tolerate a babysitter, not even his grandparents. They'd taken him to many, many therapists to cure him, and due to a lot of bumbling and incompetence by said therapists, his neuroses became more impossible to manage.

All this had led to, when he was fifteen, his mother's brother taking him in at his home in Iowa. First it was for a summer, then the rest of his high school and undergraduate career. A practical, patient professor at Iowa State University, Uncle Harmon walked Adam first through a transition of moving and then to a therapist who actually knew what he was doing. There Adam was finally, properly diagnosed and began to struggle in a healthy way with the limitations his mental illness placed on his life.

He'd grown considerably in his attempts to manage his mental health, but not yet far enough to deal with the thorny issue of retrieving his abandoned items from his former living space.

In the end, he talked himself over to Crispin House by reminding his anxiety and OCD that since he still had things present in the house, he still in a way belonged there, and so no panic was necessary. This had been a strategy he'd utilized with occasional success back in Iowa when he'd wanted to visit a friend at their home; if he left a few of his possessions there, he could sometimes convince himself he belonged. It wasn't always a slam dunk, though, and at Crispin House there was one variable that meant no matter what tricks Adam played on himself, he was pretty much guaranteed a panic attack.

That variable was Brad.

He wasn't there when Adam arrived, to Adam's great relief. Ollie let Adam in with a cheery wave, smiling and inviting Adam to wander around and double-check things as long as he liked. "I miss you, man," he teased, playfully punching Adam's shoulder. "And not just because the bathroom turned into a sty about ten minutes after you left."

Adam attempted to smile, laugh a little, to basically be human in the presence of a friend who meant well. It was difficult, though, when your brain was screaming at you, *Get out, get out, you don't belong here*, the whole time you were having polite conversation.

"How's everyone doing?" he asked, doing his best to sound interested and not distracted.

"Great. Mick and Brad are out golfing right now, taking a break from Fundy. Stedman's brutal, man."

Dr. Stedman taught Fundamentals of Entomology and was known for being rigid and impossible. Adam had loved him and strongly suspected the man of being a fellow member of Club OCD. "Sorry to hear that. Give them my best."

Ollie followed Adam around casually as he found his things and put them in the box he'd brought to take them back to his apartment. Ollie was an inch shorter than Adam and absolutely adorable. He reminded Adam of the Latino actor from *Saved by the Bell*, Mario Lopez, only hotter and more stacked. He was straight, Adam was almost sure of it, even though he'd never seen Ollie date. Whatever his orientation, he was pleasant to look at and not a bad distraction from panic.

Ollie leaned against the kitchen door while Adam went through the cupboard, which had been his until two weeks ago. "Yeah, I told them he's a rite of passage your first year. As for the others, Andrew's girlfriend broke up with him, but you know how weird he is, so he doesn't care. As for Kim—well, I don't have to tell you. All he does is study, study, study."

Adam listened to the rest of Ollie's report of his former housemates' lives with half an ear as he moved from the kitchen and into the upstairs hall closet, where he was fairly convinced one of his towels had ended up, even though he'd always kept his things in his own room. He'd tried not caring about it, telling himself it was a towel and didn't matter, but it had been his favorite towel in some obtuse way, and searching for it through his discomfort seemed less upsetting than leaving it behind.

"So how has it been living on your own?" Ollie asked. "You get lonely, or just happy to have a place all to yourself?"

Adam couldn't find the towel. It wasn't anywhere in the closet, and now the closet was a mess, which meant he had to stand there and make it right. "A little of both, I guess."

"Here, let me help." Ollie took some of the towels Adam had rooted through. Adam hid his wince at the idea of Ollie folding anything correctly, but apparently not very well. Ollie smiled at him wryly. "It's okay, dude. They're my towels. I don't mind how they're folded."

Adam sighed and added *not caring about poor folding* to his already burdened list of things he was ignoring. "I know. It's just… well, you know."

"I do, man." Ollie's smile died, and he looked concerned. "Is that why you moved out? Were we too messy?"

"No," Adam said, then forced himself to be honest. He liked Ollie. "Okay, that was always a little difficult. But it was important for me to learn to live with that too, so no, that wasn't why."

Ollie grimaced. "It was Brad, wasn't it."

Adam became very focused on folding a washcloth.

Ollie shook his head. "I told him to lay off. I told him."

"It's okay. He means well. And really, it was time for me to try living on my own. It was always supposed to be the next step, and now I've done it."

"Well come visit us, you hear? I really do miss you, man. Not for the cleaning, either. You're good company."

Adam rolled his eyes. "Please. I am not."

"You are! I loved studying in the commons with you. You would be there, but you weren't in the way.

You respect people's space, you know? You're good people." He clapped Adam on the shoulder.

Adam blushed a little and smiled. "Thanks. We'll have to do coffee sometime."

"It's a date." Ollie aimed his index finger at Adam in a faux warning as he backed away toward his own room. "See you around."

Adam spent another half an hour trying to find the towel, which was the last of his items he was missing. He was stuck now too, because it was a task unfinished, a puzzle without an end, a string of ceiling tiles to count that kept adding more squares. Worse, with every minute he lingered, he increased the odds—which he calculated like a rabid squirrel inside his head—that he would run into Brad.

At four thirty in the middle of the laundry room, he did.

"I heard you were here." Brad stood on the stairs, poised like Joan Crawford in a movie, ready to give some overly dramatic line.

"Hey." Adam tried to sound casual. "Just looking for my burgundy towel."

"Did you look in the upstairs cupboard?"

"Yeah, and the hamper. Can't find it anywhere."

"Well, I'll keep a look out for it and get it back to you."

Adam tensed a little. "That's fine. I'll find it. I'm sure it's here."

Brad's put-upon sigh echoed against the concrete-block walls. "Really, Adam."

It took so, so much work to simply ignore him, to continue to search through piles of washed and unwashed laundry. He knew from bitter experience it would be better to say nothing than to engage, because to do so was like extricating oneself from goo. The more one tugged, the more one became entwined.

He should have known it wouldn't work, though. Brad had sought him out. Brad had never liked the idea of Adam moving out. Brad had been the one to instigate the breakup, but it had been Adam who left the house, and Brad never missed a chance to tell Adam how stupid that was and how it was a further sign that he was cripplingly mentally ill. Every time he saw Adam in the lab, he told him so as if he hadn't already said it ten thousand times. Having Adam captive in his own house would be too great of an opportunity to miss.

His house, not yours. You don't belong here. Get out, get out, get out!

Adam drew a steadying breath.

Brad made a tsking sound. "You're doing it, aren't you. You're freaking out because this isn't your house now. Admit it."

"I'm just looking for my towel." Adam repeated this mantra like the lifeline it was. "I won't be but another few moments."

"It doesn't have to be another few moments." Brad finished his descent and swanned over to Adam, lighting gracefully on the corner of the sorting table, folding one delicate leg over the other. "I told you. You're overreacting. You never had to move out just because we broke up."

"That's not why I moved out. It was time."

This sigh was sonorous, an arc of song to punctuate exactly how exasperating Brad thought Adam could be. "Whatever. You don't need to be like this, you know that. I mean, if you're that upset about our breaking up that you have to move out, you should see a therapist. Well, see another one."

A well-placed barb, because Brad knew Adam wasn't happy with his current therapist, not really, and also knew how upsetting it was to Adam to try to find a new one.

Adam shut his eyes, drew another cleansing breath, and let it out slowly before continuing his search.

Brad curled his lip in derision and shook his head. "Look at you. How can you live on your own when you're like this? What do you do when you have a panic attack and no one is there to help you?"

"I don't have them," Adam snapped.

"Not yet. You've been gone not even two weeks. You will have one, though. You have them all the time. And what then? Huh?"

"I don't know." Adam bunched a wad of other people's dirty clothes in his hands, realized what he was doing, and dropped them with a heavy shiver. "It's not your problem, okay? Leave me alone."

Brad pushed off the table and came to stand in front of him, his dark eyes full of sorrow but laced with irritation. "Just come home. Please. This is ridiculous."

"You know, you're right." Adam's voice shook with forced brightness. "If you find my towel, bring it to the lab. Have a good evening."

Not waiting for a reply, he all but ran to the stairs, hurrying up them as Brad called for him to wait. As Adam bolted out the door, he tossed a nervous wave to Ollie then headed down the walk and around the corner to his car. By the time he got there, his breath came in short, shallow gasps. He was a ball of sweat, and his vision was half colored red by his impending attack. With a lot of internal dealmaking, Adam drove like a nervous grandmother to his apartment, locked the door, and crawled into his bed.

Safe in his cocoon, he drew the covers up over his head, whimpering as he hyperventilated in the dark.

DATING BRAD had seemed like such a good idea at the time. They'd moved into Crispin within days of each other, and for over a year they were simply friends, bonded by their orientation, their academic discipline, and their love of Thai food. Brad had also lived in the same house as Adam, which meant they could stay up late on the couch and neck and it wasn't any trouble, because they both belonged there by Adam's rigid code of dwellings. Actual sex had gotten complicated, but they didn't have sex at first, only made out. If it had all been able to stay as it had begun, it would have been a great relationship. When they'd started dating, Brad made him laugh, made him feel safe and secure.

What had begun as concern and shepherding, though, had quickly turned sour. It hadn't taken long for Brad to start micromanaging Adam's life, smothering him with what he'd likely meant to be protection. Their relationship had been bad for a long time, at least six of their nine months together, but Adam had been so drawn in by Brad's desire to care for him, to protect him and guide him, that he couldn't quite quit the crack cocaine Brad had become, even though he knew the illegal substance would probably be healthier. Which was why when Brad broke them up and Adam knew a brief moment of sanity at the severed connection, he'd made his escape. To linger, he'd known, would mean returning to the codependent pattern of yearning for someone to take care of him, to make decisions for him, to decide what was good and bad for him so he didn't have to, even if that came at a cost of his self-esteem, his friends, his fragile sanity.

Instances post-breakup such as this were the most challenging. As usual Brad had tried so insistently to pull him back, never realizing how desperately Adam wanted to return. It was like a sugared donut. Sugar had long, long been Adam's enemy, wiring him too hard and fast, making him crash into a sea of anxiety he couldn't hope to control. Sugar was bad. But donuts looked so good, even though he hadn't tasted one in fifteen years. They always seemed the most wonderful, wicked sin Adam could think of.

Brad was a donut whose taste still lingered in Adam's mouth. As Adam lay under the covers, shivering and weeping, he told himself no matter what he thought he wanted, he could under no circumstances have another bite.

Adam needed something else to eat. Something not-Brad. Adam needed to date someone, or at least fantasize about someone level-headed. Someone who didn't try to control him, who was kind but gave him space.

Someone, say, who was big and burly and liked to fuck in laundromats. And gave spankings.

Adam emerged from the covers slowly, eyeing his phone, which he'd laid on his nightstand. He did have Denver's number. He hadn't used it, figuring Denver hadn't really meant for him to text, that it had been nothing more than a polite gesture. Yet he did have the number.

Maybe sending a text to Denver would get Brad out of his head. It was the kind of exercise his therapist in Ames would have set up for him: simply sending the missive could be healing. It wasn't a real risk, either, because Denver wouldn't text back. He wouldn't reject Adam, he just wouldn't care.

Yes. It was a good idea to text Denver. He picked up the phone and started composing before he could psych himself out of the act.

Hey there. This is Adam from the Laund-O-Rama. Not sure if you remember me, but wanted to say hi.

Adam's finger trembled, but it only took him twenty seconds to hit Send. He sat in his bed clutching the phone for a long time, heart pounding, adrenaline pumping. God, that had been unnecessarily terrifying. But he'd done it, hadn't he? Yes. He had. He'd wanted to babble about how his backside had hurt for thirty-six hours and made it difficult to sit, but he'd liked it and found it nicely distracting, and he'd wanted to find a way to ask about why that was, but he'd had the good sense not to do any of that, had stuck to polite conversation only. It was practically a *breakthrough*.

Did he feel healed? Maybe. It was a break in the pattern, which was good, so, yes. Maybe—

His phone dinged, and he nearly dropped it in surprise. He yelped when the notification display said he had a text from Denver Rogers.

Sure I remember you. Thought maybe you forgot about me. What you doing tonight, baby?

Adam had to put the phone down on the end table and dive under the covers again. Holy shit. He'd texted back. What was Adam supposed to do now?

He had no idea. Except that he had to reply, obviously. *And not about spankings.* Adam reclaimed the phone with trembling hands.

Nothing much. What about you? Are you working?

He studied his response for a moment. Lame, yes, but also benign. Surely this would be the end of the exchange. He considered deleting the questions, but nothing much looked too curt on its own, so he put the questions back in.

Denver answered within thirty seconds, like he'd been waiting.

Yep, working at Lights Out like always. Stop by and your first drink is on me.

Adam stared at the display. Doubt and panic tangled, and the clash wasn't pretty. Denver wasn't supposed to text back—never had Adam dreamed he'd tell him to come over!

Maybe he wasn't. Maybe this was him being polite. He calmed. That had to be it.

Another text came through. *What time do you think you might stop by? I'll watch for you.*

MAYDAY. MAYDAY. Adam took the phone under the blanket with him, lying sideways as he stuttered out a reply. *You really want me to come?*

Hell yes. I been waiting for you to call.

He'd been waiting? Really? Adam read the text again. He didn't seem to be joking. *He wants to see me.* His anxiety paused, uneasy, but longing too. Every part of his neurotic orchestra had liked Denver.

Denver wasn't a donut. Denver Rogers was a big, meaty steak. Adam didn't normally do steak, but Jesus, was he craving beef right now.

I could swing by around ten.

See you then.

Adam held on to the phone, waiting to see if anything else happened. It didn't.

Then he realized what he'd just promised to do, what he'd gotten himself into. Going across town to Lights Out. An unknown local bar.

Alone.

To meet Denver, who had fucked him over a laundry table. Who had, allegedly, been waiting for his call.

"Oh God," Adam whispered, and went back under the covers.

"WHAT ARE you staring at?" El asked when Denver pulled out his phone at the laundromat for the fifteenth time. "Waiting for your booty call?"

Denver tucked his phone away, but not before verifying that Adam hadn't texted again. He cleared his throat. "Nothing. Just—nothing."

El grinned. "Ha. It's Bug Boy, isn't it? Your entomologist still hasn't texted you, and it's driving you crazy."

Denver shifted uncomfortably on his plastic chair. "He did text me. He's coming by the bar tonight. I'm going to buy him a drink."

"So it was a booty call."

Denver was hoping like hell it was, but for some reason El making fun of it put him on edge. He scowled and didn't reply.

He did, however, pull out his phone again.

El stopped laughing. "Man, you really are fixated on him, aren't you?"

Denver was, and he didn't like it. "I'd figured he wasn't interested, and then out of the blue here he texts. Dunno. Threw me, I guess."

"If I hadn't promised Paul we'd do a *Firefly* marathon after he got done studying, I'd swing by to see your show."

God, but Denver was glad for that marathon. "It's nothing. I've been in a mood, is all."

"So I noticed. What's going on?"

Denver had no idea. He wasn't getting laid, which wasn't helping, but it wasn't because he didn't have options. The Sea of Twink remained as full of fish as ever. He simply… wasn't interested for some reason. He frowned. "I don't know."

El stretched his feet out on his bench. "When's your next night off? Come by and we'll grill out on the balcony or something."

"I don't have one. The other bouncer quit again."

El winced. "Well, now I know what's wrong. You need to tell Jase you need a day off."

He did, he knew that. Usually he didn't mind working, but lately, yeah, he did. "I'll talk to him."

"Good." El nudged him with his boot. "So. Tell me more about Bug Boy."

Denver shrugged. "You already heard the story. Not much to tell."

"Well, tell me again. I want to be able to tell your grandchildren about how you met over a laundry table."

Denver narrowed his eyes at El. "Are you going to do that annoying thing where you try to get me hooked up because you're in a relationship now?"

El shrugged. "Maybe. Mostly I'm just bored." He scratched at his nicotine patch. "And craving a cigarette."

"You can still smoke, you know," Denver pointed out. "Paul isn't going to leave you over it."

"I know." El glared at the patches. "It seemed like it was time, though." He sighed. "And I know Paul would prefer I didn't. He worries I'll die of lung cancer."

Considering how much El smoked, it wasn't an invalid fear. "Well, good luck, I guess."

El clapped a hand on Denver's shoulder, grimacing in camaraderie. "You too."

CHAPTER FIVE

ADAM STOOD in a gas station restroom across from Lights Out, staring into a cracked and faded mirror, coaching himself out loud. "You can do this," he repeated for what had to be the tenth time. "You can do this, Adam. You can do this."

He didn't believe it any more than he had the last nine times he'd said it to himself.

Stop by, Denver had said. Stop by Lights Out, like it was no big deal. It wasn't a big deal to most people. However, Adam wasn't most people, a point driven home by the fact that he was nearly hyperventilating over the dirtiness of the restroom and how he'd be wiping off his phone with a Wet Wipe before putting it back in his pocket.

He should have set things up better. He should have said he'd stop by another night, though the same problems would exist whenever he went. At least then he could have thought up a plan. He could have figured out how to get all the Bug Boys but Brad to come to the bar with him. He could have worked up more courage so he wouldn't be swimming in a sea of Xanax.

He could have grown wings and flew.

I can do this, he told himself, trying to stop the spiral of self-loathing before it got out of control. *All I have to do is go into the bar. Walk through the door, say hi to Denver, and see what happens. It's not hard. People do it all the time, and they're just fine. I'll be fine too.*

He'd be fine. Everything would be fine.

So long as no one slipped anything into his soda.

So long as he didn't lose his cab money and have to walk home.

So long as he didn't get jumped by hooligans in the alley.

In the mirror, Adam's countenance went pale. He shut his eyes, drew a deep breath, and whispered to his reflection, "I can do this. I can do this. I can do this."

He had on his usual club shirt, its familiar fabric like armor to Adam, but it made him nervous too. He'd been vain and gone without glasses, but now he obsessed about his contacts, whether he'd washed them enough, whether they had rolled back into his eyelids, whether they had defied factory tests and glued themselves permanently to his cornea.

The contacts, he knew now, had been a horrible mistake. He hadn't counted on being this nervous when he'd put them in.

He should have waited to go out with the Bug Boys. Safety in the swarm, that was the joke, or it had been. That group, for him, had been fractured since Brad. The lab, the friendships, everything. He wasn't ever sure if it was real or his imagination, if the others truly didn't talk to him as much now or if that was simply how it seemed. Maybe they'd all been part of a fantasy of inclusion. Or maybe he was making his life a melodrama for no reason.

Feelings aren't facts. He had this taped to the top of his bathroom mirror, over his kitchen sink, and a few other places now that he lived alone.

It was true, though, that he didn't have anyone to go with him to Lights Out. The Bug Boys always went to bars closer to campus. If Adam asked them to go to Lights Out, they'd ask why. Which theoretically shouldn't be bad, because they didn't care that he was gay. In reality it would be, because they wouldn't understand about Denver.

Adam wasn't sure he understood about Denver.

Taking a deep breath, he tugged at his shirt, blinked to ensure the proper placement and lubrication of his contacts, and left the bathroom, using a Wet Wipe to turn the doorknob. It was a little hard-core OCD even for him, but he was determined not to let his disorder get a single foothold tonight. While things had been lonely since he'd left Crispin House, they'd been downright miserable since his encounter with Cowboy. All he could think about was how good it had felt. Not just the sex, but the way Denver seemed to be able to shut off his monkey mind like nothing else. He wanted that again. He wanted that so badly he ached.

You're using him, his conscience whispered, and not for the first time.

Adam still wasn't sure whether or not his conscience was right. Was he using Denver, or trying to? Did it matter if he did, if Denver consented? Really, it wasn't like they had some kind of deep and abiding

connection. They'd fucked in a goddamned laundromat. They hadn't exchanged vows.

He refused to feel guilty over being largely at-
tracted to Denver's sexuality. After the head-fuckery of
Brad, Adam was more than ready for some fuck-and-
go. Certainly Denver looked like the kind of guy who
would be relieved to find out they weren't doing the
relationship thing.

Adam still had butterflies when he got in line to
enter the bar, but thanks to his drugs, he'd evened out.
He could do this. He could totally do this. He was independent now, no more Brad. He lived on his own, and
he'd never thought he could do that. He'd done his own
laundry, which had gone a bit south, but then decidedly
north.

This was about sex, pure and simple. He wasn't
trying to find a new Brad. He was angling for more hot
sex. The new, independent Adam.

Or something.

JASON DAVIS was the owner of Lights Out, and
while he wasn't exactly El Rozal, he was still on the
short list of people Denver would call should shit hit
the fan. He liked to think that went in reverse and that
this was why, when Jase had found himself shorthand-
ed, he'd asked Denver to step up and take over the open
shifts. Which up until now, Denver hadn't minded.

Thing was, El was right. It was starting to eat at
Denver, never having a night off. It'd be nice to have an
open evening every now and again to do… stuff. So before his shift started at nine the night Adam was due to
drop by, Denver ducked into Jase's office to talk to him.

"Denver. Hey." Jase leaned back in his chair.
"What can I do you for?"

"Wanted to see if you'd hired me a buddy for the door yet."

"Sadly, no." The corner of Jase's mouth quirked up. "Your dominion over the twinks can continue unabated, at least for now."

Denver propped an arm on the doorway. "Actually, I was kind of wanting a day off. Not a big deal, just… you know. Shit to do."

Jase threaded his fingers over his chest. "Or someone to do. Do go on, Mr. Rogers."

Denver glared. "Jesus. You and El got the same damn disease."

"You used to always tell me you couldn't work the door enough. What else would you do in the evening besides surf for tail? Might as well get paid for it. So something about that has changed." Jase's eyebrows waggled. "Denver's got a boyfriend."

"Forget it," Denver murmured, pushing away from the door.

Jase didn't follow him, but he hollered after Denver as he went back to the floor. "I'm heading home here in a minute, but I'll check the schedule tomorrow and see what I can work out. Tell loverboy to hold on tight, you'll be ready for the picnic in the park soon."

Denver flipped him off without turning around and headed to his post at the door.

Adam lost some of his courage during his time in line at the door of the bar. It wasn't a long line, but it was enough to make Adam doubt himself. Maybe Denver didn't actually want to see him. Maybe he'd been playing it nice. Or worse, maybe he figured they were done and really was simply going to buy Adam a drink, and he'd done all this for nothing. What if he made an idiot of himself? What if everyone found out? What if—what if—?

"Hey, stranger!"

The what-ifs died in their tracks as Denver Rogers's meaty hand clapped on Adam's shoulder. Just the sight of six feet whatever of meaty muscleman was better than all the anxiety medication in the world. Denver Rogers wore another tank top, though this one was gray and read *Tiny's Gym* in faded blue ink. One of the straps stretched low enough to almost reveal one dusky nipple. Denver's arm bulged, muscles rippling as the hand he'd placed on Adam lingered, kneading gently before sliding down, teasing Adam's waist and then the curve of his ass.

"H-hi." Adam tried to push his glasses higher up his nose only to remember he wasn't wearing them. *Say something. Say something. Say. Something.* "I made it," he blurted, then inwardly cringed.

"That you did." Denver winked at him as he reached for the ID of the guy behind Adam. "No glasses tonight?"

"No. I... no."

Adam stood there stupidly, unsure what to do, but just as he was about to stumble back into the crowd and die from a cocktail of anxiety and mortification, Denver's hand caught him, holding Adam in place beside him.

"Sorry." Denver nodded to the throng. "When it rains, it pours, I guess." His thumb brushed against Adam's arm before letting him go. "So how are the pollinators?"

At first Adam thought he was asking about Brad and the other Bug Boys. Then he got the joke. "Oh. Ha. Pollinators. They're still... pollinating."

Denver laughed and kept checking IDs, and Adam stewed quietly in his own uncertainty. He would have gone and found a place at the bar or at a table, but Denver blocked his exit, so he stood there, feeling dumb. He supposed the upside was Denver seemed to want him there.

This would be a good moment for witty repartee. Brad would come up with a quip that would make everyone laugh, a cutting cynicism that summed up the situation and illuminated it at the same time. Adam tried to think of something, but witty hadn't ever been his forte.

Did he even have a forte?

"There." Denver eased onto a stool he pulled out from behind the door before leaning back to observe Adam. "Usually all I do for the first few hours is sit here on my ass until someone gets drunk enough to kick out. You brought a herd with you tonight."

"Oh, I came by myself," Adam said, not realizing Denver had been teasing until he'd already spoken.

Denver just smiled. Somehow Adam was sure this wasn't how it was supposed to go. He'd focused so much on getting in the door without bolting, he'd forgotten to plan how to behave once he was inside.

Denver nodded at the bar, adjusting his hat with the same motion. "I believe I promised you a drink. What's your poison?"

"Oh. Um, a mineral water, please. Or just water."

"Mineral water," Denver repeated, sounding like he thought this might be a joke.

Adam grimaced. "Yeah. Sorry. But regular water is fine too."

He tried to leave it at that, he truly did. But Denver was looking at him funny, and the stress of the awkwardness of the moment was already heavy. The cork popped off Adam's mouth, and he stood beside himself, helpless, as his neuroses emptied out between them like upturned trash.

"Sorry, I take a lot of medication, and I can't drink while I'm on what I took to get here, though I do drink, just not today. I don't like soda. Sugar is bad for me, especially when I'm nervous, and I can't do artificial sweeteners, so that's why water. I mean, I'd ask for herbal tea, but that's weird in a bar, and would they even have it? Coffee is worse. I used to do tonic water, but it has sugar in it, and like I said, it makes me funny, so that leaves water. Or soda water. I try for mineral water because it sounds festive and it doesn't seem as rude as asking for water because I still have to pay for it, but then sometimes they don't have it and they think I'm all fussy, which I guess I am, but I don't try to be. So really any water would be fine, just so long as it isn't alcoholic and not with sugar, real or fake, thank you very much. I'm sorry."

Verbal vomit spent, Adam drew a breath, waiting to see what Denver would say. He hoped it was something, because he could feel tide number two of unnecessary information creeping up his throat.

Denver blinked a few times. He didn't speak, but he winked as he slid off his stool and went to the bar, spoke a word with the server, and came back with a can of LaCroix, which he held out to Adam.

Adam accepted the drink with his face aflame. "Thank you."

Cracking the can open, he winced at the noise, then focused on taking a drink. It was plain mineral water, which was usually his favorite, but with LaCroix was not. It tasted like bitterness. With bubbles.

More people had come to the door, and Adam watched them move through as Denver checked their IDs, occasionally greeting someone or making a remark of recognition. Adam scanned each new arrival, weighing and assessing them by looks and manner. This was more the local bar rather than the college bar, which he'd already known, but it was interesting to see how the patrons parsed themselves out. It was soothing, categorizing people, like sorting his moths.

This one is a bear, big and burly, but has a heart of gold. Not much education, but he doesn't seem to need it. This man is overeducated, using words as weapons to fend off others. This man is a student, and he is with a pack of students.

There were a few undergraduates, one of whom Adam thought he'd seen in the biology building. The students moved in a swarm, finding safety in numbers, but of course that came with conformity, unity. Adam pegged the tall blond one as the leader, though from the look of the pink-haired one behind him, his territory was in question.

"People-watching?" This came from Denver as he reestablished himself on his chair. "This is a good spot for that. Jase and I often place bets on who's going to go home with who." Denver's eyes slid to Adam. "Or whom, or whatever. Sorry. Not used to flirting with a graduate student."

Adam couldn't decide where to bloom first. Denver was trying to impress him? Flirting? There was flirting happening here? He clutched his LaCroix happily. "I'm an entomologist, not a grammarian. I always mess that up anyway. That and the 'you and I' when it should be 'you and me.' Moths don't use grammar, thankfully."

Denver's seizing on the topic was almost visible. His body even turned. "Right, you said that's what you study, moths."

"Yeah. Hawk moths are my focus, but I'm obsessed with the entire family of Sphingidae."

"Well, tell me about them," Denver urged.

Adam gave him a long look. "You don't want to hear about hawk moths."

Denver eased deeper into his stool. His expression shifted subtly, but whatever it was made the hair on the back of Adam's neck dance. "Tell me," Denver said, his voice sliding into a soft drawl, laced with a thin lash of command, "everything you know about hawk moths."

Adam blinked, confused, uncertain. *No*, he wanted to argue. *You're making fun, or you will.* No one wanted to hear about moths, for fuck's sake.

Except he couldn't speak, not those words, because That Look was back. He recognized it from the laundromat. It was the same look that had made Adam feel perfectly fine about letting his pants hang at his knees while he got felt up and then fucked up the ass in front of anybody who came into the room. It was the look that had smoldered in the back of his brain as he'd gotten ready to come tonight. It was the look that had convinced him to overcome everything in his way.

Now it demanded he talk about moths. So he did.

He started hesitantly, worried this might be a trap, but all Denver did was listen. His face changed as he digested facts, and sometimes he asked questions. Especially about the hummingbird hawk moth.

"So you mean I might have seen one of these things, thought they were a bird, but they're a moth?"

Adam nodded, trying not to be too eager, but it was hard. "I can show you a picture sometime if you want.

I mean, they don't actually look the same holding still, but when they hover, absolutely."

Denver pulled his phone from his pocket. "Can we look them up? If I type in 'hummingbird hawk moth,' will it show up?"

"Oh yes."

Denver fumbled for a second with the browser, then handed it to Adam. "Here. You find me a good one."

Heart fluttering like one of the moths, Adam pulled up a page with some of the best examples he knew of and showed them to Denver. He got exactly the reaction he was looking for.

"Wow." Denver flipped through the photo gallery with wide eyes. "They're really big."

Adam considered this comment. "Well—yes, for a moth, but hummingbirds aren't big either. Plus people view them at a distance. It's the movement, see, that makes them so special. They can swing, and not many can do that. Only three nectar feeders have developed this: hummingbirds, some bats, and the hummingbird moth."

"Is that what you study? Their movement?"

"Well, in a roundabout way. I'm more interested in their genes. But it's really boring to non-entomologists."

Denver's eyes danced. "I love being bored."

Again, Adam hesitated. This never happened, and he knew damn well Denver didn't care about moth genetics. "There are almost fifteen hundred different kinds of hawk moths, but there's no real study in the phylogenetic framework. How they've evolved, and why, how they're related."

Despite all logic, Denver seemed genuinely intrigued. "So this helps you what? Figure out how to protect crops?"

"Well, yes, but not in the way you might think. I mean, biology should always be study for the sake of studying, but this discipline could have actual purpose. We're losing pollinators. Why? What's driving them? Is it evolution? Is it us? Is it something we haven't yet discovered? What can we learn by understanding how they evolved in the first place? Could that help us halt their die-off? Could it help us in some other way?" He realized he'd gotten carried away, flushed, and stopped talking.

Denver finished checking an ID and glanced at Adam impatiently. "Well, don't leave me hanging, boy. You sounded like you were on a roll. Tell me more about how your bugs will save the world."

God help him, Adam did.

CHAPTER SIX

For someone who didn't know a damn thing about flirting, Denver thought he was doing a pretty good job.

He could follow some of what Adam was saying, and in its own mind-numbing way, it was cool. He wasn't half as interested in the moths as he was the way Adam lit up like a Christmas tree when he talked about them. Denver found himself wondering how the hell someone came into such a thing, studying moth family trees or whatever, and then he realized he could ask. That proved almost as entertaining as the rest.

"My uncle got me into it. He's a professor at Iowa State University and lives just outside of Ames. He's into wine—grows grapes, bottles it, sells it. Everyone in his family works there, and it's a job for them, but to him it's a hobby. I helped out while I lived there as well, though not as much because I was focused on school. He wanted to do everything organically, which was hard since they live next to a golf course. He kept bees too, in part for the grapes, but he's the one who introduced me to the idea of pollinators and how important they are. I made a state fair project out of it, used it to land a scholarship and everything."

Denver could just see Adam getting caught up in bees and grapes. He had a dopey focus about him, like he was the kind of guy who'd need to be reminded to stop and eat. "So what do you do when you're not studying moths?"

The question seemed to embarrass Adam. "Not much, I suppose."

"No pollinator bowling leagues, huh?"

He'd meant it as a joke, but something about the comment had Adam looking, if not ashamed, forlorn in a way that hinted at more to his story. "Mostly the entomology grad students hang out together outside of classes and grad work, yeah."

"You say that like that doesn't include you."

Adam reached over his shoulder to rub at his neck. "It used to. I... had a falling-out with one of them, and it's been hard to be with them since. Plus I moved out of the house we were all renting." He looked pained. "Sometimes I wonder if that was smart."

"Moving out on your own? Why, money tight?"

Adam shook his head. "No, it's not that. It's just... harder, being on my own. Harder than I thought."

"Sometimes hard's good," Denver pointed out.

"Sometimes."

A scuffle near the bar drew Denver's attention, and he stepped away from the door to loom ominously. Once things settled back down, he returned to his station, where Adam stood huddled against a support pillar, eyeing the dance floor with a mixture of envy and fear. He looked so lost, not quite out of place but definitely rudderless. Denver couldn't decide if he wanted to wrap him up in a blanket or fuck him into security. Maybe both.

Denver noticed Adam rubbing his neck again, except this time it was more than a nervous gesture. He seemed focused on his shoulder.

"You hurt yourself or something?" Denver asked him, motioning to where Adam kept rubbing.

"Oh—no, not really." Adam pulled his hand away as if he'd been caught cheating. "Had a lot of data entry today. Makes me sore."

"Here," Denver said, motioning to the stool, "have a seat."

He liked the way Adam did what he was told, not arguing, only sitting on the stool and looking expectantly at Denver. If Denver had thought he could get away with it, he'd have tacked on a *good boy*, but he wasn't sure yet how that would play. So he simply positioned himself behind Adam and put his big hands on those beautiful, slender shoulders, then kneaded once, experimentally.

With a whimper, Adam went boneless and sagged back into Denver's hands.

Denver smiled and fell into the massage, keeping one eye on the floor and one on the door while he worked his entomology student over. He loved the way Adam felt in his hands, so slight and frail he could break him in two, but at the same time strong, his muscles resisting and fighting before ultimately relenting to Denver's touch.

He missed the glasses, he'd admit.

He loved everything about Adam, though. On so many levels Adam was the same as every other twiggy

youth Denver picked up at Lights Out, but in plenty of
other ways he wasn't. To start, Adam wasn't the usual
barely legal Denver took home. Even when his tricks
weren't still wet behind the ears, they tended to be
young of brain if not literally young of body. El liked
to make jokes about how a month's worth of Denver's
tricks could probably combine their brainpower enough
to run a can opener. Not Adam.

It was weird how even now as Adam melted into
Denver's kneading hands, he maintained an unusual
sense of awareness. The man's brain never turned off,
always analyzing, assessing, weighing. When Denver
had to stop his massage to check an ID, Adam popped
right back into alertness, moving aside to make room
for Denver to pass. What Denver really liked was the
yearning he felt in Adam. It was wrapped up in that
intelligence somehow, making him different than the
needy, greedy twinks who wanted Denver to top the
shit out of them, but on their terms. They wanted a daddy in a way that made Denver want to hand out cards
for a therapist.

Adam... well, Denver wasn't sure exactly what
this guy wanted. Adam kept trying to project he was
fine when it was very clear he was one coal away from
full-on hot mess, but half a nudge from Denver and he
all but purred.

It made Denver want to put Adam on his knees.

For the moment he had to settle for sliding his
hands under the body-hugging sparkly white tank,
toying with Adam's nipples from behind, pressing his
erection into the small of Adam's back. He wished he
could get out of work before three, but he knew damn
well there was no chance. Jase had already gone home,
probably to fuck his happy little acupuncturist before

bed, which meant he was counting on Denver to lock up and make sure the new guy running bar didn't serve his friends a few rounds after closing like the last kid had done.

Denver nibbled on Adam's ear. "You got early classes or anything tomorrow?"

He loved the way Adam unconsciously tipped his head to the side to give Denver better access. "Not until the afternoon. Just lab stuff in the morning. No rush."

Denver's cock swelled to life at this welcome news. "Good. I don't want to have to hurry when I fuck you." This remark made Adam gasp and go even limper in Denver's arms, and Denver smiled into his neck, trailing a corded muscle with his tongue. "I'm gonna eat your ass, moth man." Adam squeaked like a mouse, and God, but it took everything in Denver not to bite down on that shoulder and make him cry out harder. "Gonna spread you wide on my bed and lick the shit out of you."

Like someone had set him on a spring, Adam jerked, not out of Denver's arms but damn close. "Oh— I—" He broke off, bit his lip, and scuttled away from Denver's hands. "I... I'm sorry. I can't go back to your place."

Denver paused, digesting the curveball. "Okay. I don't mind going to yours."

If anything, Adam twitched harder this time. "No! I mean—" He turned his face away, but not before Denver caught a look of abject misery and self-disgust on Adam's face. "Never mind. Just... forget it."

Adam stood up, looking like he had every intention of walking away.

Denver didn't mean to grab Adam as hard as he did, only catch his shoulder and turn him around, but Adam moved faster than Denver anticipated, and Adam's foot snagged on the edge of the stool. After tumbling off-balance, they landed pressed together on the opposite side of the vestibule, Adam's face flat to the wall with Denver's big, burly body pushing hard against him.

"Sorry," Denver murmured and started to pull back.

"Oh God, don't go," Adam rasped, turning his head slightly to one side. "Don't stop, please."

Denver paused.

Adam's eyes were closed, his face contorted in an indiscernible expression, but his words were easy to interpret. Well, the *need* was. What exactly Denver wasn't supposed to stop, however, he couldn't figure out. Was he supposed to hold Adam? Push into him? Shove him into the wall again?

Deciding to give that last one a go, Denver drew back enough that he could—somewhat hesitantly—shove Adam back into the wall.

Adam moaned and went slack, his taut ass pushing back against Denver's increasingly interested cock.

"Oh my God," Adam whispered. "Oh my God, that's so hot. I wish you could fuck me right here. Right against this wall."

Denver's cock went from confused to driving the bus in point four seconds. Reaching around, Denver grabbed Adam's junk and used his knee to spread the other man's legs apart. "You like being watched, huh?"

"Safe." Adam's voice was tortured, his cock thickening rapidly beneath his tight jeans. "I like being safe."

Denver laughed. "Being slammed against the wall in the vestibule of a gay bar by a man you can't go home with is safe?"

He realized as soon as the words were out of his mouth that he shouldn't have said them, even before Adam lost some of his softness, self-conscious once more. "I know, I'm strange."

The door opened behind them; Denver shifted closer, shielding Adam as he craned his head to nod the newcomers through. "Maybe. But I kind of dig it."

Adam eased slightly, and when Denver's hands began to roam over sensual territory again, Adam yielded, relaxing deeper than he had before.

Denver nuzzled his ear, nibbling at the soft flesh. "You're careful about who you go home with. That's smart. More guys should be."

Adam closed his eyes, head lolled back onto Denver's shoulder, and when he spoke, his voice was so subdued he almost slurred. "It's not that I don't want you."

"I figured that one out." Denver cupped Adam's erection, teasing his fly undone with his thumb.

"It's just not… safe to be alone with someone like that. That alone and vulnerable."

Had something happened to Adam? Was that why he was so nervous, bopping around like a rabbit? The idea made Denver hot to find whoever had hurt Adam, made him so afraid, and pound them into oblivion. He pulled Adam in tighter, turning his fondling of Adam's cock into a caress. "You tell me what you want, baby. Tell me what is safe, and I'll give it to you."

"This." Adam's hands rose up and back to clutch at Denver's head, knocking at his hat and rubbing against the bristles of his cheeks. "God, this."

"In the hallway, right by the door?"

"Yeah. Against the wall, you behind me. They can see me, but they can't touch me, because you're here. Like with the laundry. You won't let anyone fuck with me."

The words rushed through Denver, making his whole body swell with pleasure, pride. "Just me." He pulled Adam's cock out of his pants and stroked him meaningfully. "I'm going to fuck with you, though. Fuck you, baby. Right into the wall."

"Yes." Adam's hands clutched harder at Denver. He was so lost he was barely there. High on mineral water and Denver. Denver fucking loved it.

"I want to fuck your mouth." Denver growled this into Adam's ear, stroking him harder. "I want you on your knees in front of me, looking up while I fuck that sweet mouth."

Fingernails cut into Denver's neck. "Yes."

God help him, he almost did it right there. It wouldn't be the first time someone had fucked on the main floor, maybe even at the front door. He could have whipped it out and rutted fast, burying into Adam like he was asking for, knocking some good moans out of him so enough people heard to look and admire. The very idea of it filled him with such a rush it made his teeth ache, made him want to turn animal and just do it. But even if Jase wouldn't hang him for it, or the cops, who felt the need to nip in and make sure the world wasn't coming to an end via public exposure, he didn't want people seeing Adam that way. He got the feeling this wasn't something Adam did on a regular basis, and he wasn't sure Adam understood that if Denver fucked him against the wall, others would try to repeat the performance when Denver wasn't around—they'd ask, but again, he just had this feeling that Adam didn't quite know how to play this game.

Adam had decided Denver would protect him, so Denver would. Resisting the urge to fuck him into the wall, at least right here, seemed to fit into that scenario.

He kept Adam snug against him as he walked into the bar, waving at Kevin to get his attention. *Taking a break*, he mouthed, jerking his head at the storeroom.

Kevin paused in midpull of a draft, looked meaningfully at Adam, who was breathing hard with his cock hanging out of his undone pants. Kevin rolled his eyes. But he nodded too, which was all Denver needed. Pushing aside drunken patrons and a few who made approving or jealous sounds as they got a good look at what Denver was doing, Denver covered the distance to the storeroom door.

The harsh fluorescent lights cast Adam in a sickly, pearlescent glow. His hair had been done in that carefully mussed style, but now it was simply mussed. His lips weren't swollen, but they were damp and parted. His eyes weren't bloodshot, but they were unfocused and drunk with lust. No terror, though. Not a drop of fear lit those pretty brown eyes.

Denver ran his thumb over Adam's lip, soaking in the image. Then he placed one of his huge hands on the top of Adam's head, pushed him onto his knees, and gripped his hair, drawing his head back as he pulled out his cock and ran it over those sweet, parted lips.

This was a pretty damn good image too.

WHEN DENVER pushed the hot length of his cock into Adam's mouth, Adam moaned and slid into quiet ecstasy.

He didn't even mind the taste of the latex because all he could think of was how it was Denver's thick, fat cock filling him, fucking deeper and deeper into the back of his throat. That he hadn't had to ask, that Denver had simply whipped a condom out and put it on himself before sliding in farther than the very tip of

Adam's lips—God, it did something primal to Adam.
It made him want to whimper like a dog and suck on
Denver's beautiful hairy balls to show his gratitude.

Adam didn't pull off, but he did whimper. He'd
already figured out that Denver liked whimpers.

"Yeah." Denver's fingers anchored in Adam's hair,
holding so tight it made Adam's eyes water. "Yeah,
baby. Love it when you make noise for me. Show me
how much you like it when I fuck your hot mouth."

Adam moaned again, throwing himself into it this
time so it came out this almost tortured thing through
his nose. It made Denver hiss and thrust so hard he cut
off Adam's air for a second. After a quick convulsion—
you can't gasp when someone has his cock in your
windpipe, it turned out—Adam's next moan turned
into a shivering kind of scream. He also shuddered and
clutched hard at the backs of Denver's thighs. He didn't
even make the move on purpose—he just chased after
that cock and pulled it that deep again.

Denver's rough grunt of approval made Adam
close his eyes, but before he could ride away in pleasure, the grip on his hair jerked, and he looked up. Denver's dark eyes bore down on him.

"Eyes on me."

Adam obeyed, trying to nod, but he couldn't, so he
blinked and fixed his gaze on Denver, watching as he
thrust. In, out. In, out. Adam's lips were strained and
numb from the latex, his tongue sore from pushing hard
against the bottom of the thick rod in his mouth. He felt
so fucked. So beautifully fucked. Like he didn't matter
at all, like he was just a mouth, here to be the place
Denver fucked in and out of. Screw moths, screw his
dissertation. Nothing mattered except that he kept his
eyes up and his mouth open wide. His OCD and most

of his anxiety had checked out and gone to bed, having decided that at least while Denver was in charge, they didn't need to play. They trusted Denver too.

Adam was so relieved and happy he wanted to cry.

"Good boy," Denver murmured, and Adam whimpered again, the emotion behind it coming from the base of his balls. Denver fucked in rhythm, his fingers tight on Adam's scalp. "You like that, huh? When I tell you you're a good boy?"

Adam tried to nod, but he couldn't move, aching with pleasure at his incapacity, and he worked Denver's cock a little harder with his tongue in thanks.

Denver smiled, the hand holding his dick at Adam's lips stealing away to pet his face. "You are a good boy, Adam. You're letting me fuck you real nice. You're so good, you're not leaving this room until you've come so hard you can't stand. You hear me, boy?"

Adam moaned in answer, eyes falling briefly closed in his euphoria. He opened them in a flash, fixing them back on Denver's own. Denver laughed and stroked his cheek.

"Yeah. You're a real good boy." He fucked a few more times, pushing in so deep it almost hurt. Denver's eyes danced with devilry. "Want to do something more for me? Something I'll really enjoy?"

Fingers digging into Denver's thighs, Adam moaned and sucked so hard he saw stars.

He was rewarded with a hand roughing up his hair. "Okay. You said you trust me, which I'm taking seriously. You have to *completely* trust me for this." His fingers never stopped stroking. "You're going to take a breath and open your throat, baby, and I'm gonna fuck way down into it. *Way* down. You won't be able to breathe until I pull out, and I'm gonna stay down there a second, because your throat will spasm around me, and it'll feel really good. Then I'll pull out and you can breathe, and then I'll fuck you again. You're gonna have to focus on me and let go, trusting that I'll take care to let you breathe. It's important you don't panic, because if you do, I'll have to stop fucking your throat." He cupped Adam's cheek. "Say no if you don't want this. Say no if you change your mind during too— I'll give you my hanky to drop, same as the underwear. But if you decide you want this, if you do what I say, open wide, let me fuck you deep and breathe when I pull back, it'll be great for both of us. You think you can do that, baby?"

Adam could hardly hear Denver, because his pulse pounded like a hammer at his ears. The reminder that he barely knew Denver, that he could die while Denver choked him to death with a cock, sent his panic into the ceiling and made his OCD lift its head uneasily. But he clamped on the panic. No. He wanted this. He wanted this so much. He wanted to give this to Denver.

Not for Denver, but for *himself.*

He nodded, got a firmer hold on Denver's meaty thighs, and drew in a full, steadying breath.

Denver grinned, a nasty grin that made Adam's balls ache. "Yeah. Gonna fuck your throat, baby, and then I'll fuck your ass with my mouth." He withdrew a red handkerchief from his back pocket and passed it over. "It's clean. Ball it in your left hand."

Taking the handkerchief, Adam did as he was instructed. The material felt soft and soothing along his skin, and when he squeezed it, it felt like he was holding Denver close.

Adam drew in another breath. Then another. In, out. In, out.

Denver guided himself into the back of Adam's throat, all the way until Adam's nose rubbed into Denver's groin.

"Breathe."

Adam filled his lungs.

"Hold."

Pushing forward, Denver smashed Adam's nose into the hard plane of his body and closed off the airway of his throat. Adam couldn't breathe at all.

His throat did spasm, just like Denver said. He couldn't help it, he kept attempting to swallow and breathe over and over, nothing happening until Denver withdrew with a satisfied groan. Adam's gasp was automatic and noisy, like he was surfacing from a swimming pool. His heart pounded so hard it hurt.

Denver smiled at him, stroking Adam's swollen lips with his dick. "Good job. Think you can do it again?"

Still sucking air, Adam nodded. He could do this. He would do this. His heart beat triple time, but there wasn't any fear, he realized. Only... *excitement*. He tipped his head up, met Denver's eyes, and took a long breath through his nose.

Denver plunged again.

It was almost meditative, being throat-fucked. It was beyond simply holding still while Denver used him—it felt like survival, real survival. It didn't make any sense—he'd have thought his anxiety would be through the roof, but it practically hummed. A *game* of life and death, with someone safe.

Fun. This was *fun.* Emotion surged through him, not panic but need. It held him still, kept him counting the seconds until Denver pulled back, and Adam took good air before the cock closed it off again. It made him so subservient to Denver's fucking that he forgot to think about showing up Brad or to listen for noise from the door. His mother could have walked in and he'd still have focused on clutching that handkerchief and waiting for Denver's cock between breaths.

Denver began to move faster, maybe even a little deeper. "God, that's so fucking hot." He pumped a few more times, then rested at Adam's lips, teasing them while he breathed.

That time Adam had coughed, spitting up a wad of built-up saliva, but he was ready for another round. He wanted it. He needed it.

The hand at his hair kneaded. "You don't have any gag reflex at all. You just sit there waiting for it. Jesus. I'm not going to last, you're so hot. Only way you'd look better is with my cum dripping off your face." Adam moaned. Denver grinned. "Oh yeah? You wanna wear my spunk?" Adam tried to nod, but he couldn't move. Denver thrust deep, and Adam let his eyes unfocus while he waited for another chance for air. "Okay, baby. Gonna pump real hard in a minute, then I'll be ready."

When Denver finally pulled out, Adam's gasp was a sob, and he shook, part from use, part from a kind of pleasure that made him want to collapse on the floor and cry.

Then he felt the first blast, and he held still, waiting for the rest.

Brad had come on him once, on his back, when a condom had broken and Brad had been too impatient to get another. Adam remembered lying there, feeling the hot fluid land on him, cooling instantly, marking him, soiling him. He remembered waiting while Brad got a tissue, Brad bitching about getting it on the sheets.

He'd felt used and branded, and he'd loved it—and he hadn't said a word about it to Brad, nor had he ever found the courage to ask for such treatment again.

Denver came like a geyser, cum glopping out first on Adam's cheek, then his nose, then his mouth and his eyebrow. He shut his eyes tight to protect his vulnerable contacts, but other than that, everything about Denver coming on him turned him on harder than he'd ever been in his life. His own cock throbbed, and he tried to chase after Denver's tip to catch the rest with his tongue, but Denver stopped him. "Kind of defeats the point of you sucking on latex if you eat it, baby."

Adam blinked up at him. He was a little shocked at himself, not just because he'd forgotten and wanted to lick the cum but because he still wanted to, even after being reminded. The thought was arresting. Had he burned his anxiety out? Or did it have a big fat cum fetish?

Denver tucked himself away. He kept smiling down at Adam, looking proud. Not of himself, but of Adam. It made Adam want to purr.

"You did good. Real good. I got rough there at the end, but you took it."

"I loved it," Adam whispered, throat raw.

Denver stroked his hair. "I know." He winked and tugged Adam to his feet. "Come on. Time for the good boy to get his reward."

Adam hadn't had anything to drink but the LaCroix, but he listed and weaved as he followed Denver to what looked like a break room table in the middle of a tower of beer boxes. Adam held up his hands as Denver stripped off his shirt—careful not to disturb the drying cum—and undid his pants all the way, tossing them to the floor. He laid Adam on his back on the table, putting his ankles in his own hands. The gesture opened Adam, his cock bobbing and his clenching ass gaping for Denver's view. Denver smiled down at it in approval.

Then he sat in the chair at the end of the table, lifted Adam's ass in his hands like a loaf of bread, and drew it to his mouth.

Adam cried out as Denver rimmed him, tugging on his ankles and laying himself farther open. Denver grinned over the moon of Adam's upturned ass, shoving his thumbs inside and pulling Adam even wider.

"You look good wearing my cum," Denver observed, working his thumbs in. He paused to bend to Adam's ass and ram his tongue inside, wiggling it and making Adam gasp and cry like someone on a porn shoot. "You look good holding your ass open too. Real good."

Adam made a gurgling sound and felt a spurt of precum leak out of his cock.

Denver's grin made another one follow. "You like dirty talk. I knew that from the laundry, but you *really* like it, don't you. You like having your throat fucked, like having somebody come on your face, like being my late-night snack all sprawled on a table. You're a dirty boy, Adam." He licked the long length of Adam's thigh. "I really, really like dirty boys. I like to eat them right up."

He applied his mouth to Adam's hole once more, and Adam tipped over into some kind of crazy lust state, babbling in tongues, thrusting into Denver's mouth, nearly pulling his legs off in an attempt to open himself wider. Denver drove him further and further to the edge, saying "Mmm" and "Tastes so good, baby, tastes like a good, dirty boy" until Adam thought he might actually come without anyone touching him.

"Tell me what else you like," Denver said when he lifted his head.

"Spanking." The confession tumbled out of Adam on a rasp. "I love spanking."

Denver paused, running fingers over Adam's crack. "I noticed. You get spanked a lot?"

Adam shook his head, squirming as he tried to get Denver to touch him more. "Only by you. But I liked it."

"Difficult to sit down later, was it?"

Adam nodded, his cock leaking as he remembered. "That night and part of the next day too. It was very focusing."

"Should I spank you now?"

Yes, oh, please, yes! "Only if you want to."

Adam gasped as Denver slowly licked the length of Adam's parted crack. "As if I'd ever say no to making these cheeks pink. If I do that, though, I'm going to want to rearrange you again."

A happy purr rolled through Adam. "Then I want you to rearrange me again. Because I only want you to spank me the way that you want to."

Did Denver growl? He might have growled.

What he did do was help Adam off the table and arrange him so that Adam had his hands on the floor, his legs spread, and his ass turned up over Denver's lap. Except Adam's hands weren't precisely on the floor. First Denver produced some sort of butcher paper from a roll and laid it out, telling Adam to put his hands on that. "It's a pretty dirty storeroom."

Adam did, kissing Denver's jean-clad thigh on his way down.

It felt good to lie there, letting Denver massage his backside, cupping his cheeks, fitting his palms against the globes in preparation for the strikes.

"I think tonight, since you were so good, I want to give you a nice reward." Denver began to slap each cheek lightly in rhythm. "One hundred spanks, fifty on each cheek. I'll switch cheeks every five strikes, pausing to finger every ten, and when I resume, it'll get harder. I'll slowly add fingers, up to four. If you can't take four, you'll tell me to stop." He picked up the handkerchief again, this time stuffing it into Adam's mouth. "You'll do that by spitting this out. Nod if you understand."

Adam nodded, heart pounding with excitement and slight apprehension. He'd never taken four, and Denver's fingers were thick.

Denver teased the rim of Adam's hole. "The lube I have here will really help. It might make you feel a little dirty inside, because it's thick. That okay?"

Dirty. Groaning into the handkerchief, Adam nodded enthusiastically.

"Excellent. I'll get started, then. I'll count, since you can't. *One.*"

Closing his eyes, Adam relaxed his body and gave himself over to the blows. He didn't let himself marvel about how surprising it was that he liked spanking this time; he didn't want to take any of his focus from this feeling. God, but it was glorious. The burn wasn't there yet, only the sharp sting, but Adam knew the burn would come.

One hundred. He was pretty sure he'd feel this session far longer than he had the last one.

When the first round of spanking stopped and Denver slipped his index finger inside, Adam huffed, pushing reflexively against the invasion. Denver hadn't been lying—there was something thick inside him now,

thick and wet, moving all around as he wriggled his
finger.

Adam whimpered and clenched as Denver withdrew, then took a sharp breath as the second round of
spankings came, harder as promised.

Denver ran his free hand lovingly down Adam's
spine as he continued to deliver the spankings. When
he added the second finger, he spoke over Adam's
whimpers and squirms. "You're so pleasing. I hadn't
meant to do half of what I'm doing to you, not yet, but
you're so obedient and ask so nicely to be done, I can't
help myself. You're hot, honey."

Even if Adam would have known what to say to
that, he couldn't, not with the gag in his mouth. That
turned him on even more, and as the third round started, he felt like he was unfolding into some new level
of pleasure he hadn't known existed, layers of his skin
peeling off and sending him into space, powered by the
sensations Denver delivered to his ass.

Adam never spit out the gag. The fourth finger was
rough, but something about that only fueled him more.
The pain burned every nerve ending, white fire that
danced in his toes and fingertips. Tears streamed down
his face, and his cock was so hard he thought he'd come
any second.

Best of all was that Denver had started talking
dirty—so incredibly dirty. "You're unleashed now,
boy. Look at you go. I sure as hell am looking at you.
Ass as red as an apple. Greedy hole stuffed full of my
fingers. I can feel that thick cock against my leg, ready
to pop because this has turned you on so much. What
a night you had. Pushed against a wall. Throat-fucked,
then sat there as I came on your face. Held yourself
open so I could eat you out. Now you're getting good

and fingered while I make your ass so red you'll be sleeping on your stomach and standing for a good two days. You're nice and slutty, Adam Ellery. A good, obedient slut. Would you like to come now, my good, slutty boy?"

Groaning around the gag, Adam nodded enthusiastically.

Shifting his legs, Denver made it so Adam's cock hung free, but also so he had better access to Adam's nipple, which he rolled between his fingers. "I'll do the last ten now, and when I hit one hundred, I want you to come. Come as hard as you can, keeping the gag in your mouth."

These blows were so intense each one stole Adam's breath, but the sharp pinches and tugs on his nipple helped him focus, carrying him toward the end, sending jolts of pleasure to his cock so that when Denver hit one hundred, Adam orgasmed automatically, jerking and thrashing until Denver thrust into his hole again, pressing against his prostate and anchoring him at once.

"Good boy," Denver soothed Adam as he drifted back to earth, smoothing lotion over Adam's tender skin. "You did such a good job. I wish I had my camera handy so I could show you how pretty you look, your ass all red, lube leaking out of it, your legs spread open and trembling." He kept tracing circles across Adam's ass and lower back. "You'd look good with a dildo in your mouth too. I'd love to truss you up, plug every hole. Dildo in your mouth, plug in your ass, and tie your legs open. Take a good look at you before I spanked all that lovely skin."

Adam's heart raced as he absorbed the wicked litany Denver described. He'd never done anything like that, had barely fantasized such things until the night at the laundromat. This was a brand-new door inside him, a secret place he hadn't so much as considered he could explore before.

No way could this be the end.

Much as he wanted to vocalize this thought, Adam couldn't move, let alone speak. Even when Denver hoisted him up and repositioned him so he straddled Denver's thighs—carefully, so as to not rest on his reddened ass—even then Adam's best effort was to gaze imploringly at Denver as he allowed his arms to be draped around the other man's neck.

Smiling, Denver removed the gag from Adam's mouth. He traced Adam's bottom lip with his finger. "Can I kiss you?"

Adam nodded and leaned forward, aiming for Denver's face.

Denver captured him, sucking on first the lower lip, then the upper, coating them with moisture the gag had taken away. When he delved inside, he ran his tongue along the inside of Adam's lip too, then the upper, and then, finally, he tangled with Adam's tongue, thrusting alongside it, mimicking what he'd done with his cock. Without thinking, Adam made his tongue flat and went pliant so Denver's tongue could fuck him better.

When Denver broke away, he kissed Adam's nose as he stroked his cheek tenderly. "You're something else, moth man." Denver continued to touch Adam's face. "I'm going to call you a cab. You think you can get yourself dressed?"

Adam considered this, then nodded. "In a minute." He'd have liked an hour to lie there feeling fucked-out, but he supposed that wasn't very practical.

Denver's fingers strayed to Adam's hair. "I work late most nights. But maybe sometime we could meet for an afternoon? Or something?"

Adam tried to reach for Denver's shoulder, but he couldn't make his hand lift higher than the other man's elbow. "Or something."

CHAPTER SEVEN

DENVER HAD to work early Thursday night, which meant it was still light out when he locked the door of his apartment. It was a gorgeous Colorado fall day, so he planned to walk, but it was chilly too, so he carried along a jacket. When he came out into the main room after hanging his coat in the back, Jase was bartending for the spotty afternoon crowd. He took one look at Denver and glared, folding his arms over his chest.

Denver chuckled and tipped his hat forward in a salute as he straddled a barstool. "Afternoon, boss."

Jase rolled his eyes and leaned on the bar after he passed Denver a tall glass of tap water and a bowl of popcorn. "I hope you at least disinfected the table after."

Whatever. Denver grinned around the rim of the water glass. "You can dock my pay for the half hour if you want."

"What's this?" one of the customers demanded. It was Rob, an older gentleman Denver was pretty sure used to teach at Tucker University. He had no hair left except for a ring of gray and a wispy white tuft in the back that stood straight up, making him look like a wrinkled elf. A wicked one at the moment, his eyes lit with hope of scandal.

Jase jerked a thumb at Denver. "The Hulk here left his shift at one to go fuck the living hell out of a twink in the storeroom last night."

"Wish I'd have seen it," a second old man said. He looked almost wistful.

"Next time I'll send someone in to take pictures. Maybe I should take Den off the door and hire him to do peep shows with his tricks."

Denver laughed and played along with the ribbing, but when Kevin showed up at eight and Jase went back to his office, Denver followed and hung in the doorframe until Jase looked up at him.

"Hey, Jase—could you do me a favor?" He jerked his head at the main room. "If Adam—the guy I had in the storeroom—comes back in, could you save your ribbing for me and spare him?" He wanted to explain why, but he didn't have the words, so he left it at that.

Jase's eyebrows went up. "Damn. So there *was* somebody you wanted a day off for, huh?"

"Adam's kind of special." He rubbed his chin, frowning. "I mean, he's smart as fuck. He's a grad student studying moths. But he's—" He cut himself off, lost again. Not shy. Skittish? Goddamn, this was why Denver stuck to weights.

"Special to you." Jase smiled. "I get it. You might want to talk to Kevin, though. He enjoyed spreading your story."

"Story's fine. I just don't want anyone making Adam uncomfortable, because it's easier to do than you think. But yeah, I'll tell Kevin to give Adam space."

"Your boy coming back tonight? As much as I don't mind your backroom adventure as a one-off, I'd prefer you kept your extracurriculars to your house as a general rule." Winking, Jase waved him away. "Go man the door. Oh—and by the way, you're clear for Sunday, if you still want that day off."

It wasn't a bad evening—Thursday nights were frat boy night by some official decree, drawing the gay house at Tuck U and the stragglers from the others at both campuses. It always blew Denver's mind that any frat boys could be openly gay. Not that he was ever even remotely lined up for Greek life, period, but still. A lot of these guys' straight buddies came with them on frat night, out of solidarity or extreme reverse machismo. Those latter were easy to spot, as they ended up hanging out with him at the door, assuming he was straight since he was stacked. That was always a good time, because eventually Denver would hit on them and make them freak out.

Though every so often he got laid that way. He wasn't sure if there were more gay men per square inch now in the younger generations or if they were just curious.

He had a few fish on his line that night, a bicurious tagalong to one of the frats and a sweet bubble-butt, dark-haired twink that normally would have had his crank going hard, but Denver kept holding out hope Adam would show up, and no way was he having hamburger when he could have steak. Adam stayed away, though, and he didn't text or phone either. So on Friday morning after a late breakfast but before his workout,

Denver did something he'd never done before, not since leaving Oklahoma City.

He called first.

He'd considered texting, but he couldn't figure out what the hell to say. Dirty come-ons were the only thing he could think of, and they didn't feel right. Not yet.

"This is Denver," he said, when Adam answered with a hesitant hello. "How you doing?"

"Hey." At the brightness in Adam's tone, Denver relaxed. "I'm good. What about you?"

"Not bad. About to go work out, but thought I'd check up on you. Busy with moths, are you?"

"Yeah. A project is due this afternoon. I was all set to be done last night, but the data got corrupted." He sounded frustrated and a little anxious.

"Don't let me keep you if you're busy."

"Oh no, it's fine, really. I need to take a break or I'll go nuts."

A pause stretched out, and Denver wasn't sure how to fill it. "Well, good," he ventured after a minute.

"So. What are you doing today?" Adam asked.

"Hitting the gym, then laundry late this afternoon, unless El comes and we go after he closes the shop. Then work at nine."

"Laundry. I wanted to go this morning, but I'm stuck here now. And I don't want to run into those frat boys again."

"Come when I go," Denver offered. An innuendo rose to his lips, but he let it pass. He wasn't sure quite why either.

"God, you have no idea how much I'd love to, and not just because you're starting to make all utility tables erotic. But I don't know when I'll be done. It might not be until after dinner."

"Well, I can go tomorrow too. No big."

"Except tomorrow I have to work in the insectary." He sighed. "It's okay. I'll rinse out some shorts in my sink."

Denver thought furiously. "How about I bring you some dinner before I head to work? I'll text about six to see where you are and come by with some takeout at seven."

"Oh gosh. That would be awesome, but I don't want to put you out."

Denver rolled his eyes at the ceiling. "It ain't putting me out. I gotta eat too, you know. Besides. I want to see you."

He panicked a little at that, thinking it sounded too needy or weird, but it must have been good, because Adam went all soft and gooey. "You do? You want to see me?"

"Well, yeah. I been dying to hear how the moth stuff turns out."

Adam laughed. "I bet you are. Okay, I'll look for your text at six. That ought to motivate me to get my crap done, if anything will."

"Sounds good. Talk to you then."

When Denver hung up, he was grinning from ear to ear, and the smile still lingered when he got to the gym.

FOR ADAM, the worst part of needing to redo the data he'd lost was that it meant having to spend the day with Brad.

He didn't want to be one of those in their group, one of the exes who made everything difficult by refusing to be in the room with his old boyfriend, and he'd been working hard not to end up in that place by simply removing himself from the equation most of the time.

Like doing his data late last night so he could turn it in immediately Friday morning. The problem was Brad kept wanting to talk things through, to make them okay, and Adam didn't want to be okay. He wanted his space, because so many things about what had gone wrong with Brad were snarls inside his head. He couldn't tell what he was justified to feel and where he was being a princess.

The entire time the two of them were in the lab together Friday, all Brad did was create more of those snarls in Adam's head.

"I'm not attempting to get us back together, but we need closure on this." Brad leaned over Adam's workstation, putting his hand on Adam's notes. "Come on, hon. I still care about you."

"Right now what I care about is this data." Adam shoved Brad away and glared at the columns of numbers, willing himself to focus so he could plug them back into the spreadsheet.

"It's not due until midnight."

"Well, maybe I have things to do before midnight."

Brad snorted. "What, laundry?"

Adam's ears heated, and he kept his eyes on his computer screen. Brad probably didn't mean to sound as smug as Adam perceived him to be, but Adam couldn't help it. He hated feeling like the loser Brad was trying to mother. "If you must know, I planned to go out."

The thrill of Brad's surprise was worth the lie. "Out where? I know you don't have a date."

"You know, do you? Because I'm so pathetic?"

"Because I know you, Adam. Better sometimes I think than you know yourself." He pushed a stool into

Adam's thighs. "You've stood all day long. Your legs have to be killing you. Sit down."

Brad nudged the stool hard enough to buckle Adam's legs, forcing him to sit. Adam's tender ass touched the stool for a few seconds, then popped off it again, and Adam only barely managed to swallow his hiss. "I prefer to stand." He could sit on something soft, but not these stools. If Brad weren't around, he might indulge himself so he could explore the uncomfortable squirming sensation, but that was absolutely *not* something Brad got to witness.

Sighing in annoyance, Brad plunked down on a stool across the table from him. "Seriously. You act like we aren't even friends anymore. Any of us."

Maybe it was petty, but Adam didn't want to be friends with Brad. "I just need some space and some time. Okay?"

Brad frowned. "You didn't have to move out of the house to get that, you know. I still can't believe you're over there in that skanky complex."

"It's actually very nice, mostly. And yes I did have to move out, because this is your idea of giving me space. Now, come on. I really do have to finish this."

Brad pursed his lips, a pouty gesture Adam used to find adorable and now drove him nuts. "Trying to talk about what happened isn't failing to give you space. Neither is pointing out that someone with clinical anxiety and OCD shouldn't go off and live on his own."

"I am not two steps from a fucking institution."

"No. But I've seen you have panic attacks because the cereal was out of order. You shouldn't be on your own."

Adam had to physically hold himself back from crumpling his notes into a frustrated ball. "Brad, fuck off."

"Fine. I'm fucking off. I'll just let you sit here and obsess over your lab data before you rush off to your plans."

He said he was leaving, but Brad lingered, nostrils flaring, his tight brown-black curls quaking with his indignation before he rose from the stool and flounced off. He really did flounce, queening out as only Brad could.

Once he was out of sight, Adam let himself sink forward, his forehead falling to the center of the table. He breathed in for a minute, trying to shut out the feelings of guilt and recrimination Brad had stirred, as well as the confusion.

That's why I can't be around you. Because I can't tell where you're right and where you're wrong. And I'm starting to be afraid if I don't figure it out now, I never will.

CHAPTER EIGHT

WHEN DENVER finally arrived at Warren Hall with two bags of Thai takeout, it was almost seven thirty, which was half an hour later than he'd told Adam he'd be there. He'd made it to campus on time, yeah, but he'd neglected to factor in searching fifteen minutes for a parking spot and having to haul ass across the green to get to the biological sciences campus. The delay put him off his game, but even on time he would have felt uneasy in this place.

A guy who never finished high school probably wasn't supposed to feel at home on a college campus.

What really goosed him, though, was that East Cent was supposed to be the "friendly" campus. There were two universities in Tucker Springs: John D. Tucker University, the private school where all the mind-bogglingly rich children of Colorado and elsewhere went, and Eastern Centennial State University, the land-grant college. As a college Tuck U wasn't known for much beyond their jazz program, though locally its campus was considered a great place to get looked down upon. East Cent was friendly. East Cent hosted community fairs and folk fests. East Cent let the public use their community gym for a small fee, including their swimming pool.

East Cent was still a university, though, full of smart young people being, well, smart. On the way over to Warren Hall, Denver passed two rallies (one for the New Libertarians campus group, and another by raw vegans, whatever those were) and overheard more fifty-dollar words than he knew existed. Two young men Denver would have pegged as total preening twinks were having a heated discussion about Kant verses Jung but stopped to openly drool over a well-endowed sorority princess as she passed by. Even the flyers on the bulletin boards were intimidating.

He felt too big too, which was not something he normally experienced. Usually his size, which he'd worked hard to achieve, made him feel safer and more secure. Not on East Cent's campus. Here his size made him feel freakish and strange, even more of an interloper than he already was.

Denver tried to be inconspicuous as he navigated the maze of corridors to the entomology department, though the fact that he had to keep checking his phone to follow the directions Adam had given him didn't help any. When he finally arrived at the green lab door marking his journey's end, Denver schooled his expression, determined to be easy and light.

Pushing the door open, he came face-to-face with a tall, lanky young man with olive skin and tight curly hair whose nostrils flared at the sight of Denver. "Can I help you?" he demanded in a tone that made it quite clear he had no intention of helping Denver in any way at all.

Even with his hands full of takeout and cell phone, Denver could have snapped the guy in half without a moment's thought, but still he cringed inwardly. "Looking for Adam Ellery."

The man softened slightly. "Oh. I had no idea Thai Kitchen had started a delivery service." He got out his wallet. "How much?"

Jesus H. "Uh." Denver glanced down at the bags in his hands, as if they might contain a way out of this conversation. "Paid for already. He in here?"

The dark-haired man rolled his eyes and held out his hands. "I'll take them to him."

Whether it was one push too far or what, Denver couldn't be sure, but he pulled the bags out of the boy's reach and treated him to the look he saved for guys with pathetically obvious fake IDs. "Adam?" he called out a little louder. "You in here, babe?"

It was a particular pleasure to see his tormentor's eyes go wide and his mouth gape open at *babe*, but it wasn't anything compared to Adam himself coming around the corner. Adam beamed, transforming from harried ball of nerves to blushing beauty at the sight of Denver.

"Oh, hi! Sorry, I'd been watching for you but got caught up in something. Come on back."

The dark-haired guy appeared to be choking on his own tongue. "Adam. Is this some kind of joke?"

Adam instantly went back to harried and upset. "What are you talking about, Brad? I'm not joking. I'm eating dinner. And I thought you said forty-five minutes ago you were leaving."

Brad aimed a finger at Denver. "That. That is a joke."

Before Denver could even think how to react, Adam went red-faced. "Oh my God. Brad, get out. Seriously, get the fuck out of here."

"He called you babe."

Denver raised his eyebrows at Adam, who seemed to be discovering new levels of mortification. With his dinner companion too paralyzed to speak, Denver stepped in and addressed Brad. "You jealous, sweetheart?"

It really was a pleasure to watch Brad sputter, but Adam clearly wasn't much happier. With a nod to Brad, Denver navigated around him and shifted the bags so he could put a hand on Adam's waist. "Food's getting cold. Show me where to put it down."

Though he was ready for another round with Brad, the other man left in a flurry of muttering, meaning Adam and Denver were alone in the lab.

"I'm so sorry." Adam's cheeks were still aflame. "I had no idea he would be such an ass. I can't believe I ever dated him."

"Ah. An ex. Now everything makes sense."

"Not just an ex. *The* ex." Adam was a study in shades of blushing today; currently he was blotchy scarlet. "He's the only other guy I've ever dated or been with, period."

Why the hell that bummed Denver out, he wasn't quite sure. A joke to soften the blow escaped him, so he busied himself laying out the cartons and to-go flatware. "Did you get your project finished?"

"Yes, but something about it feels off. I'm turning it in anyway, but I'll never forgive that server for failing me." He leaned over the counter, looking at the spread of food with naked lust. "God, I could just put my face in this. I never did get lunch."

"Well, dig in," Denver encouraged, and Adam did.

He didn't relax as they ate, though, looking like a spring ready to go off. "I can't believe what an ass Brad was. I'm so sorry."

"I take it he doesn't like that you left him."

"That's just it. He broke up with me. Well… actually, it's complicated. He broke up with me, but I moved out." His blush crept back up his neck. "Sorry. You don't need to hear my petty drama."

They'd lived together? Denver hated this more every second. "Don't people normally move out when they break up?"

"Oh—no, we didn't live together. Not like that. A bunch of guys from the entomology department share a house over on Finlay Avenue." Adam had been wolfing his curry, but now he stopped to glare at the container of drunken noodles between them. "I moved out because I couldn't stand being in the same house with Brad, but in some ways he's more annoying now than before I left. You'd think I was his son, not his ex." Adam tossed down his fork. "The worst part is I know he means well. And I begged for this in a way, because I always let him manage things for me, before. But I don't want it now, and I have no idea how to turn it off."

Denver had no idea what to say to this. He knew what he wanted to say: that Brad should fuck off. With a sideways broom handle. Obviously he couldn't say *that*, however. He tried to think of what El or Jase would say, to channel that instead, but he couldn't figure that out either.

Adam kept going, caught up in his tirade. "I want to be independent. I know it must look weird, me being me and moving off on my own. And yes, some days it's very hard. But it feels good. Doesn't that mean it's okay? It should. Except sometimes spending four hours scrubbing the already immaculate floor of my closet feels good, and there's nothing admirable about that."

The conversation seemed to be taking on levels Denver wasn't sure he was qualified for, but he tried his best. "Look, I met Brad for five minutes and I can tell you, he's an ass. You aren't. Getting away from him can't be all bad."

"I'm such a mess, though." Adam, head bowed, glanced guiltily over at Denver. "You have no idea. I keep waiting for you to see even part of it and run screaming." He pushed hair out of his eyes. "I know we're just fooling around. But I really like you. You're fun. I don't feel like I'm a mess when I'm with you." His eyes hooded a little. "Plus you make me feel hot. Like, seriously fucking smoking. With Brad I felt like a clumsy fish. You tell me to bend over, and it's like everything in me lets go. I wish I could feel like that all the time. Either that or have sex with you twenty-four seven."

That made Denver grin, but not much because he didn't like how out of sorts Adam was. "You're too hard on yourself. Everybody's a mess one way or another. Everybody's got dirty laundry they don't want other people to see. The trick is figuring out how to not care about it. Make peace with it, accept it as part of who you are."

Adam snorted and dug into the noodles. "You sound like my old therapist in Ames." He twirled his fork thoughtfully in the carton. "He'd like you, I think."

"Good. 'Cause I like you for more than just fooling around." That felt so bald he reached for a dumpling to cover his awkwardness. "So. Washing your shorts in the sink tonight?"

"I guess." Adam said this with extreme derision. "God help me, all I want to do is get drunk."

Denver bumped him with his elbow. "You can, you know. It's still legal. It's also Friday night. Long tradition there."

"Yes, but getting drunk at home alone is too pathetic even for me."

"So come to Lights Out. Get drunk and let me watch, and I'll make sure you get home."

Adam seemed to consider the idea a moment before shaking his head. "I can't stay out that late. I have to get up at seven in the morning to work in the lab."

"Then I'll get you home by midnight, Cinderella."

"How? You can't leave work."

Denver paused with a fork halfway to his mouth and lifted his eyebrow at Adam.

Adam eased back down. "Sorry."

"I could leave work, but I was thinking more along the lines of calling a friend of mine and his boyfriend to hang out with you. You'd like Paul especially, I think. It would probably be a relief to El, because Paul's studying for some vet tech thing and driving El up and down the walls. They could both use some time away. What do you say?"

He said all this casually, like he wasn't going to keep shifting the deal until Adam said yes. He couldn't say why he was so attached to the idea of Adam coming out tonight, of watching him get drunk. He knew he couldn't fuck him this time, not at work. He didn't care. He wanted Adam there, even for a while.

He had no idea what any of this meant. And he was determined not to think about it.

Adam bit his bottom lip, then nodded. "Okay. But I'll take a cab home."

The hell he would. But Denver didn't feel like arguing that right now, so he smiled and pointed to Adam's plate. "Finish up, and we'll head out."

IT WAS dumb, Adam knew, but he was nervous all the way over to his apartment, even though Denver made it clear he was staying in the car. Still, he had himself ramped into a frenzy, which was why when Denver spoke, he had to ask him to repeat himself.

With more patience than Adam deserved, Denver said, "Bring out the things you need washed for tomorrow. We'll run them in the bar's washing machine while you're drinking."

Okay, so he'd heard him. The problem was Denver wasn't making any sense. "What? You can't do that."

Denver leaned over the console between the seats and looked Adam in the eye. "Get the clothes you need washed and get dressed for a night out. I'll call El while you're gone."

He turned back to the steering wheel, fishing his phone out of his pocket and punching in a text, pretty much ignoring Adam. With not much else left to do, Adam got out of the car and walked, somewhat dazed, into his apartment building.

That Denver hadn't tried to come in had thrown him. He'd been going back and forth the whole time about whether or not he should let him, mostly telling himself he should get over his idiocy and just be human for a change. It wasn't like Denver was going to jump him, and if he did, it'd be in a way Adam wholly approved of. The idea of Denver not even asking was weird. Good, he was pretty sure, but off-putting.

He obsessed over Denver staying in the car the whole time he showered and changed clothes. What did it mean? Was it because of what he'd said about not liking to take guys home? How had he known it was because he couldn't stand to have anyone in the house, period, who didn't live there? Had Denver figured that out? Had someone told him? Did it show?

Maybe Denver didn't know he planned to take a shower and wouldn't be just a few minutes. Maybe Denver would knock on the door in the middle of Adam's shower or while he was getting dressed, and when Adam acted like a freak at the door, he'd get disgusted and change his mind about being with him.

Adam moved in double time, going as fast as his neuroses would allow.

On his third pass through the apartment to make sure all his appliances were off, everything unplugged, he spied his laundry hamper in the corner. It was overflowing, which was upsetting enough, but then he imagined what would happen if he went out to Denver's truck without a bag of clothes to wash.

Five minutes later he emerged, plastic bag full of underwear, socks, and a T-shirt he could stomach being washed with whites in hand. The look on Denver's face as he lifted his head from his cell phone—gaze going right to that bag—told Adam he'd been right to bring the clothes.

"You really don't have to wash them," he said as he got in the car. Images of dirty, filthy basements and scum-stained laundry machines swam in his head.

"I know. But I want to. Jase won't mind. I've done it before, and I'll just tell him it's my stuff." He glanced at Adam, a whisper of a smile at his lips. "You nervous about me handling your underwear?"

Well, now that he brought it up, that wasn't his favorite thing either. He should have gone with that, but he was nervous about the evening, nervous about getting drunk with strangers, nervous about why Denver hadn't tried to come into his apartment, and so he told the truth. "Actually—I hope you're not mad—I'm kind of one of those neat freaks. I know it sounds dumb, but is it a clean machine? In a clean area?"

"Cleaner than that damn laundromat we met in. Jase is pretty much a stickler for cleanliness in general."

Adam relaxed a little. A lot, to be honest. "Okay." He cast a quick glance at Denver. "Thanks."

"Not a problem." He shifted his grip on the steering wheel, keeping his eyes on the road. "Can't imagine it's easy, working that hard at school. Grad school no less. They should give you guys maids or something."

"God, I wish. More like we're the maids." He eased into his seat. "A friend of mine is doing a residency at a hospital in Denver. His day makes my schedule look like a cakewalk. Another friend of mine is on his way to getting his doctorate in pharmacy. Once he took some all-day test, and in the middle of it he called his girlfriend and broke down on the phone. He was so nuts she called 911. The professor was angry, said they'd disrupted the test."

"Jesus."

"Yeah." Denver had the windows down, and Adam rested his arm on the door, drinking in the cool evening air. "My profs aren't quite that crazy, but they definitely have the ivory tower going. The only thing in the world they pay attention to is school. Which kind of bothers me. I'd thought I wanted to go into academia, but it's not what I imagined it was going to be. Too much politics, too many power plays."

"What is it you want to do when you're done?"

"I don't know yet. Maybe something in research for a company. Except I don't want to end up working for Monsanto or somewhere like that."

"How close are you to being finished?"

"That's always the big question when you're a doctoral student. At this point it's whenever I'm done with my dissertation. Hopefully within a year, but we'll see. I still have plenty of research to gather, let alone organize and write up."

Denver shook his head. "And you wonder why you get stressed out. I never worked like that in my life. Couldn't if my life depended on it."

Adam's focus shifted to Denver's bulging muscles. "I couldn't work out like you do. You must spend hours at it." The mental image made his cock swell. "God, I bet that's hot."

This made Denver laugh. "Well say the word, and I'll get you a front-row seat."

"Don't tempt me." Adam smiled too. "Seriously, do you work out every day?"

He nodded. "I do a rotation of things, some at home, some at the gym."

"Does it get boring?"

"Naw. Feels good. I've always been one of those guys who has to move and use his body. I'd go bananas behind a desk."

"No, you'd turn into the Hulk and tear the desk apart. Which, for the record, would also be hot."

Denver's hand stole over and rested on Adam's thigh. "So my muscles turn you on, baby?"

Adam let his knee fall into the console, giving Denver better access. "Oh yeah. I bet you could bench-press me."

Denver's hand crept higher, massaging the crease of Adam's leg at his groin. "Little thing like you? Wouldn't break a sweat."

At this point Adam's cock pressed into Denver's hand. "I wish you didn't have to work."

"Me too, baby. Me too." Denver palmed Adam through his jeans. "I'm off Sunday."

Adam mentally indexed his schedule. "I'd have to stop by the lab for a few hours in the morning, but other than that, it's only me and the endless dissertation notes." And cleaning his apartment, and the rest of his laundry. Which he did have to do, or his OCD would ensure he had hell to pay. He'd make time for Denver somehow, though. He had to. It was practically therapy.

Denver's thumb rubbed insistently against the hard ridge of Adam's cock. "It's a date, then. You keep this bad boy ready for me."

Just that touch had Adam nearly ready to pop. "That's not going to be a problem."

AT THE bar, Adam intended to politely decline hanging out with Denver's friends. He'd make small talk for a few minutes before giving an excuse to leave. Once again, however, reality did not fall in line with his plans. To start, Denver wasn't working the door like last time but was tending bar—upstairs. Adam hadn't even known there was an upstairs. It was very nice, actually, old and beautiful with a gorgeous balcony patio, and this was where Denver's friends took him to sit. They didn't let him dribble some small talk and escape either.

"So you're in entomology?" This came from Paul, a slender strawberry-blond white man around Adam's age with eyes like a lost puppy. He made Adam feel calm just looking at him.

"Yes. I'm doing my dissertation on hawk moths."

El, lean, lanky, and moderately muscled, was Latino, and far more assertive than his boyfriend. He raised his eyebrows as he propped his feet up on an unused chair. "Those sound scary."

"Oh, they aren't," Adam assured him, and before he knew it, he'd wandered into a monologue on his favorite subject.

Paul and El humored him, but it was clear they didn't find it all as fascinating as Denver had. Eventually El led them into a new conversation. "You from Colorado originally?"

"Yes. Sterling, though I finished high school in Iowa and my parents are in Minneapolis now." Adam stirred his gin and tonic. "What about the two of you?"

El leaned an elbow on the table. "Born and bred Tucker Springs. Paul hails from Nebraska."

"Oh." Adam didn't know what to say after that, and he started to worry about the lull in conversation, but Paul picked it up.

"So you and Denver are dating?"

Adam blinked, unsure of how to answer. *Were* they dating? "I—maybe?"

El laughed and shifted in his chair. "They're dating."

Adam couldn't help noticing El kept fussing with a bar napkin and that he had nicotine patches all over his arms.

A loud shout at the bar drew Adam's attention. Heart skipping a beat, Adam saw Denver balancing a shot glass on his bulging left biceps while a highly inebriated man tried to grab it with his mouth.

"Feel like doing a shot?" El asked, his tone dripping wickedness.

"Oh yes," Adam whispered.

The next thing he knew, he was propelled toward the bar. To his surprise, Denver hesitated before he'd perform the trick for him.

"You're on your second gin and tonic, yeah?" He frowned at Adam, measuring him with his gaze. "How much does it take to get you wasted? I don't want you to go to your gig all hungover tomorrow."

The idea that Denver was tracking his consumption moved Adam and made him feel protected and calm deep inside. He smiled. "I know it sounds weird, but if I stick to hard liquor and get plenty of water, I'm usually fine."

"All right. One shot, and you're drinking two big glasses of water between every G&T from now on."

"Okay." Adam gripped the bar, gaze glued to Denver's guns, wondering if he could get a few licks in too.

He needn't have worried. Denver leaned over the bar, propping up his muscled arm as he had before, but when Adam got ready for the shot, Denver shook his head and waved him back.

"Nope. You're doing a different kind." He waved at the patrons to Adam's left. "Clear out, boys. Adam here's gonna do a Murphy."

The bar erupted in oohs and catcalls, and as the men emptied the barstools, Denver slapped the bar and motioned to Adam. "Up you come. On your belly."

Adam's pulse pounded as he climbed up to lay down as instructed. He felt strangely exposed and instantly aroused, especially when Denver's arm moved scant inches from his face. "Oh God," he whispered.

"Hands in your back pockets," Denver instructed, and once Adam had his palms cupping his own ass, Denver's hand rested on the curve of Adam's right ass cheek, massaging him openly to the delight of the room. "Now. Joe here's going to set up the shot, and all you gotta do is lift your head and grab it with your mouth."

Adam quickly learned this was easier said than done. Denver had—he assumed—deliberately kept his arm far enough away that no matter how Adam strained, he couldn't quite reach it. Once he came close, but only succeeded in getting peach schnapps spilled all over his face, which made the room erupt in laughter.

"You got something on your lips," Denver commented and bent down to Adam's face.

Adam vowed he'd spill all his shots after that, because Denver licked every drop of schnapps off his mouth, nose, chin, and lifted Adam's head by the hair to get at his neck. The room went wild, and normally it would have made Adam feel uneasy. But Denver was right here. Adam felt safer than he'd ever felt in his life.

"Let me move you closer," Denver said as Joe set up the second shot, and Adam gasped, then groaned as Denver pressed firmly into his perineum under the guise of pushing him forward. He kept his fingers there too, making a show of holding him in place by massaging the back of his balls until he spilled the second shot on himself too.

This happened again during the third and fourth rounds, but on the fifth Denver actually steadied him, and Adam successfully grabbed the rim of the glass with his teeth, tipped his head back, and downed the shot. The room erupted in cheers, and Denver helped Adam off the bar.

"Water time," he said, patting Adam's butt.

"Yes, sir," Adam replied half in a daze. He cast a longing look at Denver, wishing like hell the man wasn't working so he could ravish him in some dark corner. Or a lit corner. Adam really didn't care.

Instead he was hauled back to the patio with El, Paul, and a tall glass of water. Paul beamed at him and chatted about how fun that looked, but El studied Adam so intensely eventually Adam gave in and asked him what was wrong.

"Nothing," El said at last. "Just thinking it all finally makes sense." He absently touched a nicotine patch on his shoulder. "Be good to him, would you?"

Adam thought that comment made no sense, but he didn't argue, only nodded and took a big drink of his water, because he could see Denver watching him out of the corner of his eye.

CHAPTER NINE

ADAM NEVER got to make out with Denver Friday night, which was disappointing, but Denver did feel his ass up before nudging him into El and Paul's car to be taken home. He also reminded him to be ready for Sunday and handed Adam a department store sack of clean, folded laundry. Adam had leaned out the window, aching as he watched him disappear.

He'd gotten to bed without trouble, though, and wasn't terribly hungover in the morning, and as an extra bonus, he had clean underwear. In a better mood than he'd thought he'd be, Adam dressed and hauled himself to campus.

Brad didn't have to work the insectary that Saturday, but Adam knew he'd see his ex at some point during the day. Sure enough, Brad appeared just after Adam's shift ended as he went to the Quadrangle dorm cafeteria for a late lunch. Brad was in the lounge of the Quad, talking intensely with several of the Bug Boys, but when he saw Adam, he broke away to stalk over full of righteous indignation.

"What the hell, Adam. What. The. Hell."

"I'm hungry, and I'm going to lunch." Adam sidestepped Brad and continued toward the cafeteria. "If you want to have public hysterics, you'll have to follow me."

"It's not just me, you know." Brad clomped up the steps after him. "The whole house is talking about it. We're worried about you."

They were worried? This got Adam to pause and turn around. "Why? What's there to be worried about?" That was his weakest defense, and Brad knew it. *What danger is there to worry about that I've overlooked?*

Brad folded his arms over his chest. "We're worried about your *inappropriate* relationship."

Adam snorted and started walking again. "So everyone's worried because I'm getting laid."

"By a fucking *Neanderthal.*"

Adam turned around again, out of patience. "He's not a Neanderthal because he's cut. Stop being a snob."

Brad's nostrils flared. "He's not your type."

"Why, because he's not you? Jesus, when did you turn into such a self-centered ass? You were my first for a lot of reasons, but I'm not going to pine over you for the rest of my life."

"You've been weird ever since you moved out. Are you having some kind of breakdown? Not that I'd be able to tell, because you won't return my calls or let me come over. You're probably staying up late lining up your silverware and double-checking your shoelaces are still tucked in."

A low blow, delivered at too high of a volume and in too public of a place. Adam resisted the urge to look around to see who was listening. "I don't let anyone come over. And I'm not having a breakdown. I'm doing well, except for the fact that you keep stalking me, insisting I'm not."

"I'm not stalking you. I care about you." A hitch caught in Brad's voice, and a sheen of tears cut through his anger. "I didn't break up with you because I didn't love you or didn't want you anymore. I broke up with you because you won't address your mental illness."

Adam knew people were staring, and the knowledge that he was a spectacle made him want to crawl into a corner and draw his shirt over his head. His panic started rising, and he could feel the threat of an attack becoming acute. "Will you kindly keep your voice down?"

"I won't." Even as he said this, though, Brad took Adam's arm, pulled him off to the side, and began speaking in harsh whispers. "I'm not going to stand by and watch you self-destruct."

Adam ran his hand through his hair, drawing one deep breath, then another. "If you make me have a panic attack in the middle of the Quad because you won't leave me alone, I'll never forgive you."

"Fine. I'll go." Brad's voice quavered, and Adam knew he'd go off and cry in the single-stall restroom down by the dorm entrance. "I just hope muscle boy knows what to do when you freak out. I hope someone still wants to comfort you once you've driven off all your friends and you're all alone."

On that dramatic parting note, Brad flounced off. The rest of the Bug Boys cast uneasy glances Adam's way, but Adam didn't linger. After a few more steadying breaths, he headed into the cafeteria, moving slowly and carefully and staying close to the wall.

But the damage, unfortunately, had been done. When he entered the cafeteria, the discordance of too many voices assailed his ears and mingled with the chaos already whirling inside his head. The doubts Brad had planted, deliberate and accidental both, swirled within him, coalescing in whispers that caressed his brain, slowly dragging him down.

He's right. Denver would turn tail and run at your first panic attack. What were you thinking, leaving Brad, even as a friend? What if everyone hates you and you're completely alone? They probably do. Who would want you?

What if you get sick and they've abandoned you and you have no one to call when you're dying? What if someone breaks into your apartment and you're alone with no one to protect you? What if you don't unplug something and start a fire and burn in your bed because you forgot to check the fire alarms? What if someone else in the building starts a fire? You stayed on the ground floor, but what if your window freezes when you try to get out? Or what if the lock fails and someone comes in and rapes you? What if the worst happens and you die miserable and alone without even Brad to comfort you?

What if, what if, what if, what if what if what if—

"Are you okay?"

The speaker cut through Adam's chaos enough for him to lift his head, but the room was still spinning and out of focus, his vision framed in red. "Panic attack," he whispered before surrendering to it again.

Slender, careful hands pressed against his shoulders, steadying him with significant strength. "Easy. Deep breaths. Focus on the sound of my voice."

Adam did, as best he could.

Long brown hair swayed into Adam's vision, floral perfume drifting in its wake. Those strong hands shifted, one moving to his chin to lift it slightly. "That's it, keep breathing. Keep going. You're doing great."

Adam's vision cleared as his breath steadied, and he became aware he sat on a bench beneath the coatracks, staring into the beautiful, made-up face of a woman who appeared to be in her early thirties.

A woman with an Adam's apple.

The need to not let his panic in any way be construed as his rejection of her help gave him an anchor to cling to. Adam forced a wavering smile. "Thanks. I—ah… thanks. Ma'am."

Smiling wryly, she held out her hand. "Louisa. And you're welcome."

He accepted the handshake. "Adam." Nodding at the cafeteria line, he added, "Can I buy you lunch?"

"Absolutely, but not until you can convince me you won't fall over when you try to stand up."

"Give me a minute, then." Adam patted the space beside him, and Louisa sat. "So. What are you studying?"

She snorted. "Gender studies, of course. I'm finishing up my master's in social work too. I'd like to go into counseling, specializing in therapy for transgender persons." She smoothed out her pencil skirt as she crossed her ankles and tucked them to the side. "You?"

"Entomology grad student."

"Lovely. Do you TA?"

"Yes, though I've had to cut back because I'm trying to finish up my dissertation so I can review next summer. It's research intense, and I don't have enough data yet to really begin writing my defense."

"Ah, yes. Such fun, I'm sure."

Adam drew a steadying breath. "Okay. I think I can stand now." They rose together, and the room only spun for a moment. "Yeah. I'm cool."

"Excellent." She indicated he should go in front of her, and he knew she watched him carefully as he eased his way over to the line. "Ooh, they're having vegan mac and cheese."

"Are you vegan?" Adam asked as he reached for his tray.

"No, but have you had that stuff? It's amazing. Pricier than the other, though." She waggled her eyebrows at him. "Sorry, I'm not a cheap date."

Adam laughed. "It's okay. You're worth it."

They chatted idly as they made their way through the line. He noticed too that Louisa garnered plenty of lingering glances and frowns. Few of them were friendly.

They sat together near the windows, where Adam fell to his lasagna for several minutes. Clearly half his attack had come out of hunger.

"Thanks," he said again as he dug into his food. "I knew I was going to run into Brad, and I tried to get myself ready, but I think I need to give myself better prep."

"Brad is the one who was shouting at you in the hallway?"

Adam nodded with a grimace. "Yes. He's my ex."

"Oh, those. Aren't they fun?" She smiled wryly. "So, are you a single adorable entomology grad student who isn't put off by a trans woman?"

Adam thought back to El's question at the bar. "I can't figure out if I'm single or not, but I'm definitely gay. Total Kinsey 6. Sorry. My lab building is next door, though, and I love buying lunch at the Quad for beautiful women. Even if they're expensive dates."

Louisa laughed and pushed playfully at his shoulder, and in that moment she was so lit up, so feminine, so beautiful, so warm and open and lovely that Adam was truly sorry he didn't swing her way.

TINY'S GYM was a locals' place. It didn't have the bells and whistles of the LA Fitness near Tuck U, nor was it open twenty-four seven like the Anytime Fitness locations scattered throughout the town. It was a basic gym. Treadmills by the windows, rows and rows of free weights in the middle, weight machines along the back wall. Ten years ago Tiny had bought out the Mexican grocery next door and gotten himself a serious classroom space for all the hippie group fitness that repaid his investment within the first year and now did nothing but roll in the dough. Tiny's didn't have luxury locker rooms or ambience, but it was friendly, it was located on a side street off the Light District, and it validated its members' parking.

It was also run by an openly gay burly little bear who worked the gym floor like a used-car salesman. Everybody loved Tiny, including Denver.

When Denver hit the gym Saturday afternoon, it was even more packed than usual. Every treadmill and elliptical was occupied, and the waiting list on the clipboard at the front desk was half full of names. The weight machines were almost as busy, and the free weight area bustled with activity, mostly men of various bulk grunting and preening to outdo each other. As Denver approached, however, nearly all activity ceased as every regular smiled and waved and offered him some sort of greeting. He wasn't two reps into his first routine before Tiny himself came over to greet him.

"Denver! How's it going, man?" Tiny, who stood a head shorter than Denver but was almost as wide in the shoulders, clapped Denver hard on his left biceps.

"It's going." Denver replaced his hand weight and leaned on a support pillar beside him. "How about you?"

Tiny's grin strained the dark patch of chin pubes tickling his bottom lip. "I'm here for the usual, big guy."

Denver rolled his eyes and outwardly gave the appearance of one jovially put-upon, but inside he braced for the usual unease whenever Tiny approached him, because he knew where this discussion was headed. "I told you, man. I just wanna come lift."

"Bullshit. You're gonna end up giving free advice to everybody who shows up the whole time you're here. Same as always. I don't know why the hell you won't let me pay you."

"Because I ain't going to get certified," Denver reminded him.

Tiny held out his hands. "Full tuition and a twenty-thousand-dollar sign-on bonus if you agree to sign a three-year contract with me. While you get your degree, I'll put you on the books and find something for you to do so you're still pulling a salary. And you get free membership, obviously. Hell, I'll throw in membership for all your friends if it'll get you on board."

"At the rate you're going, by Christmas you'll propose marriage on top of it," Denver drawled.

"Will that win you? Because I'll do it."

Denver surveyed Tiny's stocky frame in mock consideration. "Naw. You ain't my type." He headed toward the stacks of weights. "How come you're so hot to hire me, Tiny? You got plenty of already certified yahoos running around trying to get your attention. I know 'cause I've seen 'em."

"None of them know weights like you do. I'm getting memberships from guys who want to build just because you come here. You wouldn't believe how many times a day I get asked when you're likely to come in next. Now imagine what'll happen when I put you on advertisements as an on-the-floor trainer and PT for hire." When Denver only frowned at him, Tiny sighed. "Thirty thousand. I can't go higher."

Denver became very focused on attaching the weights to his bar. "It ain't money that's holding me back, Tiny. I'm not interested is all. I told you that already."

"You tell me that every time, but I don't believe it." Tiny pursed his lips and shook his head. "I know you want to do it. I watch you with the guys you help. I know you aren't some kind of noble idiot who won't take payment. I know you aren't looking to go out on your own either. So what gives? What's holding you back?"

"I gotta get back to my workout." The knots in Denver's belly were starting to affect his voice.

"Is it that you hate school that much? That you don't want to go? It doesn't take hardly any time, and you can stretch it out depending on where you take the classes. Some you can do over a weekend, but I think you'd feel more confident if you took one of the six-month deals. I'll take you however I can get you."

Yeah, it was the school part that tripped Denver up. The GED he doubted he could pass before he even considered studying physiology and all the other crap he'd never be able to do. He didn't say anything, though, just kept adjusting his weights.

Tiny sighed. "I'm not giving up. I'll wear you down eventually. Think how nice it would be to go hang out at Lights Out without having to work there. How nice it would be to have your evenings free and get paid to do what I already know you love to do—with a real salary too."

For the first time since Tiny had started his offers, Denver did think about it. He thought long and hard about how it would feel to be able to go flirt with Adam whenever he felt like it, how much sexier he'd look to a grad student as a personal trainer than a high school dropout working bouncer at a bar.

It would feel fucking great, is what. But it was all a fantasy, because there was no way Denver was going to do it. No way he *could*. So he tucked the fantasy away, dusted his gloves, and got back to the much less agonizing task of deadlifting four hundred pounds.

CHAPTER TEN

"YOUR EX sounds like a real ass."

Louisa made this observation as she and Adam sat in Mocha Springs Eternal, sipping a vanilla latte and green pomegranate tea. Their lunch had turned into a stroll across campus and had landed them in the Light District, where they decided they'd both very much needed some coffee, or in Adam's case, tea. They were in one of the side lounges, Adam sprawled in a love seat and Louisa in a wing chair. A local band consisting of a bassist, fiddler, and harpist fussed about setting up at the other end of the coffee shop.

Adam dunked his tea bag three times, held it still for three seconds, then dunked it a fourth time before removing it and placing it carefully in the extra cup he'd requested for just this purpose. "Brad can be annoying, yes. But he means well, I know that. I mean, I'm no angel. And he's right. I have a metric ton of baggage."

"I assume you've heard the one about the road to hell and how it's paved?" Louisa sipped her latte and eased deeper into her chair. "By your own admission his meddling makes you worse. Would you have had a panic attack today if he hadn't jumped you on the way to the cafeteria?"

Probably not, no. "He wasn't always this way. He was very patient with me at first. I'd started to doubt I'd ever have a boyfriend, but then there he was. Before he messed with my head, he helped me."

"Just because he helped you over a hurdle doesn't mean you owe him for life, Adam. You don't owe him anything at all. That's not how relationships work."

"You don't understand. Brad put up with a lot. I mean, a lot."

Louisa sighed. "Yes. My last boyfriend did too. He had to hear his Louis was about to become a Louisa. Do you think I owed it to him to continue living as a man because that's what he preferred?"

Adam grimaced. "Obviously not."

"Same goes for you. Brad helped you find your feet in relationships. Then you wanted to take your personal relationship with yourself in a different direction than what he was accustomed to, and he objected. Are you trying to tell me you can't choose a different path because Brad doesn't want you to?" Her hand closed over his, which was the first time he realized he'd been tapping his finger. Not only tapping, but in what Brad had called his SOS tap, a staccato burst of energy that usually meant a panic attack was around the corner. Louisa's gaze softened. "I've been trying to read you, but I'm training to be a Licensed Independent Social Worker, not getting a PhD in psychiatry. You have OCD, right?"

Adam shut his eyes. "God. I'm that obvious? You've known me four hours."

"I knew my mother for twenty-eight. Obsessive-compulsive disorder and I are old acquaintances." She let go of Adam's hand with a gentle pat and eased into her chair again. "There was a light switch at the bottom of the stairs and the top of the stairs in our house, two switches on the same circuit. My mother insisted the downstairs switch had to be pointed down at all times when the light was off. My sister and I would humor her, but my father thought it was ridiculous and forced her to endure it off and upright. He also wouldn't let her rattle the drawers to make sure they'd caught or sweep the driveway with the whisk broom because she thought it cleaned better than the floor broom. I was glad he stopped the sweeping, but the rest was hard to witness. I would hear her sneaking out of her bedroom in the middle of the night to fix the switch because she couldn't sleep with it pointing the wrong way. She had panic attacks too, but you weren't allowed to touch her during one or comfort her in any way. She was a counter too. She counted everything. Cracks in the sidewalk. Tiles in the ceiling. She never went to therapy or took medication either, not while we were still speaking."

"You're not speaking to your parents? I'm sorry."

Louisa shrugged. "It's their loss. And frankly, at this point it's a relief. They wanted me in conversion therapy when I thought I was simply gay, but as soon as I came out as transgender they couldn't bear to see or speak to me. So I have my family of choice now." She sighed. "Sadly, they're all back in South Dakota."

"I'll happily fill the OCD void, if you're accepting applicants for that position."

She pushed at his knee teasingly, but Adam saw softness and even mistiness in her eyes too. "I'll gladly take a friend who happens to have OCD, yes." She retrieved her latte. "But we were talking about you. I heard all about your ex. Now I want to hear about this hulky muscleman from the laundromat."

Adam cradled his tea mug, staring wistfully into it. "God. He's a fucking house, he's so big, and he's so sexy it hurts. He works at Lights Out as a bouncer. And a bartender. He said he could bench-press me, and I don't doubt him."

Louisa raised an eyebrow. "Is he—how shall I put it delicately—a simple man?"

"You mean is he dumb as a box of rocks? No. Not at all. I mean, I don't know that he'd rival Stephen Hawking in any way, but he's grounded like I've never seen anyone. Easygoing, but nothing gets by him. He's so nice too. Last night he brought me dinner, fended off Brad without so much as raising his voice, then arranged for me to go out with some of his friends so I could relax. I have no idea if he's book smart or not, but he's brilliant in other ways. Attentive and kind too. He monitored my drinking so I didn't get hungover for this thing I had to do this morning, and he made sure I got home safe."

"Well, if he makes you happy, I say mazel tov."

Adam sipped his tea, then voiced what had weighed on him all week. "He doesn't know about my OCD. I worry what he'll think when I tell him."

"Why do you have to tell him? It's not communicable. Let it come up when it comes up."

"Yes, but there's one very knotty problem." He'd started tapping again, and this time he stilled himself, though his mental tapping didn't quit. "One of my tics is that I have a problem with people being in each other's spaces, particularly in places of residence. I can sort of fake it in someone else's house, but not in mine. It was a huge issue when I lived with the Bug Boys. I could handle it if they were with their guests, but if I found a girl in the kitchen in the morning? Full-on panic. There were a lot of fights over it."

"So go to his house."

Adam bit his lip. "I don't know. I fake it when I'm in someone else's house. I'm not relaxed. I worry about what's plugged in and what isn't, whether or not things are on that shouldn't be. I know things are messed-up and out of order, and it upsets me. Normally it ends there, but I have no idea how I'm supposed to make out with someone when I know the soup cans aren't alphabetized by type and the shoelaces aren't tucked inside the shoes in the closet. If they're even in the closet at all."

Louisa frowned thoughtfully. "Yes, you're right. That's a tricky one. Well, sit with it. Don't panic. Strategize. Do you have a therapist here in town? Have you brought this up?"

No, he hadn't. He could only imagine what she'd say if she heard about Denver. "I'm afraid she won't like how I met him."

"Then you get another therapist." Louisa's hand closed over his again. "You can also take your time and let this unfold as it will."

Though the words nearly gagged him, Adam voiced the fear that lay beneath the others. "I'm afraid he won't stay interested long enough for me to figure it out."

"Then he isn't worthy of you, Adam." Louisa squeezed his hand. "Try trusting that he'll be patient and that you're worth the wait."

Adam laughed bitterly. "You do know OCD is the doubting disease, right?"

"Yes. But I also know its sufferers take comfort in abstract rituals. Dunking your tea bag isn't going to make him wait any more than telling yourself so in the mirror every morning. You might as well adopt the habit that has the potential to serve you."

Adam nodded, then turned his hand to squeeze her back. "Okay, here's the real reason you can't hate Brad: if he hadn't goaded me into an attack, we wouldn't have met, and I'm starting to think that would be a real tragedy. At least for me."

She smiled. "For me too."

THE FIRST thing Denver did when he called Adam on Sunday afternoon was ask him about his laundry. Something about the way Adam kept talking about it when he put him in El's car Friday night, the way he kept trying to drunkenly plot out when he'd do the rest of it and the merits and disadvantages of each time— well, Denver had decided it wouldn't be bad to follow up, even if he wasn't sure quite why.

"I did get it done," Adam told him, and to Denver's relief he seemed pleased to be asked. "I went to that place on the south side like you suggested. It was quiet and very, very clean, and there wasn't a frat boy in sight."

"They rob you blind?"

"Yes. Almost five dollars a load, and they made me buy special soap because the stuff I'd brought was the wrong type. But I didn't mind. It was worth the extra money to feel okay about doing laundry. Thank you so much."

The last misgivings about asking died away, and
Denver eased back in the seat of his truck, smiling.
"Anytime, baby. We still on for our date?"

"Absolutely. What are we going to do?"

What Denver wanted to do was take Adam back
to his place and fuck him silly, but something told him
this wasn't going to work out. "I wondered if you'd like
a drive up into the mountains."

"I'd love to. I've never seen the springs."

"Well, we ain't going there, because it's not much
more than bubbling mud. I will take you to Sherman
State Park. Unless you don't like hiking." Denver panicked when Adam's pause went on too long. "We can
do something else. That was just an idea."

"I'd love to hike," Adam said carefully. "Can you
tell me a little about the area? Like, what will I expect
to see and find?" A sad sigh drifted through the line.
"The dangers? Even the remote ones?"

Denver considered this. "Huh. Well, it's mostly a
reserve. There's a couple of easy trails, stuff for families and grandmas, and those don't go very far." They
were kind of boring too, but Denver didn't think he
should mention that.

"What about swinging rope bridges or other poten-
tially unmonitored and loose things? Sheer cliffs and
ledges?"

Ah. Adam was afraid of heights. "Yeah, the easy
trails are all connected by a rope bridge. There aren't
any cliffs and ledges, though, unless you go off the
marked paths, which I don't know enough to do. There
are some midlevel trails, which are basically just long."

"What about animals?"

"Well, it's the wild. Technically they list deer,
coyote, rabbits, and elk, but all the standard Colorado

wildlife are fair game. Moose, badger, bears, mountain lions—"

"Oh God!"

Denver gentled his voice. "You do know this is a state park? There's rangers every ten feet. I've never seen a bear or lion there, and anyway, if you do, it's not instant death. You're safer from bears if you stay away from tourists who don't know better than to feed them or leave out their picnic stuff, and even then all you have to do is make a lot of noise and not hunt at night. Lions don't want a damn thing to do with you. If you see one, count yourself lucky. You can encounter both of them here in town too, you know."

"Oh God."

This wasn't going well. "You can also get struck by lightning or hit by a meteor." The line went very quiet. "Adam? You there?" When the pause went on too long, he sat upright. "Adam?"

"I'm here." He sounded like he'd run a mile.

"How about we go bowling?" Denver suggested.

"I'm sorry," Adam whispered.

"It's okay." Denver wished he could hold him.

"I want to see the park. I haven't been anywhere but Tucker Springs. I flew into Grand Junction, took a cab here, and that's it."

"What? You haven't been into the mountains at all? Boy, how long you been in Colorado?"

"Three years. I know. It's pathetic."

"It's a crime, is what it is." Denver tapped his fingers on his leg while he thought quickly. "Tell you what. How about a compromise? We go into the mountains, to the park. I'll drive you wherever you want to go. We don't ever have to get out of the car unless you want to use the restroom or get something to eat." There was another silence. "Adam?"

"You'd do that for me?"

"Of course I would. Hell, Adam, I don't care where we go. I just want to spend the day with you."

"I'll be ready in ten minutes," Adam replied, soft and melted.

Denver glanced in his rearview mirror at his truck bed, which was technically clean for trucks, but he remembered how fussed Adam had gotten over pretty much everything he encountered unless Denver was fucking him. Which was what he had in mind for the truck bed, admittedly, but first he had to get him to lie down in it.

"Give me half an hour," Denver said, started his engine, and headed for the car wash.

CHAPTER ELEVEN

SHERMAN PARK sat about twenty minutes south of Tucker Springs. A state park founded in 1932, it was expanded in 1989 when the Corey Reservoir was made by flooding the Corey Ranch on the far southern side. The park was one of the great examples of Colorado's varied climates: it snowed plenty up in the mountainous parts, but down by the reservoir in the summer, prickly pear bloomed. People came from western Colorado to camp at Sherman, but because it was buried deep in the mountains and didn't have any of the sexy things to attract tourists, overall Sherman was a private place for those who loved it.

Denver wasn't exactly a nature nut, and he was a native of Arkansas, not Tucker Springs, but he loved the mountains, and he loved Colorado. Tucker Springs was a nice place, and the fact that he was smack-dab in the middle of three state parks and three national forests was icing on the cake.

He drove Adam the long way to the park, taking him on back county roads with vistas of the valley, showing him spots he thought were unique and worthy of someone who hadn't ever been in the mountains. Adam seemed to enjoy it, leaning forward on the dash and pushing his glasses farther up his nose as he tried to give himself a panoramic view. When they finally toured the park itself, Adam looked like someone had given him Christmas.

"It's so beautiful. I feel so small, like I'm nothing—but it's not scary. I don't know why. I should feel isolated and freaked-out, but I don't. I suppose it's because you seem to know what you're doing, where you're going."

"I did a lot of driving around when I first came here, kind of like this, actually. Every now and again I like to drive up 550 into the mountains, past Baldy Peak and Brown Mountain, to really feel them, you know?" It felt like he'd said too much, but he got caught by the naked longing on his lover's face, a look made sexier by his glasses.

Denver glanced at the clock on his dashboard. "What time do you need to be back?"

Adam blinked like he'd forgotten he ever had to go home. "I don't know. I have to teach at ten tomorrow morning, and I should check the lab before I go."

All right, then. Denver adjusted his hat and settled into the seat. "We'll stop at Ouray for a bite, and then you and me, baby, are going into the mountains."

Adam put his hand on Denver's shoulder, his mouth agape. "Really?"

"Really," Denver assured him and grinned. Reaching over, he tousled Adam's hair. "Hope you like fresh fish, because I know this great little bar."

Adam did like fish, it turned out, especially rainbow trout. He snarfed up his first serving and looked so hungry Denver ordered him another, ignoring his protests that he didn't need it, and Denver felt justified when Adam ate that down too. Adam was relaxed in the bar, and full of smiles.

Until he went to use the bathroom.

He went in and came back out like someone had put a spring on the door. His face was so white Denver thought someone had tried to jump him or something, but when Adam was finally able to talk, he said, "Dirty."

Denver checked it out himself—it was pretty gross, yeah, but not the worst he'd seen by a mile. The sink was stained, the floor was sticky, but other than that it was just old and poorly kept as most men's bathrooms were. It was apparently too much for Adam, who not only wouldn't go back in but had retreated into himself, looking embarrassed and ashamed and miserable.

"We can find another bathroom," Denver assured him as they got into the truck.

"I'm sorry." It was about the thirtieth time he'd said that.

"Not a big deal. I've never cared for the idea that men's bathrooms have to be such cesspits. We'll find another one."

He couldn't, not with any kind of ease. The only other option seemed to be a gas station whose bathroom wasn't any better. This set off another round of apologies and, for reasons Denver could not understand, made Adam shiver, as if Denver would beat him or something for daring to ask for a clean bathroom.

Pieces fell into place for Denver. Someone had bullied Adam. Someone had made him feel that everything he did, everything he wanted, was wrong, that any request for special treatment was unreasonable and should be punished. Whether or not it was Brad the idiot couldn't be determined. It could have been a parent. In fact, as he watched Adam melt further and further down, he suspected whatever haunted Adam was old and deep.

It made Denver quietly furious.

He shoved that anger to the side for now and focused on comforting and calming Adam. "We'll find something. Ouray doesn't have the only toilets in the world."

"I'm so sorry. I don't have to go that badly." This was a bald lie. When Adam wasn't cowering into himself and looking torn between abject misery and stark panic, he squirmed uncomfortably in his seat.

There wasn't anywhere else immediately apparent, which didn't help matters. Certainly there wasn't any five-star hotel with a butler-serviced men's room, but there wasn't even an outhouse by the side of the road. Denver was annoyed with the universe. All he needed was one goddamned clean men's toilet. Was this too much to ask?

As they made their way into the mountains themselves, they were officially past any hope of anything unless Denver drove them to Telluride. Which he could do, but he had the feeling there'd be a greater cost to Adam than a burst bladder if they went that long.

A small side road was ahead, something nice and isolated. All at once he had an idea.

"Adam, are we talking draining the lizard here?" When Adam looked at him blankly, he added, "You just have to piss?"

Humiliation stained Adam's cheeks, and he pushed his glasses higher up his nose. "Yes. I'm sorr—"

"No worries," Denver cut him off and drove onto the side road.

He took them deep into the woods and partway up the slope of the mountain. It appeared to be an abandoned lane to some house or cabin, as soon the pavement ended and Denver's Nissan bumped and bounced along a rutted dirt road.

"Where are we going?" Adam asked, panic rising.

"Looking for a levelish spot—there." The road opened out to what had been a turnaround, and Denver stopped in the center of the space, parked the car, and killed the engine.

"Denver?" Adam's voice was almost a squeak.

Denver put a hand on Adam's shoulder and massaged, soothing him with body and voice both. "Okay. This isn't ideal, I know, and if it's too weird, we can go back. But give it a try, maybe. This is what we're going to do. We're going to get out of the truck. I'm going to stand by the back bumper, and you're going to water the front tires. Or whatever it is you decide to pee on."

Adam's eyes practically filled his head. "You want me to pee outside?"

"Hell of a lot cleaner than those bathrooms. I got some Wet Wipes in the glove box if you want to wash your hands after."

Adam relaxed a little, but he seemed to be waiting for some other shoe to drop.

Denver did his best to show he was barefoot. "There's no rush. It's a pretty spot. Bearless too, as much as I can gather, and anyway, I'm right here. I'd stay nearer the front while you go, but I had a feeling you'd rather piss in peace. If you want, though, I'll hold it for you." He winked.

Adam bit his lip before his next words burst out of him. "Why are you doing this?"

Denver half considered lying and saying some-thing glib like *because I thought you had to pee*, but he didn't think it would mollify Adam. So he went with the truth. "Because it seems important to you, and be-cause I like taking care of you."

That softened Adam somewhat. "I'm sorry I'm such a freak."

"You're not a freak. Quirky, yeah. You seem like you've got some skeletons in the closet, a couple you really don't want out maybe, but they weigh on your mind. I get that. I been there. Hell, I'm still there on a few counts. You don't need to apologize for asking for what you need. Maybe trust, though, that I like giv-ing you what you need. Maybe that makes me happy." Adam looked near tears. Denver stroked Adam's cheek. "I'm gonna go stand at the back bumper. You sit here and think about it, and if you want to try using my tire as a toilet, you do it. Or if not, you can holler at me to take you back to Tucker Springs, and we'll get you to your apartment and go bowling after all. Or we can cut the difference and find somewhere decent in Telluride. Whatever you want, baby."

He kissed Adam on the forehead, gave his shoulder one last squeeze, and got out of the truck.

For a long time, nothing happened. The door to the truck didn't open, but neither did Adam stick his head out and ask Denver to take him home. After doing some tire watering of his own, Denver figured he'd give Adam another ten minutes, then he'd check on him.

In the meantime, he leaned against his truck and enjoyed a beautiful Colorado day.

Just before he was about to return to the cab, the door opened. Denver turned enough that he could glance at what was happening, and out of the corner of his eye he saw Adam slink out, shut the door, and head to the front of the truck. Ridiculous as it was, Denver held his breath, letting it out in a silent sigh, a smile playing on his lips as he heard the unmistakable sound of piss hitting dirt. The door opened again—Wet Wipes, Denver realized with a wider smile—and then closed.

A minute later, a quiet Adam appeared. "Thank you."

"Not a problem." Denver tipped his hat. "So. You want to head deeper into the mountains, or meander towards home?"

"Actually." Adam hugged the corner of his side of the truck like it was a lifeline. "I wondered if we could stay here a little while? If that would be okay?"

Denver tried not to look surprised. "Sure thing. This clearly isn't a maintained road. I thought it was a little too remote for anything but nature's toilet for you."

"No. I mean—yes, it scared me at first. But not now. Do you think—would it be okay? Do you want to?"

Whether it was the softness, the meekness, or the Adam-ness of it all, Denver didn't know, but the guy made him melt. Hell, he'd walk to Durango barefoot in the dark, if Adam asked like that. "Sure thing, baby." He smiled and reached for the latch to the tailgate, lowering it slowly. Adam sat down on the edge, and Denver followed suit—scooting back, because he was a heavy fucker—but he drew Adam up beside him. He figured they were going to talk a bit. Maybe Adam would even tell him what it was that upset him so much. It felt like that part of the movie, and he was fine with that. Hell.

Maybe he'd unload his own closets. This was a good place for that, and with a good person. For the first time ever, the idea didn't scare him. He was almost looking forward to it.

Adam turned around so he could face Denver, and Denver rested his elbows on the truck bed. He smiled at the consternation on Adam's face. It was all but busting out of him. Denver didn't want to rush him, but he did want to encourage him. "It's okay, baby. Tell me what's on your mind."

Adam hesitated a second longer. Then he reached out, put his hand in the center of Denver's chest, and leaned in close.

"I want you to fuck me. Right here, right in the open where bears or mountain lions could eat me. I want you to hold me down and fuck every hole I have and make me scream." His fingers tightened over Denver's shirt. "Spank me again too. I want everything you'll give me, Denver."

Denver blinked, dizzy as his softened center gave way to lust. "Okay."

Adam smiled. Then he took Denver's face in his hands and seared his mouth closed with a burning kiss.

CHAPTER TWELVE

IT WAS terrifying, being this exposed, and Adam wasn't talking about the fact he was buck naked and ass up in the flatbed of a pickup, his glasses tucked safely in the cab. He was out in the woods, in the mountains. On a dirt road where he had just—God help him— peed. He was beyond civilization except for the truck, surrendered to nature, its chaos and dirt and death surrounding him.

Denver surrounded him too. He knelt in the truck bed, fully dressed, exploring the exposed and quivering pucker of Adam's asshole with a laziness that implied he had all damn day to do so.

"So pretty and pink, baby. Flex it again for me."

Holding on to the edge of the truck, Adam dug in his knees and did as he was told.

He received a grunt of approval and a stroke down his thigh as a reward. "Yeah. You like me looking at

you like this, don't you, all naked in the middle of nowhere, playing with your hole. Don't you."

Adam couldn't quite tell if that had been a question, but there didn't seem to be harm in answering. "I
do like it. I like everything you do to me."

More stroking, with more tenderness. "But you
like me telling you what to do most of all."

Yes, he did. It gave Adam an incredible rush. "I
do." He rubbed his thumb against the metal of the
truck. "The spanking is also nice."

"Yes. I'm aware of how fond you are of that. And
you said you hadn't done that before me?"

Adam shook his head. "I knew other people did
it, but I didn't get why. Now I feel about it like my
aunt did about chocolate. I think if I didn't get it after a
while, I'd go crazy. I love the feeling."

"Endorphins." Denver's hand cupped Adam's ass.
"You can play fun games with spanking sessions. Some
people like to meet up just to be spanked."

Adam imagined meeting Denver in the back of
Lights Out, bending over Denver's lap, getting spanked,
then leaving. It felt wicked and sexy, but…. "It would
be too lonely for me. I'd want to stay and talk to you."

The kiss on the crease of his ass made Adam star-
tle. "Should I start with a spanking now? Or end with
one again?"

"Can you do it during? I like it when you make me
feel so mixed-up I don't know who I am."

He wanted to tell Denver how special it was that
he could make Adam feel that way, how rare it was for
him to be able to trust someone and for his OCD to
trust them too, to let go. He couldn't do this without
making confessions he wasn't prepared for, though, so
he didn't say anything.

"All right." Denver slapped Adam's rump like he was a horse. "I'll keep you on your toes. For now, I'm in the mood to see more of you. Reach back and pull yourself open. Play with yourself and give me a show. I'll squeeze some lube in there for you to grease yourself, and then I'll sit back and watch you finger your ass, stretching it good. You gonna do that for me, baby? You gonna fuck yourself so I can watch?"

Adam could scarcely speak for his arousal. "Yes, sir."

Denver grunted and took a healthy pinch of his asscheek. "I like it when you call me sir."

Adam liked to call him sir. It felt like surrender. It felt like saying, *Yes, you're in charge, and I will do whatever you ask me to do.* It was freeing. Like all the doubt got washed away for a few minutes, and he could be okay. The opposite of standing in front of his mirror and scolding himself into safety. Denver didn't scold him.

He just fucked him.

Except for right now when Adam, apparently, was to fuck himself, which he did with abandon. Letting go of the edge of the truck to rest his head on the soft, clean mat Denver had spread out, Adam balanced on his knees, reached both arms around his body, and dutifully played with his asshole for Denver's enjoyment. He pulled his cheeks apart and flexed his hole, quivering as Denver squirted lube inside him.

Denver's swat against Adam's ass was playful as he pushed the viscous liquid inside. "Sounds great, doesn't it? Makes you feel filthy."

It was impossible for Adam to answer. His whole focus was on Denver's hand on his cheek, still resting on the skin. Would he spank him now? Even a little?

Chuckling, Denver smoothed teasing circles over Adam's flesh. "So greedy for it. You'd let me do anything to you to get your spanking, wouldn't you?"

"Yes." Adam didn't hesitate to reply, and he loved how answering made him feel. *So dirty. Make me answer more.*

Denver pressed a kiss at the base of Adam's spine, tender and sweet. But when he spoke, his voice was thick with drawl and wickedness. "Fingerfuck yourself good and hard, boy, and earn that spanking."

Whimpering, Adam rushed to comply, his arms like rubber, his hands shaking. A loud, thick *squish* broke the silence as he pushed two fingers inside himself. Adam could feel the lube moving inside him, distributing inside his passage.

"I like that sound." Denver gave him a sharp smack on his asscheek. "Pull all the way out and push in so I can hear it again."

Adam did, over and over, learning the angles that produced the best auditory effects. When he particularly enjoyed them, Denver would grunt and give him a slap, so he worked to make them sound as sloppy and loud as possible. At one point Denver made him pause to add more lube, and Adam balanced as best he could on his head and knees, holding himself open with both hands while Denver filled him. When Adam resumed fingering himself, however, something else nudged at his asshole.

Denver. Denver's fingers were there too. Inside.

With his other hand anchored in a firm grip of Adam's cheek, Denver explored alongside Adam's fingers. "Let's stretch you nice and open. Oh, yeah. Hear that sloppy sound. You feel that, boy? You feel all that squirming inside you?"

Adam whimpered and grunted what he hoped sounded like a yes. He had to take deep breaths and push against each thrust, focusing hard on relaxing the muscles around the invading digits. It was so much pressure, but also so unnerving because he could feel the touch everywhere. His own fingers were along for Denver's ride, tangled with each thrust. The clearing was full of the sound of excessive lube moving. *Schump. Schump. Schump.* He could feel it running down his thighs, dripping onto the mat below him.

I'm so slutty and filthy.

"I want to pump harder inside you and spank you. Make you fuck yourself until you're stretched and make your cheeks red. I want you to think about getting stuffed and spanked at the same time. I want you to look at me with the hungry eyes you did for spanking and ask for this too, because it was so good."

Adam wanted to just wait for this wonderful experience to start, but eventually he realized Denver wanted his permission. "Yes, please, do that."

The handkerchief went into his hand again. "You know the rules. Drop it if you feel like anything's too much, and I'll stop right away."

Like Adam was going to do that, but he held the handkerchief anyway. The fucking was a little rough, almost uncomfortable, but as soon as the spanking started, he had a different idea about the discomfort and he understood what Denver meant. They were such nice, hard spankings, and the thrusts were a nice counterpart, so much so that when Denver switched hands to spank the other cheek, Adam had his finger inside himself before Denver did.

"You're making me happy, boy," Denver said, rubbing his thumb against Adam's perineum.

Adam only relaxed deeper into his sexual haze and tipped his ass higher.

He stayed in that blissful, pink space, full of hard fingers and sharp spankings, and then abruptly that ended. Denver withdrew his fingers, pulled Adam's out as well. Before Adam could recover enough to ask what was happening, something cold, stiff, slick, and huge nudged at his entrance and into his fucked-out passage.

It wasn't Denver's cock. It was some object, a dildo he presumed, but for a moment the spell broke and Adam began to panic, imagining a host of insane, idiotic things Denver never would put up inside him and yet could. The pleasure it gave fizzled under the weight of doubt.

"Please." He gripped the mat to keep from reaching for the object. "Can I see it?"

Wordlessly, the object was removed. Through the pornographic tent of his legs, Adam gazed at the black silicone cock and balls that Denver held. Large and long and fat, obscenely so.

"This okay?" Denver drawled.

Adam stared at that monster cock. He'd had dildos in him, but he was always careful about where they came from. "Can you tell me what type of material it is? Has it been used before?"

"It's a high-quality-grade silicone from a manufacturer I respect. This particular one is brand-new. I had a feeling you'd want something that hadn't been used before. I ran it through the dishwasher without detergent before I brought it here."

That was… that was almost perfect. Adam wanted to cry. He didn't let himself. Crying wouldn't get him that dildo back inside him, and it wouldn't get him more spanking. "That sounds fine. Please fuck me with it."

Grinning, Denver ran the tip down Adam's crack. "Will do."

The dildo was big. It felt like a mountain inside Adam, and it made him grunt and bear down against it, his body at war with whether it wanted to swallow or reject it. Denver insisted he take it, however, pushing even when Adam wiggled away. He held Adam's hips still and forced it in.

"If you don't want to take it, drop the handkerchief."

Adam did want it, so he made himself take it, making increasingly desperate noises as the fat, long dildo worked into his ass, inch by terrible inch. When Denver finally stopped, Adam was panting and shaking and so hard he thought he would explode.

"Good boy," Denver said, pushing the base deep so the balls tickled Adam's perineum. "Feel good, baby?"

Adam's only available response was a grunt and a faint wiggle of his hips. When Denver tapped the base, Adam cried out.

Laughing, Denver patted Adam's tender ass. "For taking all of it, you get a reward. You want some more spanks with this big dildo up your ass?"

It was so difficult to speak. It felt like the dildo was in Adam's throat. "Yes, sir. Please, sir."

When Denver licked the strained crack of Adam's ass, his knees threatened to buckle. Denver chuckled and kissed his way around the base of the dildo. "I'm going to spank the dildo too. I hope when I do, you scream."

Adam's brain short-circuited at the very idea that some of the spankings would land on the dildo base, so much so that he was tense during the ones he'd longed for, the ones on his ass. Some of them landed on his thighs too, which was new—everything felt so sharp and biting in this anticipation. The blows made the dildo push in deeper, so what would it feel like when he—?

A sharp, sudden smack against the base of the dildo made Adam see stars and cry out, a loud, single note of surprise. It broke as another blow came right after, and another.

"No, no, no—" Adam's hips undulated helplessly against the assault, the tip of the dildo moving against something inside him that made him feel primal and terrified. It made him want to grunt and rut like a pig. "No, *ah, ah, ah*—"

"Drop the handkerchief if you want me to stop. Release it from your hand."

Adam didn't want to let go of the handkerchief. He didn't know what he wanted, but it wasn't that. "I'm going to… I'm going to…."

"Do it." Denver kept spanking the base, increasing the strength of the blows, sending that tip farther in. "Let me see what you're hiding."

"Feel like an animal," Adam managed to whisper.

"Show me your animal."

Adam had no choice. He clawed at the mat, arched his back, pushed against Denver's relentless spankings until he was insensate, head lolling as he begged Denver in a slurred, guttural voice not to stop, to drive it in rougher, faster.

He wasn't sure when Denver began fucking him with it, pulling the dildo out and slamming it deeper than the spankings were taking it, but Adam kept egging him on, lost to his lust, knees wide, elbows dug in and hands against the front of the truck as he tried to take more and more.

"Baby, you're my sweet, greedy bitch," Denver said.

Adam grunted and pushed against the dildo.

He thought for sure he'd get to come, but Denver wasn't done torturing him. Just when Adam was so ramped up he was ready to pop with a breeze, Denver stopped and produced some straplike thing that fixed at Adam's belly button and held the dildo in place so he could turn Adam around and sit him down astride his lap. Adam moaned, drooling as his sensitive cock bushed against Denver's belly. When Denver took him in hand, Adam nearly came on the spot.

"Don't," Denver instructed, squeezing him as if to keep the cum inside. "Sit on me, baby, and let me make out with you while you have that big fat cock in your ass. Talk to me. You like that in you, baby? You like having that big fat cock in you after I fucked you with it?"

"Yes," Adam slurred. "Yes, sir."

"Such a good boy." Denver stroked Adam's neck as he leaned into his hand. Denver's hands drifted to Adam's chest, teasing his nipples. "You haven't had a lot of people tell you that you were a good boy, have you, baby? You've had a lot of people tell you that you were wrong."

Somewhat, yes, but mostly it was criticism inside Adam's head, the nasty voices of his own mind. He tried to explain that, but he could only stare stupidly at Denver.

Denver didn't seem to mind. He rubbed Adam's nipples, tugging them into sharp points, until they had the same kind of pain Adam knew in his ass, until they ached like Adam's cock.

Denver smiled at him, twisting one nipple gently. "You're such a good boy. A good man. A hot, sexy, slinky man who can take that huge-ass cock, because you can bear a lot, can't you, baby. You love getting fucked in the face. You love it when I fuck you hard against the wall or a table. You love being fucked, love letting go. And I love catching you, baby. Love it so damn much. I'm not sure what you're seeing in a dumb muscleman, but I'm glad you do, and I'll try to keep you as long as you'll let me."

Adam began to think the monster cock was the only thing holding him up. He wanted to tell Denver he liked him for more than his muscle, that no one had ever been this patient with him, that he was pretty sure the only reason he'd been able to piss on a tire was because Denver had told him he could, that no one had been able to calm him like Denver could, sometimes simply by drifting into Adam's thoughts. But he was too strung out from everything, too full of cock, too full of cum and lust and everything in the world to speak. So he just stared into Denver's eyes and listened. Stayed quiet for him. Obeyed him, because his directives were fast becoming lifelines.

The idea that Denver might be interested in continuing to give them to him was more than Adam could comprehend.

Adam pressed his lips to Denver's, nipping his lower lip briefly before sucking on it and stealing inside for a proper kiss. Denver responded with a groan and taking firm grip of Adam's nipples, tugging and twisting them as he swallowed Adam in a kiss of tongues and growls and enough intensity to make Adam shake.

Denver unbuckled the dildo strap with one hand, freeing Adam, and the dildo slid out of Adam with a hard *thunk*. While Adam continued to devour Denver's mouth and delight at the wicked things he did to his remaining captive nipple, Denver undid his jeans and slipped a condom on—Adam heard the wrapper. The second it was in place, he pushed Adam onto him, sheathing himself deep.

Adam rode him, digging his fingers into Denver's shoulders while he pumped himself up and down on his lover's cock, as Denver dipped his head to suck at his nipples between kisses and murmured encouragement. "Yeah, baby. So hot. That's it, take it. Ride it."

Adam did his best to do as he was told.

Before either of them came, Denver turned Adam around, first to spread him wide across his thighs and ride Denver's cock backward, then forward onto his forearms, ass up so Denver could push into him in earnest.

"Gonna give it to you like you asked," he promised as he began to piston fast, making Adam groan and melt deeper into the padding. "Gonna pound you until you scream, until you beg, until you can't stand and I have to carry you back into the truck. Gonna spank you while I do it, on your already red and sore ass."

He did too. He fucked relentlessly, driving Adam to the edge of release and back again, until Adam begged Denver to please let him come, please, please. He punctuated his thrusts with smacks against Adam's cheeks, his hips, until Adam was raw and weak with kneeling, until his thighs screamed too. Then Denver stopped spanking and reached around to jack Adam as he thrust, and once Adam shuddered through his release, Denver followed, pulling out and coming all over Adam's ass and back.

While Adam recovered, he heard a pop and smelled the sharp disinfectant smell of Wet Wipes before they were applied to his back, his ass, his thighs.

"Was that good, baby?"

Adam couldn't speak. Spreading his thighs wider so Denver could wipe him, he whimpered.

Denver laughed and finished cleaning him. "I love how you let me get you dirty. Other dirty things make you nervous, but when I make a mess on you, it's okay. That makes me feel so good."

Adam wanted to explain, to tell him OCD was funny that way, that logic didn't apply, that it seemed to be the utter randomness of the neurosis that made it magic. He couldn't speak, though, so he held still and let Denver tend to him.

He managed to kiss Denver, though, as he helped him get dressed, and then, as promised, carried him to the cab. Settling into the seat, Adam let his body throb in happiness and use as Denver maneuvered the truck back to the highway.

Adam was asleep before they got there.

When he woke, his ass burned in what he'd come to cherish as a spanking afterglow. He also noticed it was dusk and they were turning into Tucker Springs.

"I missed it," Adam said, chagrined, as he reached for his glasses. "I missed the ride into the mountains."

"You were so tired and looked so comfortable. I didn't want to wake you. We'll go again sometime if you like," Denver told him as he headed down the side streets to Adam's apartment. "We could go up to Bridal Falls—I've never been but always wanted to."

Adam remembered what Denver had said while they'd been making out, about how he'd try to keep Adam as long as Adam would let him. What did that even mean? What was he supposed to do with that?

"We don't have to go either," Denver said, when the silence dragged on.

To hell with it. "Denver," Adam asked, "are we—are we dating?"

Denver hesitated. "We can be."

"Do you want to be dating?" Adam pressed.

He laughed nervously. "Well, yeah. But you have to forgive me if I'm a little rusty." He glanced at Adam. "This'd be my second official relationship too. And the first one wasn't very great."

Denver being bad at relationships boggled Adam's mind. At the same time, the idea that Adam was special enough to be dated, to be Denver's second relationship the same way he would be Adam's, made him feel special, strong, and safe. His anxiety, though, kept him from enjoying the moment completely. "I'm sorry I was such a case today."

"Nothing doing. Hell, I'm glad for the whole bathroom disaster. I'd been trying to figure out where I could take you so I could make out with you in the back of that truck. You solved that nice and tight." He reached over and rubbed Adam's knee affectionately. "You're a good boy, Adam. Don't let anybody tell you different."

You're a good boy. Adam picked up Denver's hand and kissed it, holding it lovingly to his lips.

When they got to his place, Denver gave him a long, hard, cock-stirring kiss good night, but he didn't even ask if he could come up. That was another hurdle they'd have to cross, if this was going to go anywhere beyond fucks on side roads and back rooms of bars. He didn't know how long Denver's patience would last, how many OCD neuroses it could tolerate.

As he unlocked his door and went around plugging in the things he'd need for the night, Adam vowed to extinguish the fires he'd brought to the relationship as quickly as possible.

CHAPTER THIRTEEN

A WEEK and three days after his Sunday outing with Adam, Denver did laundry with El at Tucker Laund-O-Rama and received a thorough ribbing, because he'd confessed to his friend on the phone that he was, officially, dating someone.

"Denver Rogers, dating. And a grad student at that. My, my, my."

The ribbing was good-natured, though, and anyway, El was probably going to get married any second now. "Yeah, well. I saw how much fun you were having and figured, why not."

"Are we going to double-date now? Have barbecues on the patio? You never did come over, you know."

Denver hesitated with some towels halfway into a washing machine. "Well. We could do the double dating, but the other might be a problem. And actually, I been meaning to pick your ear about that."

El raised an eyebrow. "He has a thing against bar-becues? Patios? If he's vegetarian or something, we can work with that."

"No." Denver grimaced and glanced around the room to ensure they were alone. "The thing is, he's fun-ny about coming over to my place. And I can't go to his. At all."

"What the hell?" El demanded.

Denver held up a hand. "No. Don't. There's some-thing more to it, I can tell. I work hard not to bring it up, but last night I suggested very casually we have dinner at my place, thinking we could have us some nice des-sert on the couch, and you'd think I asked him to go to a war zone. And that's the thing. It's like it scares him."

"And it's not sex?"

"Fuck no." Denver got hard thinking about all the creative places they'd had sex. "It's something about my place. Or his place." He paused, hating that he had to voice this out loud, to share Adam's business with El, but he needed advice. "I think something happened to him. I think somebody abused him or freaked him out bad. Because it's about being alone in an apartment with me. I don't think it's me either. I think it's guys he's dating, period."

"You said he had another boyfriend, an ex that was driving you batshit."

"Yeah, and I think he might be part of the problem. It's bigger than that, though, I swear. But something's up, that I know. I can't figure out how to get around it. I don't want to bring it up and upset him. But I can tell it's the elephant in the room, that our not-going to each other's places is upsetting him because he thinks it'll upset me. What the fuck do I do, El?"

El leaned against a set of dryers and looked thoughtful. "That's a tough one. You probably need to let him bring it up. Nothing says you can't lay the groundwork, though. Make sure he hears you saying you're understanding or some shit like that."

"I been trying."

"It might take some time."

"Yeah." Denver dumped the soap into his machine, punched it up to start, and watched the water gush into the clothes through the door. The thing he'd been thinking about for a week now rolled around in his head like the clothes in front of him until finally it spilled out of his mouth. "I was thinking maybe it would help him if I told him something about me."

El paused before speaking carefully and casually. "You mean, something sensitive?"

Denver hooked his thumbs in his belt loops, eyes on the machine. "Something about me kind of like what I think happened to him."

The confession hung in the air, heavy and awkward. He and El were buds. They didn't talk about this stuff. They flipped each other's shit and used each other to avoid things like responsibilities and reality. Even now with El doing the grown-up thing of cohabitation, they were still each other's escape. That simple statement felt like a violation of some unspoken agreement that they'd keep things light.

Denver hoped to hell it was okay.

"I think," El said after a long silence, all traces of his usual sarcasm gone, "it might not be a bad idea. But that you should only do it if you feel like it would help you too. There isn't much worse than not being ready for something and doing it for someone else for the wrong reasons."

Denver couldn't help stealing a glance at El's arms, looking for the now-ubiquitous nicotine patches.

El laughed, but it was almost sad. "And then sometimes there are things we'll never be ready for but do anyway, because they're important to the people we love."

Laughing too, Denver eased off the machine and nodded to the benches. "Come on. I want to hear how Paul's exam went and all the naughty little ways you celebrated."

"You know I can't kiss and tell," El replied.

"If you do, I'll tell you what I did to Adam behind the ice cream shop."

Both El's eyebrows went up this time. "Deal."

ADAM CLUTCHED at his too-hot mug of tea, grounding himself in the scalding sensation against his palms. "I have to tell him."

He didn't have to look up to see Louisa's frown. He could hear it. "I thought we went over this. Several times."

"I know. But I really do have to tell him."

"Why? At least, why do you have to tell him in a way that makes you this upset?" Louisa's lacquered nails tapped against her latte mug. "OCD is part of who you are, Adam. It's not all you are, but it's part of you. Let it come into the conversation naturally."

"It can't, because I can't get past the whole other-people's-houses thing. I hate it. Yesterday I swore up and down I'd go with him to his place, that I'd bring it up, that I'd face it because it was dumb and I shouldn't let something like this rule my life. I've brought it up with my therapist, leaving out the public sex. She's urging me to take it slow." Louisa held up her hand in a *you see*? gesture, but Adam just waved it away. "Neither of you understands. If I don't fix this, I'm going to lose him. I can feel it. Ow!" he complained as Louisa flicked him hard in the center of his forehead.

"Adam Ellery, I thought you were smarter than this. You know damn well that's your anxiety talking, trying to convince you there's a monster under your bed."

"But there is." Adam was getting agitated now. "Nobody gets it. My anxiety? It's not always wrong. My first good therapist back in high school told me anxious brains are common because the people who have them are survivalists. Cavemen who worried about where the next attack would come from were usually right, because there was an attack. My biggest problem is there isn't a problem, so I invent them. Sometimes I don't have to, though. Sometimes I'm right. This is one of those times." Louisa crossed her arms over her chest, and he sighed. "Okay. It might not be as dire as I'm afraid of. But it's time to fess up. I can feel it."

Louisa relaxed a little. "If he's the right man for you, you know he'll be okay with it."

Adam turned his cup exactly ninety degrees to the right, then to the left, then to the right again. "You know, I don't even think that's what upsets me anymore. I think that's what I've been telling myself, that I'm afraid of him leaving me. Really? I hate that I have to do this at all. I hate that this is who I am. I hate that being wiggy about who is in whose house is something that can control me. I hate that most of the time my anxiety and my OCD wins. And before you tell me I can work on it, make it better, I know. I've come a long way from the wreck I was in high school, from being the kid my whole family had to move for. Except sometimes it's difficult to be the one always working so hard." He sighed. "I'm aware everyone has their struggles. I'm sitting here bitching to a trans woman. It's just…." Unable to articulate his frustration, he ran out of steam.

Louisa caught his hand and squeezed it with a firmness that centered and grounded him. He looked up at her and saw not censure, not pity, just deep, passionate empathy.

"Sometimes," she said in her pretty, quiet voice, "being the one who has to work extra hard to come even close to what is effortless for everyone else truly sucks. Is that what you were trying to say?"

That centered feeling stretched out, the roots of his experience twining with hers. "Yeah."

They said nothing after that, only held hands and finished their beverages in quiet, mutually frustrated communion.

CHAPTER FOURTEEN

THREE DAYS after his confessional with Louisa where they'd strategized all the many ways he could bring up the subject, Adam texted Denver and asked to meet him that night for dinner. To make sure he couldn't back out of it, he mentioned that he had something he wanted to tell him.

Nothing dramatic, he added, in case Denver thought this was a Dear John meeting. *Just something about me that I want you to know about.*

He sent the text, and after a few minutes of anxiety sent another.

The something about me isn't a huge deal either. I'm not an axe murderer.

A few minutes after that he added yet one more.

Sorry. I'll stop texting you constantly.

After that he felt he couldn't text again, so he stewed in his own personal cocktail of paranoia. Eventually it resulted in his scrubbing down the lab, first with the disinfectant spray and paper towels, then with a brush he found in the back to clean grime out of the most remote corners, and finally a toothbrush he stole from someone's locker. When Brad came into the lab, Adam was using the toothbrush to scour the table closest to the microscopes in precise, tiny circles.

"Don't," Adam bit off when he saw who'd entered the room. "Don't say anything. Don't start anything. Just. Don't."

Brad went to his lab station without comment, but he did indulge in a withering glare.

After a wary minute of watching to be sure Brad truly would leave him alone, Adam went back to his obsessive cleaning.

Brad didn't say anything to him, but the rest of the Bug Boys were another story. They came in shortly after Adam had convinced himself Brad would leave him alone—Mick, Ollie, Kim, and Andrew.

"Hey, Adam," Ollie called, but his smile was a little dim. "What's up?"

Adam slid the toothbrush out of sight as subtly as he could. "Nothing much. What about you?"

"Kim wanted to check on some lab work." This came from Mick, a southern Idaho native with a blond buzz cut and gosh-I'm-a-good-boy permanently tattooed on his face. "We're here to make sure he gets out sometime before next Tuesday." He waggled his eyebrows at Adam. "We were thinking of going bowling later. Do you want to come?"

"Are you kidding?" Brad spoke before Adam could. "Bowling is too full of germs for Adam."

"Lay off, Stanton," Mick warned. He turned back to Adam, tucking his hands in his pockets. "What do you say?"

It was a challenge to bowl, yes, but Adam had done it. He appreciated being included too, but Denver hadn't texted him back yet. He shook his head. "Sorry, I have plans. Otherwise I would."

Mick replied before Brad could explode again. "Well next time, then. Even if you just hang with us. We miss you."

Adam smiled, and he meant it. "Thank you."

Ollie nodded at him. "Yeah, well, don't be a stranger."

They all left then, even Brad, who cast Adam one last brooding look over his shoulder before he hurried after the others. Adam stared after them for a while, imagining what it would be like to still be living with them, knowing it was wrong for him but forcing himself to play out the scenario. Though he knew he was better off on his own, he worried that he might be somehow mistaken in his assessment of the situation.

That was the crux of obsessive-compulsive disorder. It was a disease of doubt, or rather a crippling failure to deal with the fact that the world was crowded with uncertainty. No decision could ever be the right one, because there was no such thing. No person could be the right person, because there wasn't anyone who fit that bill, not with a guarantee. Life had none, except that at some point everyone living would die. As far as Adam was concerned, that horrible yaw that remained was maddening, often beyond his ability to cope. And thus the toothbrush. Why that made things better, he couldn't say. He was only grateful that it did.

Sometimes he wondered what it would be like not to have OCD. He wondered what it would be like to never have to explain to someone he cared very much about why he couldn't enter their home without a panic attack. That state of mind was a fantasyland he could never visit.

Yes, everyone had their issues, but surely it was easier to be that free, to not be beholden to panic and paranoia. Surely it was better. Surely neurotypical people never had to confess stupid things that probably would make their boyfriends break up with them.

His mind circled the drain of doubt, spinning on self-recrimination, and thus he whiled away the hours, scrubbing down every visible surface of the lab until, at last, his phone chimed to alert him he had a new text.

If you were an axe murder, I'd still want to meet you for dinner, Denver wrote. *Text all you want, and I look forward to hearing whatever it is you have to tell me.*

He was just being nice, Adam knew that. But after an afternoon of intense cleaning and three near panic attacks while waiting for this response, he couldn't help it. He cried.

DENVER WAS wiping down a weight bench, trying not to worry over what he feared Adam was going to tell him at dinner, when Tiny came up behind him and slapped a friendly hand against Denver's back.

"Hey, big guy. Tell me some good news about how you're going to come work for me."

Denver gave an eye roll to cover his discomfort. "How about I tell you how I saw pigs flying this morning?"

Tiny grunted as he sat down on the other end of Denver's weight bench. "I heard a rumor," he said, his voice full of innuendo.

"Oh yeah?" Denver continued to wipe down the bench, but his ears were pricked.

"Yeah. I heard somebody nobody ever thought would settle down has been seen multiple times with the same guy. Some cute little grad student from East Cent."

Yeah. A cute little grad student who has something he needs to tell me tonight. Denver cleared his throat. "That's kind of a funny story."

"It's cool, man. Great, even. I like you getting serious. Means you might not drift off on me before I can pin you down." When Denver groaned, Tiny held out his hands. "Hey. How many guys in this economy have somebody begging to give them a job? Hell, how many of them have that and a cute grad student? You're charmed, buddy."

"Well, charms, they wear off. Give me a little more time and neither one of you will want me." Denver hung the disinfectant spray bottle back on its hook and tossed the wad of used towels in the trash.

He headed for the locker room without saying goodbye to Tiny, without so much as slowing down for anybody in his way.

Emotions he'd been barely holding back since getting that text began to churn like the blades of a blender in his gut, and he leaned against a line of lockers, breathing through the chaos. He'd known it was going to come to this. He'd known it all along. It was why he didn't get attached. Why he shouldn't have let himself get that way now. Why had he let down his guard? Why had he forgotten everything he'd learned in Oklahoma City?

Why the hell had he thought, even for a minute, that this time would be different?

After peeling off his clothes, he tossed them into the bottom of his locker, grabbed a towel, and headed for the showers. He'd scalded off the worst of his panic under the spray and was reaching for his soap when he heard Tiny's voice at the door.

"Is that why you keep turning me down?"

Blinking the water away, Denver glanced toward him. "What?"

Tiny leaned against the doorframe and folded his arms over his chest. "What you said about charms wearing off, how you hinted that if I spent enough time with you, I wouldn't want to hire you?"

Denver didn't want to do this. Muttering, he ducked back under the spray.

Tiny's voice rang out despite his quiet way of speaking. "The things I admire in you, Denver, aren't things that are going to fade away. You're loyal, hardworking, and kind to people, even when you think you're being big and bad. You get people to respect you, maybe at first by being as big as a house, but you keep it because you're a good man. I bet your grad student sees that too." He paused, then added, "It's okay to accept that from people, you know. Respect and friendship and everything else. You've earned it." His voice went so soft Denver had to strain to hear it over the shower. "No matter what somebody else has told you."

Shutting his eyes, Denver nodded his acknowledgment—and thanks—and buried his face in the water, though his emotions never got any higher than the top of his throat.

CHAPTER FIFTEEN

ADAM MET Denver at The Wrangler, a local steakhouse west of the Light District. It played loud country music and served microbrewed beer in steins with cow heads on the handles.

"Wouldn't have pegged this for your kind of place," Denver remarked as he held open the door for Adam.

Adam acknowledged the nicety with a blushing nod. "I felt like a steak. Hope you don't mind?"

"Hell, no. You just are always ordering salads and beans, and when you're really serious, chicken. But if you're feeling like steak, you're feeling like steak."

The truth was Adam didn't like steak at all. He knew Denver did, though, and he'd figured the whole *hey, I have a debilitating mental illness* discussion would go down better if Denver was eating something he liked. Of course now that he'd lied and said he wanted steak, he'd have to eat one too.

This realization consumed him until the waitress arrived, as he tried to decide whether or not he could bail on the smallest steak he could find—the Junior Wrangler eight-ounce sirloin—and order the chicken Santa Fe salad instead. *Consumed* was too mild a word. Worry crippled him, the decision bearing the weight of his whole existence. Could he be himself and order the salad, or did he have to lie and order the steak?

Could he confess to having OCD, or was it about to cost him his second boyfriend—the one he absolutely didn't want to lose?

The confusion and panic roiled inside Adam until he was in danger of not being able to order anything because he was going to throw up his dinner no matter what it was.

"Adam?"

The voice—Denver's—cut through enough to still him, but not for long. The waitress had come. She'd taken Denver's order and was waiting for Adam.

"Adam, are you okay?" Face full of concern, Denver reached across the table and captured Adam's hand.

He won't want you. He won't want you once he knows. He'll never hold your hand like this, never look at you with concern—only like the waitress, like you're a disease. Because you are. You're sick, and no one can ever love you. Never.

"I'm sorry," Adam whispered, pulled his hand from Denver's, and ran for the bathroom. He didn't need to eat to get sick. He was going to lose whatever was in his stomach right now.

Except the bathroom teemed with big, gruff men who regarded Adam as if he belonged on the bottom of their boot. Adam turned tail, searching for a new target.

He ended up settling on the garbage can just outside the front door, dry heaving before staggering away into the parking lot. He enjoyed a few moments of confusion, not knowing where he should go or what he should do before the panic attack claimed him. Then it was all narrowing airways and gasping for air, his brain, having melted down, passing the joy on to the rest of his body.

"Hold on." Strong arms came around Adam, guiding him to the ground, cradling him close. "Easy. Easy there, baby."

Denver. Denver was helping Adam through his panic attack. Moved and horrified at once, Adam gulped hard, panic warring with shame at Denver having to see him like this, but Denver held him fast, never wavering.

"Shh. Take it easy. I got you. Settle down."

Adam gathered enough air to whisper, "I'm sorry."

Those strong arms held him tight, stroking his hair. "Hush. You got nothing to be sorry for." They were in the middle of the parking lot, cars maneuvering around them, patrons giving them odd looks, but Denver ignored them all, focused only on Adam. "You okay? You need to see a doctor?"

For a minute he thought about lying, and if he thought there was any chance Denver would drop him off at the ER and leave, he'd have done it. But all that would happen was that he'd get slapped with a $300 copay on his student health insurance for being told— in front of Denver—what he already knew. He shook his head, waiting for Denver's frustration, his irritation, his demand to know what the hell was wrong with him, then.

Denver took this in the same stride as everything else. "Okay. If you're sure, then I'm gonna take you to the truck. That okay?"

So much shame. Nodding, Adam sank into Denver's chest. Briefly, though, because then Denver helped him to his feet and—with aching tenderness— led Adam away.

He tucked Adam into his seat belt like a child, asking him over and over again if he was okay, verifying several times that he didn't need to see a doctor. Eventually he went around to his side and got in. Adam tensed, bracing for the questions, but Denver said nothing, only started the truck and drove.

He didn't take them far—they were at some park Adam didn't know the name of but had driven by, a patch of green dominated by a small pond in the center and a dilapidated picnic area to the south. When Adam looked at Denver in confusion, this time it was Denver who blushed.

"You said you needed to tell me something, and you seemed nervous. I don't know why, but that sort of thing always seems easier by water to me."

Adam considered this through his panicked haze, thrown off course. Were confessions easier by water? He had no idea. He stared over the hood of the truck, trying to decide. Ducks floated by, quacking at one another. The pond lapped at the grassy shore. The setting sun glinted off the rippling surface of the water. He stopped panicking by degrees, his attack subsiding, leaving him simply weary.

He nodded, sinking into his seat in quiet defeat. "Yes. I think you're right."

Denver killed the engine, but he made no other move, not to get out of the truck, not to speak, not to do anything. For a long time they sat in silent communion. Eventually the impending conversation ate through Adam's peace. Taking a deep breath to stifle the new rise of panic, he spoke.

"I have obsessive-compulsive disorder."

He whispered it, but it felt like five gunshots coming through the windshield, or at least three. *I have OCD. I'm mentally ill.*

When Denver said nothing, Adam had to glance at him. He found Denver frowning, but in thought, not judgment. "Sorry, I feel like I should know what that is, but I don't. Could you explain it to me?"

This was not what Adam had expected, and for a second he suspected Denver was having him on. "Yes you have. Everyone's heard of OCD."

Denver relaxed on a breath. "Oh. Okay. Yeah." He waved his hands vaguely in the air. "You need things clean, are kind of fussy? Sure. Is that what this is about?"

Why did it hurt so much to see that reaction? Why, even though he'd expected it, did it cut him to his core? "Yes. I'm sorry."

He braced for distaste.

But once again, Denver threw him a curveball—it was he who panicked now. "Okay—but can you tell me where I screwed up? I know I'm not the neatest guy in the world, but I'm not the worst. Is it the truck?"

The truck? "What in the world would the truck have to do with this?"

"I thought maybe it wasn't clean enough." His expression shuttered. "It's me, isn't it? I don't clean up right. Not good enough."

Wait, what? Adam shook, upset and off-kilter. "Are you making fun of me?"

It wasn't much consolation, but Denver seemed as lost as he was. "Hell, no. I'm trying to fix this." He grimaced. "Which is stupid, isn't it? I'm sorry. I should let you finish. Or maybe I can finish it for you. You don't want to be with some gym rat. Right? Well, go on, then."

He'd been curt at the end, which was scary, but not half as scary as what he was saying. "What are you talking about? Of course I want to be with you. But you don't want to be with me. I have OCD. It's more than being fussy. It's a lot more. It's awful, and I'm a mess, and I've been trying not to let you see, but I'm going crazy waiting for you to figure it out, so it's better to just tell you and let you push me away now, because if I fall any harder for you, I don't know what I'm going to do—"

At this point Denver maneuvered himself in the truck so he could grab Adam's shoulders. He didn't shake him, but he held Adam in a grip so firm it felt like a vise, and when he spoke, his gaze bore into Adam's eyes.

"I ain't ever gonna push you away, Adam Ellery. I don't know how you got that into your head, but I ain't."

Adam went slack in his lover's grip, and the rest of the truth spilled out. "You don't know. You don't even know half of it. I'm awful. Nobody would want to be with me, not if they knew."

Denver let go of Adam's left shoulder to stroke his cheek, his great, fat thumb catching a silent tear.

"Try me," Denver demanded. "You just try and find the horrible secret about you that's going to drive me away."

In that one, shining moment, Adam knew something rare, something other people seemed to find so easily. Like a shooting star across the sky, in the cab of that truck, Adam knew hope. It went as quickly as it came, drowning in the great and mighty sea of uncertainty. But he remembered what it had been like, and he clung to its memory as he pried open the door guarding the secrets of his heart and allowed Denver to see.

THEY ENDED up ordering pizza, right there at the lake.

Sitting together on the bank while they gazed out at the water, Adam told Denver how he had to count the ceiling tiles in his seventh-grade classroom, having to go back and start again when he lost count because his peers figured out what he was doing and deliberately tried to throw him off course. In the middle of this story, his stomach rumbled, and Denver put a hand on his thigh, stilling him as he got out his phone. After placing an order, he motioned for Adam to continue.

Adam did, outlining every excruciating detail of his past, leading up to his diagnosis, taking him headlong into the present day.

"I'm better than I ever was," he said, feeling like he should soften this somehow, and this was at least the truth. "I mean, I struggle with it every day, and I always will. It's part of who I am." He glanced nervously at Denver. "A big part."

Denver gave Adam a stern look. "You really thought I was going to dump you because of this? Because you have OCD?"

"Denver, I'm mentally ill. I mean—I don't need to go to an asylum or anything, but there's no making it better than it is. I'm sick. In the head. And it will always get in the way. It is in the way."

Denver raised his eyebrows dubiously. "So I'm a dummy if I don't toss you over for being sick?"

Adam felt flustered. Why was this so hard? "You don't understand. OCD is in the way, and if it isn't, it will be. My OCD is why I can't go to your place or have you come to mine. It's one of my tics. That's the deal with OCD: there's no control, and that freaks us out, so our brains randomly pick rules to enforce like a demilitarized zone, and then I'm trapped."

"Wait—I don't get that one," Denver said, no teasing at all. "That's why you can't have me over? The OCD?" Adam nodded. Denver looked even more confused. "Sorry—how does that work exactly?"

Adam sighed. "I don't really understand it myself, but I've had it as a tic since I can remember. It's a rule in my head: People belong in their own spaces. I belong in my house. You belong in yours. We can't mix it up. If it gets mixed up, things are wrong, and I panic."

Denver was still frowning. "You mean, nobody can visit you? Ever?"

Adam shook his head. "No. Well—obviously they do. But I hate it. I spend the whole time calming myself down. It's a disaster."

"Your whole life? What about when you were a kid?"

Adam's cheeks burned. "Same thing. Except a lot more embarrassing, because they kept trying to convince me it was a silly thing to be upset about. Which I knew, but I couldn't stop my reaction."

"But you said you dated Brad—" Adam could see understanding dawn on Denver's face. "Ah. You shared a house. That made it okay?"

Adam nodded. "Don't get me wrong. It was still hard. He belonged in his room, you see, and me in

mine. It made him crazy. Usually he came to my room
and I sort of faked it, or tried to. He could always tell."

"You mean he told you you were an idiot for freaking out and fucked you anyway?"

Adam tucked his knees to his chest and buried his
face in them. Was that what had happened? Really?
That wasn't how he'd have described it, but Denver's
blunt speech was like lifting a veil. Had he basically
endured while Brad fucked him, waiting for him to go
away?

*Yes. Yes it was, you pathetic thing. And it was why
you went full-on whore for Denver, because finally, finally it was your turn to have the fun.*

Adam shrank into himself, overcome with shame.

Denver's hands were on him again, but before he
could say anything, a car door slammed. "Did someone
order a pizza?"

Adam enjoyed a moment's miserable wallow
while Denver got up, paid the driver, and settled back
down. When he came back, he hauled Adam into his
lap, wrapping his arms around him until he was all but
swallowed against his body.

"Okay. I have a lot to say, but I need to make sure
you're done. Is that it? Is that what you wanted to tell
me, your big secret? That everything you think is going
to drive me away?"

Adam could smell the pizza, and it made him even
more aware of how hungry he was. It seemed fitting
somehow to be starving as he waited for Denver's rejection. He was empty through and through. He nodded.

Denver nodded back. "Okay. First off, I gotta tell
you, babe. You're gonna have to work a hell of a lot
harder than that to get me to turn tail."

Adam looked up at him, incredulous. "I just told you I can't be in your house without a panic attack."

"Well, yeah. I don't see this as a big problem until it's too cold to fuck you in weird places around Tucker Springs, and even then, I can get pretty creative. But I'm also noticing you aren't living in the same house you grew up in, and this is your second place you've lived in since you got here. I'm betting there's a work-around, if we look for it."

"Well, yes, but—"

"But nothing. I ain't gonna act like that princess you used to date. I got plenty of flaws, and I have my own secrets I need to tell you, but being a prick about other people's issues ain't one of them."

Adam hardly knew what to say. After several seconds of being very overcome, he finally settled on a breathy, "Oh?"

"Yeah." Denver opened the pizza box, put two big slices on a napkin, and passed it over to Adam. "Here. You eat this, and while you do, I'll tell you some of my secrets, and when we've both got everything on the table, we'll scope it all out and decide whether or not this is something we want to make work. If not, we'll just share a pizza, kiss each other goodbye, and call it a nice run."

Adam's stomach tried to exit through his throat. "I don't want to say goodbye to you."

Denver stroked his cheek sadly. "I hope you still say that when I'm done. But if you don't, you know it's okay, right?"

Adam wanted to tell him no way was he saying goodbye no matter what. But he nodded instead, settled into the grass to listen, and because he knew Denver would get after him if he didn't, he ate.

CHAPTER SIXTEEN

DENVER WAS nervous, no question. Ironically, he was more unsettled knowing all Adam's hesitancy had been about something so simple. He would never wish bad experiences on anyone, particularly Adam, but he couldn't help wishing they had more in common between their histories. Of course, the very idea of anyone rejecting Adam because he had OCD pissed Denver off, made him want to haul ass to this Bug Barn or whatever the name of that house was and beat this Brad into a better attitude.

However, it wasn't the moment for that right now. He owed Adam his own soul-baring. Denver stared out at the lake, steadied himself, and metaphorically waded in.

"It starts pretty boring, my story." He pulled absently at tufts of grass beside his knees. "Southern boy comes out, gets kicked out, gets himself in trouble. I was sixteen and living deep in the armpit of Arkansas, and I'd have been a hell of a lot better off to wait until I was older to leave. But I wasn't terribly smart." His hand stilled against the grass. "I was pretty miserable. My stepdad liked to beat me whenever he got the chance."

"You?" Adam said this dubiously around a mouthful of pizza. He glanced at Denver's body and shook his head.

Denver had to laugh. "You think I came out of my mama this big? I used to be a runt. Shot up late at eighteen, and even then I was on the lanky side. Always had a big frame, but if you don't get enough to eat, you're still just a bag of bones, nothing more than a body to take a bruising."

Adam looked ill. "He hurt you?"

"He? Hell, baby. Everybody hurt me back then." He tapped gently at Adam's temple. "I let them in here. Let them fuck with me, let them make me feel worthless. A lot of it was because I knew I was gay, knew they had reason to hate me for being a freak. Or so I saw it at the time." He eased back into the grass, feeling it tickle his elbows. "Basically I went from fucked-up to more fucked-up no matter what I did. Once I got kicked out, I dropped school, and I started sleeping around, trading my body for a place to stay. I saw it as taking boyfriends, but none of them cared for anything but getting a piece of me. They were tricks. Then one day I met Sonny. He actually was a boyfriend. A fucked-up one, but he wasn't a trick. He took me away from Arkansas, all the way to Oklahoma City." Denver shook his head. "He spent four years screwing with my head so much sometimes I wonder that I'll ever get it straightened out completely."

He paused, wondering how Adam would react. To his surprise, Adam held up his pizza. "You need to eat something," he said gently.

Denver wasn't hungry, not with all this crap churning his gut, but he loved that look on Adam's face—quietly determined, a little bit ticked off on Denver's behalf—and he took a bite.

"The thing with Sonny," he went on once his mouth was clear, "is that he didn't hit me. I wish he would have, though, because I would have left him then. But he messed with my head instead. Pointed out all the things wrong with me. Made it clear I'd never get anywhere without him. Made me remember how much I needed him. We played, but I found out later nobody liked him, not anybody who was for real in the scene. Sonny was one of the guys giving BDSM a bad name, but I didn't know that. Anyway. We played master and slave games, where I was his slave, but I think that was our whole relationship, and not in a healthy way. He needed me to need him, or he wasn't okay. I wasn't right in the head either over it—I wanted him to tell me what to do, and I think maybe I wanted him to tell me I was fucked-up."

Denver grimaced, hating the memory of how messed-up he'd been. "I got away from him, and I came here and straightened my life up. I'd already been into bodybuilding, but I got way into it here. For a while I was more formally in the BDSM scene officially, kind of like a cleanse, to figure out how Sonny and I had been doing it wrong. Mostly, though, I built my body and kept my head straight, and I decided I wasn't going to do relationships anymore. Just fucking on the side." He sighed. "Then I met you. That's my story. I never finished high school. I let some jerk push me around for four years. I'm not really smart, and I don't have an exciting future like you do. I do think I have my head in the right spot now, but you don't have to tell me you could do a lot better than me. I already know that for myself."

Adam stayed quiet after Denver finished, not saying anything, not moving, but he wasn't tense, just pensive as far as Denver could tell. Eventually he pushed the pizza box aside and moved closer.

"A therapist I used to have always told me when our brains aren't healthy, we look for unhealthy relationships." He laughed, a soft, sad sound, and shook his head. "I think I knew Brad was wrong for me a long time before he broke it off. Part of me knew he was best at being the voice I had inside my head, telling me I was bad in all the ways that felt familiar. When we're broken, it's like it's scary to hear we might be fixable. Or maybe that we don't need to be fixed, that we can be okay as we are. That's actually hardest for me. The idea that I might have to live with being OCD." He snorted. "There's no might about it. It's my brain, and I don't get a second one. But I don't know. It's like if someone's riding you, there's hope. Like there's that one magic insult that would unravel everything and make you normal."

Denver caught his face. "Baby, you don't need to be normal."

"I want to be." This was a whisper from the bottom of Adam's soul.

It was about then that Denver realized Adam didn't give a damn about any of Denver's confessions. Denver had given him the worst, and all Adam could do was fixate on how his own dirty secrets were going to drive Denver away. It made him want to laugh, maybe cry just a little. "So what's normal, baby?"

Adam had been leaning over Denver, and at this point he came all the way down, resting his face against

Denver's chest, speaking low and quiet into his shirt. "A guy who doesn't have to talk about how OCD runs his life. A guy who doesn't have to explain why he can't have his boyfriend over to his house. A guy who doesn't have to make sure his shoelaces are tucked into his shoes before he can go to sleep at night."

That one made Denver pause. "Really?"

Adam buried his face in Denver's shirt.

Denver smiled and bent forward to kiss his hair. Life. It was so damn funny sometimes. "I got news for you, baby. That normal guy you're talking about?" Adam nodded. Denver kissed his hair again. "I wouldn't want to date him. I certainly wouldn't order pizza for him by the pond, or try to decide whether or not I'd get arrested for fucking him there."

As he'd hoped, that remark made Adam lift his head. Warily, but Denver could see the interest there too. The hope mingling with the doubt. "You're just saying that."

"The hell I am. Adam, I've had that normal guy. He's fuckable, but he's forgettable. Here's a newsflash for you: this tic of yours you're so embarrassed about, the people's places thing? It might be the reason we're sitting here right now." Denver stroked his arms. "If I could have taken you home that first night, or even the second, I probably would have fucked and run. Even as cute as you are, I would have said, 'Nope, relationships are too hard,' and I'd have stuck to my guns. But you weren't normal, baby. You were something different. You were fussy and weird and fun and cute as all hell, and hotter than sin in an oven, and I wanted you. Maybe I would have stuck by it, I don't know. You're different enough it might have been okay. But I can tell you, the OCD helped. You're telling me it's who you are, that it's part of Adam Ellery. Well, good. Because I like Adam Ellery, not-normal and all."

Adam's eyes were damp, and he looked so sweet as he leaned forward and brushed his lips against Denver's. "I like you too."

"Even without a high school diploma? Even though I was dumb as rocks and let people boss me around?"

"Maybe especially because of that." Adam traced Denver's mouth with his finger. "And just so you know… I think I'd be okay with being arrested. If you were there."

Something big and thick was lodged in the center of Denver's chest, and his eyes were itchy. He smiled, a bit of a watery one, and pulled Adam down to his mouth. "I'll do my best to keep us quiet anyway."

CHAPTER SEVENTEEN

THE NEXT month went by for Adam in something of a blur. A happy, giddy, ridiculous whirlwind of one, but it was definitely a haze of happiness that carried him through his days. He had told Denver the truth, the whole truth, and not only was Denver still part of his life, he was actively working to help make Adam feel easier. The only fly in the ointment was Adam's OCD places thing.

Denver had a plan for that too.

"Is he pushing you?" This was the first thing Louisa asked when Adam told her about The Talk. "Is he trying to get you over it too fast?"

"No," Adam assured her. "In fact, he doesn't want to get me over it at all. He wants to work around it."

He did, and the ways he tried to make Adam's OCD at peace with a new place sometimes overwhelmed Adam nearly to tears. Denver's first effort to help Adam's OCD accept him was to begin simply telling Adam about his apartment, describing what it looked like. He took pictures and messaged them to Adam. *This is my kitchen. This is where I watch TV. I'm kind of thinking about a new couch, but I need to make a little more money first.*

Other things came out in those texts too. Sometimes things that surprised Adam, made him hold still and remember he wasn't the only one wading carefully into this relationship. Like when, shortly after the text about the couch, another one came through.

I actually have a line on a good job. Really good one, doing exactly what I want.

Adam read that excitedly and replied, *Oh yeah? What's that?*

Working at the gym where I go. Then he added, *Thing is, I need to get certified.*

You could do that, Adam told him.

But I'd have to get my GED first.

Adam almost—almost—typed back that this was no big deal, what was he waiting for? Then he remembered how often Denver referred to himself as dumb, how self-conscious he got around anything to do with school. For a moment, Adam wasn't sure what to say and wanted to panic. But this was too important to spiral out on, so he forced himself to remain calm and to think.

Well, he typed at last, *as it so happens, I'm not a bad hand with studying. If you ever want to try for it, I'd love to help you.*

He was still Adam, so as soon as he'd sent that he had to add, *If that would be okay with you.*

It made him feel better than he'd known he could feel to have Denver reply, *Yeah, actually, that would be great. Thank you.*

Denver took him out to various places around the Light District every afternoon before he had to go into work, unless he had to go early. After the conversation about GEDs, he seemed to open a floodgate, telling Adam about how frustrating it was to always work late, how even though it was easy, sometimes it was too easy.

"It used to be fun because it was a great way to get tail," he said one afternoon as they sat in the truck at the park because it was too cold to get out. He goosed the side of Adam's ass. "Now it just keeps me from the tail I already got."

Said ass was still tender from a spanking session they'd squeezed in the day before, but of course that only made Adam happy. He wriggled against the seat to feel more of the burn. "Do you have to have certification to work at the gym? Could you do something simpler, maybe, in the meantime?"

Oddly enough, these questions made Denver blush. "Well, yeah. Tiny keeps asking me that too. But if I do work there, then I feel like I gotta go take the test. Which I might fail. Which I'll *probably* fail."

"Even if you did fail it—which I doubt you would, if we practiced it—you can take it again, you know."

"You don't get it, babe. I ain't like you. I'll never have your kind of smarts."

"Yes, but you have plenty of other smarts that I'm missing. And to be quite serious, studying is not difficult. I should know, as I've done a lot of it. It's not about being smart, not like you're saying. It's about knowing how to play the game. I'm good at this game. Really good. I think I'm with studying like you are with weights." The idea made him sit up straight in the truck. "Ooh! What about that? What if you teach me about weights, and I teach you about studying?"

He wasn't sure how Denver would react to it, and at first he thought maybe it had been a mistake. But slowly his boyfriend started to smile, and then he nodded, like he was warming up to some brilliant idea. "Yeah. You know? That might not be a bad idea."

IT WAS a great idea. It just didn't go as smoothly as either of them would have hoped.

To start, the gym was loud and noisy, which didn't help Adam. He didn't have a phobia about noisy places or anything, but they didn't do him any favors when he was doing something new or difficult, and his OCD wasn't ready to go down without a fight. The whole idea of using sweaty weights everyone else had used did not sit well with him. At all.

"I'm sorry," he apologized as he failed for the fifth time to pick up a stinky, sweaty weight, his hands shaking, his panic attack sliding gracefully into place.

"It's okay," Denver told him, but he frowned while he said it, and he didn't offer to take Adam back the next day.

Studying was just as difficult for Denver. They met at the library, where Adam had found a GED study guide, the very sight of which flipped Denver out so much for a second Adam thought he was going to overturn the table.

"I can't do all that! Jesus! Who the hell can learn all that stuff?"

Adam glanced down at the requirements, which he'd thought were pretty meager. "We can break it down, though. One little piece at a time."

"Forget it. This was a stupid idea, and it isn't ever going to work," Denver declared—and he stormed out.

Adam, naturally, panicked. Normally Denver would have sent a text, or not stormed out at all, but this was his anxiety, so he didn't. Adam tried to compose several different consoling messages, but they seemed lame, and he caved and didn't send any. He felt like a failure.

Then Denver did text, finally, though he didn't bring up the library. *I'm going to swing by your house at seven. Wear something you can get sweaty in.*

Sweaty? Oh God, they were going to do the gym again. Adam was trying to figure out how to say this wasn't a good idea when Denver texted again. *Trust me.*

Adam took a deep breath and sent a reply. *Okay.*

It didn't mean he didn't feel like his insides were being torn apart by a bag of cats when Denver showed up at his apartment complex, but he did as he was told and wore gym clothes. He'd also taken a Xanax.

"Looking good," Denver said as Adam climbed into the truck.

Adam smiled loopily.

He had himself all ready for the gym, which was why when Denver drove into a residential neighborhood, Adam could only frown.

"We're going to do some weight training." Denver sounded proud of himself. He pulled a fob down from his visor and hit the button. "In my friend Jase's garage."

The door in front of them went up, and Adam stared at a sparse, clean space with a bench, some mats, and some free weights showcased in the center.

"These are my weights, and a few of Jase's. I cleaned them all, and everything is disinfected." Denver gestured to the garage. "It's someone else's house, yes. But it's a garage, and the door is open. I was hoping maybe that would make things easier."

Adam wasn't sure if it would or not, but the idea that Denver had gone to such lengths to accommodate his neuroses touched him in a way that made him want to curl up against Denver and purr. "I'll certainly try," he said instead.

Despite his optimism, it was hard. The garage was practically empty, but the door into the house was right there, and random objects littered about reminded Adam that they weren't his and that he shouldn't be there. What made things okay, though, was Denver. Every time Adam tried to flip out, Denver made him focus on the weights, on the work in front of him. He used the same authority he did when they were having sex, except there wasn't anything sexy about right now. Adam had jacked off to more than one fantasy of Denver "teaching him weights," which had mostly been Denver fucking him over the bench. There was no fucking during this lesson, and no fucking around. Denver took weights seriously, and therefore so did Adam.

"You got to be careful about how much you start out with," Denver cautioned him as he taught him how to curl. "Muscles get angry fast, and they yell for a long time. Guys think they gotta kill themselves to bulk up, and it's true there's a burn, but you need to be smart or you'll injure yourself in a way you won't appreciate. Especially with arms. Your hip is in a much more secure socket, but your arm isn't. It's so you can have freedom of movement, but it comes at a cost. Rotator cuff surgery isn't a picnic."

Adam nodded through all the lectures, listening, yes, and doing what he was told, but it was so much less about weights and so much more about following the sound of Denver's voice. He began to think Denver could tell him to go into the stranger's house and lie down on the floor, and he'd do it without wondering what in the room was a fire hazard. Denver made everything okay. Everything. It made his own panic go still and quiet, ready to obey.

He tried to show this to Denver, tried to communicate his obedience, his willingness to be a good student, a good boy. He nodded and kept eye contact whenever Denver gave him a direction. A few times he even said, "Yes, sir," and he meant it from the bottom of his balls. Nothing about any of the weights lesson was sexual, and Adam didn't want it to be either, not now. This felt like communion. He didn't want it to end. If he continued to obey, he might get his wish.

Denver stroked his face, his fingers catching in Adam's hair. "You seem pretty calm. That just a front, or are you really?"

"I'm calm," Adam assured him, leaning into that touch. "You make me calm." Denver smiled, and it spurred Adam to confess the rest. "I like it when you tell me what to do and how to do it. I like it a lot. It feels like being free. I wish I could do it all the time."

Denver's eyes hooded. "Yeah?"

"Yes." Adam turned his head so he could kiss Denver's palm reverently. "Yes, sir."

Denver's hand kept stroking his face. The door was open, letting in the cool evening air. It made Adam's skin prickle. It made him want to ask Denver to close the door and fuck him. He didn't say anything, though, just kept waiting to see what Denver would say next.

What Denver said was, "Clean up your weights and help me put the stuff back in my truck."

It was a little disappointing, but Adam did it any-way because Denver had told him to. He could feel the spell threatening to slip away, but he clung to it, making it stay, and Denver helped, giving an order every now and again. He started calling Adam *boy*, too, which made Adam feel calm and good. The best, though, came when Denver told Adam to roll up the mat, and Adam said, "Okay."

Denver grabbed Adam by the arm, not hurting him, but with enough force to get his attention. "You say, 'yes, sir,' when I tell you to do something, other-wise I'm going to punish you."

Adam stilled. "Yes, sir," he said, his voice thick. "I'm sorry, sir."

Denver nodded gruffly and smacked him playfully on the ass. "All right, then. Keep working, boy."

Adam did. He never missed a cue to call Denver sir. When they were finished, Denver ruffled his hair and smiled at him.

"You did good, boy. Real good. So good that I'm going to give you a reward."

"Yes, sir," Adam replied, beaming like a puppy.

Denver gave him a stern look. "Now, what I'm giv-ing you is your reward, so if you don't like it, you have to say so. You're also going to have to do something uncomfortable to get your reward too. If it's too much, you have to tell me so I can make it better for you."

Jesus. Adam was ready to come right there in a stranger's open garage. "Yes, sir."

"All right. Now get in the truck, boy. And go ahead and play with yourself. I know this all got you hard, and I wouldn't mind watching you fiddle your dick while I drive."

Adam fiddled, all right. He spread his legs and jacked himself because Denver told him he was a good, good boy, and he was just about to come all over the dashboard when the truck stopped. Sitting up in a bit of a blur, Adam saw they were parked in an unfamiliar apartment complex. Except it *was* familiar, he realized as he thought more about it. He'd seen pictures.

This was Denver's place.

CHAPTER EIGHTEEN

"I TOLD you it was going to be uncomfortable," Denver said, his voice soothing and commanding at once. "I want you to try, though, because a good boy will try. You won't stay long. Just long enough to get your reward. Then we can go, or we can stay. Your call."

Adam wanted to stay, but whatever magic had borne him all evening had begun to wane. He took deep breaths, telling himself he could do it. It didn't work.

Then he realized he was using the wrong coach.

He turned to Denver, shaking, knowing he looked pale or green or maybe both. "I need you to tell me to do it. I think I can, but it has to come from you. I need you to boss me into your place." He swallowed. "You have to be bigger and meaner than the voice inside my head. But it listens to you. It doesn't listen to me."

Denver studied him for a long time, so long Adam thought he wasn't going to do it. Then finally he leaned forward. "Say it right."

God. God. So bossy, so fucking Denver that Adam wanted to suck his cock to show him how much he loved it. "Please boss me around, sir, and tell me I have to go into your apartment."

Denver's eyes glinted for a moment in a kind of carnal pleasure that made Adam's mouth water. Then he took Adam's chin hard in his hand and said, "Boy, you get your ass out of this truck right now, and go into my apartment. Walk in the front door, get on your knees in the middle of the carpet, and put your hands behind your back and wait for me to tell you what to do."

"Yes, sir," Adam whispered, but he was afraid.

Denver pinched his chin. "I don't care what your OCD tells you to do. I'm telling your OCD that I'm in charge for a little while. I'll make sure the fire alarm works and everything's okay. If the OCD needs something checked, it can ask me, but it has to say, 'Sir, please, may my OCD ask you a question?' and then it has to tell me and let me fix it. Then it has to let you get your reward. It can't say no. It can't yell at you or tell you that you're doing anything wrong. That's my job. You get it, boy? You're mine right now. I'm going to boss you so hard you come over it. Because you're going to come before you leave my place. You're going to learn that being in my apartment means coming hard and good and being safe. You got that, boy? Look me in the eye and tell me if you understand."

"Yes, sir." Adam's eyes were unfocused.

"Yes, sir, what?" Denver demanded.

"Yes, I understand."

"You understand what, boy?"

So hard. So hard and almost mean, but in a way that felt so safe and strong, and Adam's anxiety stopped and listened, and it let him speak. "I understand, sir, that

I'm going to go into your apartment and kneel down with my hands behind my back. I understand you're going to make me come. I understand that I'm safe with you, and that you're going to teach me that I'm safe in your apartment."

"Say, 'I'm going to learn that being in your apartment means I come like a rocket.'"

"I'm going to learn that being in your apartment means I come like a rocket, sir."

Denver pulled him in close and kissed Adam on the mouth, a rough, possessive kiss that made the last of Adam's anxiety melt away.

It returned, though, as they came to Denver's door. Adam faltered and began to shake, and Denver stilled him with a hand on his shoulder. "What are you going to do when I open this door?"

Adam tried not to hyperventilate. "I'm going to go into the living room and kneel with my hands behind my back, sir."

"Good boy. Except push your jeans and underwear to your ankles first. I feel like seeing your bare ass and dick flapping around while you kneel in front of me."

Why that made Adam calm, he couldn't say, but it did. Maybe it was the image of Denver standing in front of him. Maybe it was being naked, counterintuitive as that was. Maybe it was the shift into something semisexual, which was fun.

Whatever it was, Adam clung to it like it was his only lifeline out of hell.

When the door opened, Adam didn't allow himself to look around. He beelined for the living room, dropped trou, and fell to his knees. His breath came hard and fast, and to his incredible shame, he wanted to sob. Shame swamped him. It was his boyfriend's apartment, and he couldn't be inside it, not for a minute—

Smack!

The slap came hard—hard!—across Adam's bare ass, and it knocked him forward. "Put your hands behind your back, boy, right now, or I will make you stand in the corner with your dick in a cage."

A dick cage? The idea intrigued him briefly, but he couldn't be distracted from his panic, not even by a dick cage. Adam's hands went behind his back, but the tears he'd been trying to withhold began to fall. "I'm sorry, sir."

"You crying because you're afraid of me, or because you're scared of being here, or because you're shaming yourself?"

Adam wanted to lie, but he couldn't, not to The Voice. "Shaming myself, sir."

"That's against the rules, Adam, and I'm going to have to punish you." He stroked Adam's cheek. Then he removed Adam's glasses, put them on a shelf behind him, and pinched Adam hard on the ass. "Hands and knees. Now."

Adam felt the distinct and varied parts of his psyche gathering to try to suss out whether or not this was bad, if he—they?—should panic. Before he could figure it out, Denver crouched down and cupped Adam's face, looking him straight in the eye.

"I know you're nervous, but you said you liked giving in to me, and that feels good. Remember, punishment is part of play too, though it doesn't mean it's a game. Except I know this is serious for you, that your OCD comes with the Adam package. You listen to your bully voice, maybe, because on one level you need to follow it. You feel better when you do. Nod if I'm on the right track here."

Adam did, but it was self-acknowledgment as much as to Denver's statement. He loved rules. He loved the structure of academia. He loved the lab. He loved puzzles and problems and the laws of physics.

Denver kept going. "This is part of who I am too. I like telling you what to do, making you follow. It makes me feel good when you obey me." He stroked Adam's cheek with his thumb. "I like how your eyes go calm when I say obey. When you call me sir. It makes me proud of you, and it makes me feel so good. I like that you like to make me feel good, that you want to make me proud."

"I do," Adam said, trying to bleed sincerity. "I do want to make you proud. It makes me feel good. Safe."

"And strong," Denver added, his mouth tipping into a sideways smile.

It was so true. "And strong, sir."

"Okay." Denver sobered. "So here's the deal. If there's something you need to be punished for, if you screw up, I want to be the one who punishes you. Not your OCD. You said it trusts me. It should trust me here too, then."

Adam faltered. "That can't ever work. I screw up every day. All the time."

"Then I guess I'll just have to see you every day. We'll make a list. You can text your mistakes to me you think you need to be punished for."

Okay, that Adam had to balk at, and hard. "That feels like therapy. I don't know that we should do that. It's not right for us to mix my OCD and play too much."

Denver rubbed at his chin. "Fair point. Well, how about things between you and me, then? If you think you need to be punished for something between you and me, you let me handle the punishing."

Was that still therapy? Adam didn't know. It seemed okay, probably. How the hell he was going to bring this up with his actual therapist, he had no idea. He didn't think he could. He'd have to tell Louisa. "Okay. Except most of what I think I screw up with you is that I'm afraid I'm too messed-up, and any second now you'll figure that out and dump me."

He wasn't prepared for how angry Denver looked at that statement. "Oh, so you don't trust me? You think I'm lying to you when I tell you that I like you how you are?"

"It's one thing to say it, but look at me now, look at me here! I'm a mess!"

Denver's eyes glinted. "So you're telling me you need to be punished for being a bad boyfriend?"

Adam's cheeks colored. "Yes. Yes. I'm terrible. I'm horrible."

"And even if I don't think you're horrible, you're secretly horrible, and it's only a matter of time before I find out?"

"Yes."

"Okay." Denver pushed to his feet and slapped Adam on the ass again. "So, ground rules, Adam. No sir-ing just now. How are you with pain? Does it flip you out?"

Adam lifted his head to look at Denver, not yet sure if he should be uneasy. "I don't have panic attacks over pain, no. And I love the spanking, you know that. But what kind of pain are you talking about now?"

"Nothing you can't handle, but pain that's different enough to register inside your brain that it's a punishment, something that will allow you to let go. Here's

what I'm planning. I'm going to paddle you, Adam, because you're a bad boyfriend. That's going to be your
punishment."

Paddle. "Like fraternities use?"

"Kinda, yeah, but more professional, I guess I'd
say. It's a nice leather paddle, and especially since I
spanked you yesterday, it's going to sting pretty good.
In fact, you might cry, and if that feels good, don't hold
back. I ain't gonna judge. But if everything gets to be
too much, if you feel unsafe, I want you to say *red*,
and I'll stop. I'll give you a hanky again in case you
feel like you can't talk, so if you call out or drop it, either one will get me to end things. But know that I will
not *hurt* you. Not beyond fun hurt, or hurt you want.
I won't make you bleed. I will not bruise you beyond
what your body can take, and you won't be permanently damaged. I know exactly what I'm doing, and I'm in
control. Most important, though, is you need to remember when I'm done punishing you, it's done. If you're a
bad boyfriend on another occasion, I will punish you at
that time for that specific instance, and then that issue
will also be over. Do you understand? And we're back
to sir for this, just to be clear."

Adam did understand. "Yes, sir. Yes, please. Please
punish me for being a bad boyfriend, sir."

Denver knelt beside him and placed a large hand
on Adam's ass. "You're going to get twenty slaps, ten
on each cheek. Count them, one to twenty, and say,
'thank you, sir,' after each one." He massaged Adam's
ass reassuringly. "Remember how to stop me?"

Adam nodded. "Yes, sir." Except he was already dubious. Only twenty? He took more than that
all the time. How was this going to be any kind of a
punishment?

"All right." Denver left briefly to get the paddle, which he showed to Adam, letting him see how clean and well-maintained it was, and to get a handkerchief, which was also clean and neatly folded. Adam gripped it and braced himself on his hands and knees for the blow as Denver took up his position behind him.

"Here we go. Don't forget to count, boy."

Then it began.

Smack.

Adam's head came up on a gasp. He almost forgot to count right away, it was so intense. Sharp, *biting*, and far, far too focused. *Pain.* This wasn't the heat and burn of a spanking, this was pain, and it was only the first….

"O-one. Th-thank you, sir."

They kept coming, and Adam wanted to cry by strike three. They burrowed inside him, needles pricking into his belly on already sensitive flesh. The worst of it, though, was that he knew *why* he was receiving them.

Bad boyfriend. I've been a bad boyfriend. Bad boyfriends get spanked. Adam shuddered and hung his head.

"I need your count, boy," Denver said, his voice full and rough and overflowing with authority. "Loud and clear, and be sure to thank me."

"Seven," Adam choked, near to crying but unable to let the tears go, even though Denver had told him to. "Thank you, sir."

At eleven, he started to shout so loudly that he faltered, and it wasn't until he fell out of the space that he realized he'd been in a kind of pain haze, a beautiful zone where it was okay to yell.

Denver yanked him right back into it.

"Shouting is okay, baby. My neighbors have heard it all. In fact they've probably been wondering why it's been so damn quiet." He tweaked Adam's shoulder. "Say the count again, and no more worrying about anything but what number you're on and whether or not you've thanked me for beating the shit out of your ass."

Adam did as he was told. He did yell, a lot, and when he got to seventeen, he began to shake. It hurt so bad. He was so weak that Denver had to brace him under his belly with his knee, keeping him from collapsing so he could take the beatings. He wanted it to stop, wanted to say red so this would end, except he didn't need it to stop, and honestly he wasn't sure he truly wanted it to, not really, so he didn't say the word. He breathed hard and whined and yelped and swore and shouted and whimpered, and he counted and said, "Thank you, sir," until he'd said it for the twentieth time.

Denver smoothed a hand over Adam's back, let it travel up to his head. "Good boy. It's done."

That was when Adam finally cried.

It started as a sniffle, a burble of emotion that caught in his chest, and then it came out, soft, bone-weary sobs that made him collapse. Denver didn't embrace him, only kept stroking his back, easing his knee out and letting Adam down onto the carpet.

The carpet that was probably dirty. But it didn't matter, because the only thing that mattered for Adam were Denver's words. *It's done.* They kept ringing in his head. *It's done. It's done.* Why the hell they made him feel so good, he couldn't say, but they were more freeing than any order Denver had ever given him, any of the bossing around, any sex, anything.

It's done. And it was, it really was. Even Adam's OCD wept in relief.

He felt something cool and soothing on his ass, which he became aware was burning as if it'd been set on fire. Denver was rubbing lotion on his skin with a tenderness that made Adam ache all over in an entirely different way.

"That feels good," Adam said when he was able to speak. "Sir. I like how you always put lotion on me after you spank me, but it feels extra good this time."

"This is called aftercare." Denver slipped Adam's glasses carefully onto his face. "If you ever play with anybody and they don't do this, never play with them again."

Adam shut his eyes, surrendering to the wonderful feel of lotion or whatever it was against his skin. "I don't want to play with anyone else."

Denver's hand paused, and he reached up with his other hand to squeeze Adam's shoulder. "Me either."

They didn't say anything else through the rest of the aftercare, not until a flash of light startled Adam. He didn't realize what it had been until Denver came around to his front, grinning as he held up his cell phone. On its screen was a picture of Adam's ass. His fire-engine-red ass.

"Holy shit," Adam whispered.

Denver's grin went wider. "Beautiful, isn't it? It's redder than usual because of the paddle, and it's going to sting for so much longer and in a different way than you're used to. You're going to hurt *so* much when-ever you sit, not in an unbearable way, but in a way that makes you think of what happened here. And every time you remember, you'll think about how you're not a bad boyfriend, not anymore."

Adam thought he was going to cry again. Emo-tion choked his throat, and he kissed the closest bit of

Denver he could reach while still half collapsed on the floor, which meant he kissed Denver's elbow.

Denver bent and claimed his mouth. "Now for your reward. What I originally had in mind isn't going to work because of your ass, so what would you like, baby?"

"I don't know," Adam said, the words a lie. He knew exactly what he wanted, but he had to work up the courage to ask.

Denver kissed him again, beaming. "I'm so proud of you, Adam. Do you realize how long you've been here, how hard you let me paddle you? You're so strong, baby. You're a perfect boyfriend right now, you know that? Not a hair out of place on you, you good boy."

That was it, Adam couldn't stop himself now. "I want you to fuck my mouth again." He let his naked longing show in his face. When Denver's eyes darkened, Adam let the rest out. "I keep wishing you'd do it again, and you asked what I'd like. I want that. I want to feel like I can't breathe because your big cock is in my mouth."

Denver all but licked his lips. "Oh yeah, you can have that, baby. Good boys like you can get throat-fucked whenever they want. The only thing is, I want it to be extra special. You get yourself naked, and I'll figure out how to make it an extra good treat for you."

As Denver disappeared into his bedroom, Adam tried to scurry to his feet to undress, but it was hard, in part because his whole body was jelly, and also because his ass hurt every time he moved. His skin was actual fire.

Every flame, every burn whispered, *You're a good boyfriend, Adam.*

He did have a low-grade panic over being in the wrong house, but it was faint, and his OCD was so far over the moon for Denver that it didn't matter. He wasn't in the wrong house, because this was Denver's house.

Adam knew very well that after tonight, he belonged, completely and utterly, to Denver Rogers.

He'd just set his glasses back on the shelf and made it out of his last bit of clothing when Denver returned, an almost feral grin on his face… and a pair of leather cuffs and a length of rope in his hand.

IN THE dim lights of his playroom, Denver palmed himself and stared down at the beauty that was Adam bound in front of him. His lover's eyes were soft and fixed on Denver, specifically on his cock. His mouth gaped open hungrily.

Denver allowed himself a single moment to wonder how in the hell he'd gotten here.

His confidence rippled as he sheathed himself in a condom, as he realized what he'd been thinking. *Maybe we could get tested together so I could shoot down Adam's throat.* It wasn't the cum-shooting that tripped him up but the idea that he, Denver Rodgers, perpetual fuckup, had thought about getting tested so he could be loyal to a lover. He liked it. A lot.

But it made him hesitate.

He was used to having a guy mew and moan as he tied them up so he could do them, but he'd never taken such tender care while he did so, never stopped so many times to tell his lover he was a good boy, never meant it in the same way. It had started as something he did out of respect for Adam's OCD, but he knew it was as much for himself as it was for his lover.

Funny how OCD could cripple Adam so badly but let him get handcuffed and trussed up like a turkey. This was some fine rope work, binding Adam's arms tight to his chest but keeping his hands up and off his burning—beautiful—ass. Denver had dug up some pads that worked for knee rests, something he usually didn't bother with unless the twink asked for it, but this was Adam. Adam made him want to pamper and fuss and do all kinds of things he'd never done. Adam made him want to make everything special.

Adam wanted to be fucked in the throat because it was a treat. Holy fucking shit, Denver was in love.

He probably really was, he acknowledged as he lined himself up at Adam's lips. As the lust took over, he let the scary thought—that he was in love with Adam—take root. He thrust deep into Adam's mouth, not taking his air yet, wanting to make this last. He stroked Adam's face, loving those big brown eyes as they stared up with such naked obedience and yearning.

"You're a good boy," he whispered, and Adam mewed around his cock. Denver glanced down to make sure Adam had his hanky, then tapped his cheek in warning. "You ready?"

Adam gave a muffled cry that sounded mostly like *God yes*. Denver nodded.

Then he went deep.

It was better than the first time. Not because Adam was tied up for this round, though that was nice. Not because Adam stared up at him with liquid Bambi eyes—through glasses, as Denver had made him put them back on. It was because Adam had opened up and taken him in, *asked* Denver to fuck out his air. Adam trusted him to make it okay. Adam with OCD. Adam with all his fears. Adam, who wasn't simply someone to take to bed but someone to take home.

Denver groaned, everything in his vision out of focus except for Adam and the fire-red hanky in his hand. The world dissolved, all his shortcomings evaporating while he cared for Adam in the way they understood best. He couldn't wait until they could do this without the condom, because he wanted to leave part of himself inside of Adam, to mark him.

For now Denver nuzzled Adam once he pulled out, heart soaring as he realized Adam was beaming. "What's going on, baby?"

"I came." Adam looked dazed, stunned, and thrilled. His glasses were off-kilter too, an even sexier visual. "I totally came. Hands tied behind my back, you fucking my mouth, nothing touching my dick—I came."

He said it like he'd climbed Mt. Everest, which Denver supposed for Adam to let go like that probably was. Overflowing with pride and love, Denver kissed Adam before adjusting his glasses for him. "You did good, baby. Good boy."

"Good boyfriend," Adam murmured back, sounding proud.

Denver was proud too. And as he watched Adam basking in his triumphs, so many that night, Denver vowed he too would face his fears, no matter what shame came with them, because if Adam could conquer this, certainly Denver could handle a stupid little test.

CHAPTER NINETEEN

WHO KNEW there was so much freedom to be found in being tied up?

Adam did, was who. He'd had plenty of experience with it in the month since Denver had given him his first weights lesson, as he'd been tied up almost every day. In Denver's playroom mostly, which was good because it was January and damn cold outside. But there was a lot of playing. A *lot* of playing.

Today, for example, he was naked and kneeling with his feet tied to his wrists and a tight crisscross of leather straps binding the rest of him in place. He could move just enough to keep his knees from going to sleep, suspended between some sturdy metal piping that made a frame.

He also wore his glasses. Denver hardly ever let him put in his contacts anymore.

Denver stood before him in nothing but a pair of leather pants that made Adam's jaw hurt, "I need to get a job where I have more time free. Because I gotta get me more of this. Know what I mean, boy?"

Adam knew what he meant, but he couldn't say anything because at that particular moment he was gagged. He also had a three-inch tapered plug up his ass.

And the red hanky in his hand.

Gags and plugs had become a frequent and beloved part of Adam's life. The gag part was something he would never have considered pre-Denver. The plugs weren't a surprise at all. Adam had been born a bottom, and before Denver he'd spent a few nights jacking off with plugs up his butt, leaving them in until his morning shower. Now he often put them in on command from a text from Denver, wearing them all day to remind himself that later Denver would be removing the plug and plunging his cock into Adam instead. Some of them had cock rings and steel balls that teased his perineum and threatened to let everyone see him walking around with an erection. Some of the plugs vibrated. Some of them were so thick they made Adam gape for a while after he removed them. Plugs were fucking hot.

Gags, though, were new, nearly scary territory. Denver had a lot of gags. Penis gags that pressed varying sizes of silicone cock into Adam's throat while Denver did what he liked to him. Inflatable gags that began on the same principle but extended back farther and farther into Adam's mouth, threatening to cut off his air.

Jesus, but Adam got hard just thinking about those.

Today Adam modeled a new gag, one Adam had watched Denver take out of the box, straining against his bonds as Denver washed it in a little basin with soap on the floor between the two of them. The gag made Adam hard, but the washing made him sappy. It wasn't that he wouldn't have trusted Denver to wash it out of the room. It was that Denver knew both the opening—seeing it was brand-new and just for him—and the washing—seeing that it was clean and sanitary and safe—would be important to Adam, that he would take pleasure from both acts.

Denver winked at him as he dried off the gag. "You know I'll always take care of you, boy."

Then he put the gag in Adam's mouth, strapping it tight behind his head.

This gag, Denver told him, was called an "open-mouth gag." It was mostly a silicone ring and leather straps designed to hold Adam's mouth open. After making the comment about needing more free time, Denver pulled out the catalog he'd ordered the toy from, showing Adam the other gags. Some of them were hot, but some of them were scary, like the spider-mouth gags that had weird spikes around the ring.

Adam's was plain, and he was glad. No spikes or anything weird. He let Adam explore the catalog too—to see what else he liked, and to show him Denver already knew most of what those likes were.

It made Adam feel like purring.

"Say cheese," Denver said, prompting Adam to look up in time for the flash.

Adam squirmed against his ropes, breathing hard through his gag as he waited for Denver to show him the picture he'd taken on his phone. When he saw it, Adam whimpered.

Laughing, Denver ruffled his hair. "You want me to send it to you, boy?"

Adam nodded, trying to say yes through his gag, but it came out a kind of garbled moan.

The smell of leather made Adam drool as Denver stepped closer, rubbing the ridge of his cock against the gag. "Hmm. I might. But first, there's this text I got last week we need to deal with." He flicked through his phone, pursing his lips briefly before reading. "It says here you were late turning in an assignment. That you didn't do it on purpose, but once you figured it out, you locked yourself in the bathroom and got yourself so upset you threw up."

Adam tried to hang his head, but Denver caught his chin and made him look up. Adam didn't want to, because he knew what was coming, though he'd been hoping Denver had forgotten. He couldn't look away with Denver staring at him. He lifted his gaze to Denver's chest as a compromise, which was comforting. Big and sweaty and sexy and comforting.

"It says, Adam, that you were bad and you need to be punished. This true?"

Adam shut his eyes long enough to nod, then focused on Denver's pecs.

Denver kept his hand on Adam's hair, stroking. "So, we got a few problems here. You know that, right?"

Adam nodded. He leaned into Denver's hand, and Denver cradled his cheek.

"You told me you didn't want to have me punish you for things that weren't between us. This isn't between us. This is between you and your OCD, which you told me was off-limits. Which would be fine, except you're asking me to change the rules. Which we can do. Except when I tried to bring this up after you sent me the text, you flipped out."

Adam kept trying to escape, but he couldn't. Denver held him fast.

"So now we have unfinished business between us, boy. We're not addressing the text you sent about missing the assignment, not yet. First we're going to sit and talk about the rules and how we change them, and when. We're going to do that when we're not playing, because that's the first rule about making rules. Before we do that, though, something has happened, and I know you know what it is, because you can barely look at me."

Adam couldn't look at him, no, and yes he knew what had happened. He'd been a bad boyfriend. Again.

It had been about a week since he'd last been a bad boyfriend, but he always lived in fear of it. He knew he would be one, that he'd screw up and make himself upset. He knew he'd be punished for it and that only Denver could do the punishing. Ironically most of the punishing came from thinking he was a bad boyfriend and punishing himself first, which is what had happened this time.

Adam shut his eyes, sad and shamed, and Denver stroked his cheek. "Sometimes I wonder if you aren't doing this on purpose. Testing me to see if I really mean it that all it will take for you to be forgiven is for you to take your punishment."

That was an angle Adam hadn't thought of, and he wished he had his mouth so he could argue no, that wasn't it. He wasn't testing Denver. He wouldn't ever do that. But all he could do was make weird breathy, slurpy noises against his gag.

Denver lifted his eyebrows, looking a little smug. "Can't talk, huh? Yeah, it's hard to say what you mean with shit in the way. That was why I thought this gag was good punishment. You liked the look of it, liked the idea of it. Just like it seemed like a good idea to beat

yourself up instead of letting me do it for you. You fig-
ured I would only like it so long, huh? Only so much?
You figured you'd be my daddy this time, tell me what
I do and don't want?"

Uh-oh. Adam made desperate noises against the
gag and shook his head. The hell he was doing that.
He'd heard stories about Denver's daddies, the real
one, the stepdad, and of course Sonny the asshole.
Adam didn't want to tell Denver what to do. He wanted
it the other way around. It was just that Adam knew
he was a big fat hairy mental case, and no way would
Denver want—

Oh. Oh. Also, oh shit. He made more noises against
the gag, apologizing with his eyes since he couldn't do
anything else.

"Yeah. Now you're sorry. You're always sorry
once you figure it out, baby. Thing is, I need you to stop
trying to figure it out, at least when it comes to when
I'm going to get tired of you because you come with
extra bags. The answer, which I have told you, is not
anytime soon, and maybe never. What I am tired of is
you telling me what I do and don't want."

Adam froze.

Denver crouched in front of Adam and stroked his
face. "So now you're going to get a punishment. One
you're not going to like, baby, and I mean, you really
aren't going to like it. Use your hanky if you need me
to stop. Not want. *Need.* This is a different punishment
than our usual one with the paddle, though, so first I
need you to nod to tell me you agree you trust me to
give this to you. Except if you say you trust me when
you don't just because you don't want to disappoint
me—well, boy, if you think I'm unhappy now, you

wait until I find out you lied to me over something this important."

Adam nodded. *This* he understood. He knew his answer, but he waited for Denver to ask him properly, as it was part of the rules.

"Do you trust me that this is a safe punishment, boy?" Denver asked.

Never moving his eyes from Denver, communicating how much he did trust him with every fiber of his being, Adam nodded.

Denver kissed Adam's forehead. "Good. Now get ready, baby, to find out how much you hate that gag, how I took one look at it and knew it wasn't the one for you."

Adam was confused. So far he was loving the gag, and he wasn't stupid, he knew what was coming even before Denver undid the opening of his pants. He drooled as he watched Denver come to full hardness, as Denver slipped the condom on himself and brought the latex tip to Adam's swollen, gagged lips. Piña colada lube—Adam's favorite. Organic, flavored lube from a company that was tailor-made for OCD fetish folk. Adam twitched in anticipation, and so far he had yet to see what about this punishment he was going to hate.

Then Denver pushed inside his mouth, and he figured it out.

Blow jobs, especially ones where Adam was bound and helpless, where Denver used his mouth and throat, were everyday parts of their play, and they were Adam's favorite. But what he loved most was being able to suck on Denver, to love him with his mouth, to stroke him with his tongue while Denver blocked off his air. He loved locking his lips around Denver's cock, sucking until he was swollen with effort. In short, he loved being active.

Because of the gag, Adam was absolutely passive.

He couldn't lock his lips, couldn't collapse his cheeks around Denver's cock. In fact, he couldn't do a damn thing but grunt off his frustration.

Denver pushed in deeper, tickling the back of Adam's throat. "Yeah. You get it now? You thought this would be a great idea, but you didn't think it through. Which you didn't have to do, because that's my job. A job you keep trying to take from me. So this is what you get, babe, for taking my job away. You get what you thought was a good idea and really sucks for you. And now I'm going to make it suck even more. Pardon the pun."

Adam mewed as Denver withdrew, then moaned in complaint as Denver came at him with something that looked like a tongue depressor. It attached to the lip of the gag and extended almost to the back of Adam's mouth.

It immobilized his tongue, and he cried out in frustration.

"Yep. All you can do is sit there and let me fuck your mouth. Wait until I'm in your throat and you can't close around me like you love to. You thought you were giving up all control, but you weren't. You had a lot, and you had the illusion of none at the same time. It was perfect for you. This is the opposite. And that's why it's your punishment. I'm going to give you ten fucks down your throat, and I'm going to count them off, because you can't right now, boy, can you? You're going to take ten nasty throat fucks, and then it's going to be done. You aren't going to try to tell me how to take care of you anymore, not unless I'm actually doing it wrong. We're doing this one time, and then we're never getting this gag out again unless you're really, really bad. You got it?"

Adam got it. Saliva dripped down the side of his face, and he nodded at Denver, humbled, humiliated, and horrified at what he'd done. He wanted to be punished. He needed to be punished.

He needed, needed this to be over, settled, *finished*, and no, he didn't ever want to do this again.

It was exactly what Denver had promised. It was a grotesque parody of an act he loved. The only good part was when Denver closed off his air, because it was familiar and still had the thrill of giving over, but it was a ghost pleasure, a whisper of good in the middle of a whole lot of unpleasant. Adam hated his punishment with everything he had in him.

But he took it, and he never looked away from Denver's face. Because he was going to be a good boy again. Because even before it happened, he knew it was coming, the release he needed as much as he needed the punishment that preceded it.

Denver pulled out, unsnapped the gag, and tossed it away from Adam's face. "It's done."

Adam sagged forward, shuddering. When Denver kissed him, Adam returned the gesture with everything he had: his gratitude, his sorrow, his relief.

Cupping his face, Denver sighed. "God, baby. I don't know who hated that more, me or you. I had to keep two rings on just to stay hard." He kissed Adam softly. "It's over now. Okay?"

Adam nodded. It was over.

Denver stroked his neck. "Tell me what I need to hear."

It was easier to say than it had been in a long time. "I'm a good boyfriend." *And I'm going to work like hell to stay that way.*

Denver kissed him on the lips. "Good."

Then he pulled out his phone and let Adam watch as he hit Send on the picture he'd taken of Adam in the open-mouth gag. Boy did it have a different connotation now.

Denver worked on Adam's bonds. "Let's get you untied and figure out how we're going to work out you letting me punish you for mistakes you feel like you make that don't involve us, if that's something you're still wanting to do."

Yes, yes, it was. Adam nodded, watching his lover as he undid his bonds.

I love you, he thought, wondering if he should say it out loud. He tasted the words, but they were too scary just now, so he kept them to himself.

Denver glanced at him, smiled softly, and kissed Adam on the cheek.

Maybe, like so many things, Denver already knew.

CHAPTER TWENTY

DENVER HAD a regular porno library on his phone's SIM card, every last one of the pictures featuring Adam in some kind of bondage or with something shoved up or in him. He'd had to get a bigger card, in fact, to hold them all, and a better phone, one he could lock pictures up behind a password. He got one for Adam too, and as a present, he ordered a case with a picture of hawk moths on it.

"How in the world did you get this?" Adam cried, turning the phone over and over in his hand.

"Special order. There's all kinds of companies that will put anything you want on your phone case."

Adam had kissed him, then led Denver into the back room of Lights Out and blown him with enthusiasm. It had been a damn good gift for them both, in the end, that phone case.

Also with Adam, Denver was able to indulge in a fetish he'd never played with, not outside his own head.

Torture kink was a tricky one, because it was even more of a knife-edge than an actual knife. It wasn't that Denver wanted to hurt anyone—well, okay, he did, but it wasn't about the pain for him half as much as he wanted to see someone bound and at his mercy, to know he'd put them there and that he alone would take them out of the pickle he'd gotten them into. Some of the stuff that got his rocks off on the net was too much for Adam—ball stretching, for example. But clips? Pins? Adam liked them fine. He loved riding the edge of pain and beating it, not letting it freak him out. Being able to look at a nasty nipple clamp and know he could bear it, which of course meant that first he had to try it.

What they both enjoyed, however, were the photographs.

Denver would set Adam up, often with a nice plug and a fat penis gag, truss him and clip him, and then they'd start the pose. Adam spread out. Adam bent over. Adam appearing pained, strained, Adam's beautiful face looking so hurt, because he usually did hurt. The best shot Denver'd ever taken was on a timer, of Adam bucking up against his straps on the bench as Denver waled hard on his red, red ass. It wasn't just the action shot—though that was wicked cool—it was that he knew the cries Adam had made were all pleasure-pain. It was knowing the only thing Adam wanted on his ass was Denver's hand, that they'd reached the point where if Denver punished him, it was with a paddle or a crop, because only pleasure came from Denver's flesh on Adam's own. It was catching Adam admiring his marks in the bathroom mirror, his gaze drawn to the wide red imprint of Denver's hand.

There was the voyeurism too—they still had a thing for fucking in public, which had been tricky over the winter months. Though that became part of the fun, Adam bracing against the brick wall of Lights Out, hands in mittens and a scarf tucked over his ears as his bare ass wiggled against Denver's questing tongue. Denver got lots of shots of that one, and after a few tries he'd even managed to get a fucking great one of Adam's cheeks wide open with his tongue going in. He had plenty of Adam's naked ass open, Adam's hands doing the displaying while Denver's fingers reminded him to whom that ass belonged.

Yeah. Pictures were fucking fun.

Mostly, though, Adam was fun. Denver loved who he was when he and Adam were together, and more and more, who he was even when he was on his own.

The only hiccup was the damn studying thing. As much as he tried, he couldn't seem to get the swing of it.

He wouldn't let himself complain about how awful it was, either, because Adam worked so hard to help. After scouring about ten manuals on the GED, Adam could have opened a clinic for how to pass them. He made notecards. Spreadsheets. He had a fucking binder full of notes and charts and exercises. He tried eighty times harder than Denver ever could. And every time Denver let himself be frustrated, let it show, Adam took it as a personal failure.

So Denver didn't let himself be frustrated, not in front of Adam, and he never said no to a study session, even when he'd rather be hung upside down over a pit of starving gators and have his toenails pulled out one at a time.

Some of the shit was probably sticking, some-where, but Denver couldn't shake the idea that this was all a fantastic waste of everyone's time, especially

Adam's. He did not do school. He never had. School had forever been where he failed the most spectacularly, and he didn't even have dyslexia. He was just dumb.

Adam refused to believe it. "You aren't dumb. You're amazingly smart, so much smarter than me in so many ways." When Denver snorted in laughter, Adam turned to steel. "Don't laugh. You've seen how my anxiety traps me. But you don't get paralyzed or anxious. You just get angry. Do you have any idea how jealous I am of you?"

"You have the book smarts," Denver tried to argue, but now it was Adam who laughed.

"Yes. And if I want to hide out in libraries and colleges, I'll be just fine. Do you have any idea how hard it was for me to simply go to Lights Out and meet you that first time? How much hell I'd have been in if you hadn't intervened at the Laund-O-Rama? That's my life." He tapped his binder. "You have to get over this one hurdle, and you're going to have everything you ever wanted. I wish it were as simple as taking a test for me, but it's not. I'm never going to be cured. You don't cure anxiety. You live with it."

Denver became quiet in the middle of that speech, and when Adam finished, he stared at him for a moment longer, beginning to understand why this was so important to Adam. "So you want me to win this one for you, baby?"

Adam's face flushed, and he nodded. "If that's not too pushy."

Denver kissed him briefly on the mouth. "It's not. I'll do my best. I promise."

Despite that determination, Denver continued hitting brick walls. When they did the flash cards and Adam quizzed him, he was fine. But whenever he took the test, it was a mess. He forgot to answer questions. He sat for fifteen minutes once trying to figure out a multiple choice. The essays were beyond a joke. They were pathetic.

"I don't understand," Adam said one afternoon as they sat upstairs in Lights Out, going over Denver's latest practice test. "You know the answers to half the ones you've missed. And you know those two essay questions backwards and forwards."

Denver wanted to say that he was dumb, but he grunted and reached for his soda instead. Maybe now Adam would finally give up this idea and Denver would stop pretending he could take up Tiny on his offer.

He should have known better. Adam continued poring over the test, shaking his head. Then, in what Denver had learned was a sign that he truly had the bit between his teeth, Adam pulled out his laptop and started surfing.

"I think I might know what's going on," he murmured, eyes moving like lightning as he scanned the screen and his fingers flew over the keyboard. "But I don't want to say anything until I have a better idea."

Three days later, apparently he did.

Adam appeared at Lights Out at nine on Friday night, just as Denver was settling in at the door. He smiled as his lover approached, but the gesture fell when he saw the sheaf of papers in Adam's hands. "Babe, I can't study tonight. I'm working."

"This isn't study material. It's evidence." Adam held up a sheet of paper, looking so proud of himself he might burst. "I knew there was something else going on. Obviously it's not certain until we get you tested, but I know where to do that, and there's a grant so it's free. I made you an appointment for next Wednesday."

He thrust one of the papers at Denver. "You have trouble with the test not because you're dumb, but because you have a learning disability."

Adam might as well have hit Denver across the face with a lead pouch. "Ain't that the same damn thing?"

Now it was Adam who looked taken aback. "No! Learning disabilities are real, and they're serious. It means there's something in your brain keeping you from processing things the same way as your peers."

"So my brain's a mess. That says dumb to me."

Adam paled. "What do you think of me, then? Am I crazy?"

That made Denver straighten. "Hell, no! What the fuck, Adam? I didn't say anything about you."

Now Adam was the one who looked as if he'd been slapped. "My brain is messed-up too, and a hell of a lot worse than a visual processing disorder. If you think learning disabilities mean someone is dumb, what have you been thinking about me all this time?"

Shit, he'd stepped in it. Denver wanted out of his tangle, but it was a narrow passage, trying to explain why his brain was dumb and Adam's wasn't. "I meant that you're not broken like me. It's totally different."

"It isn't different at all. It's exactly the same thing. But if you'd rather tell yourself you're stupid, if you'd rather hide behind that, then fine. Just don't do it around me."

With that he tossed his wad of paper into a nearby trash can and stormed out the door.

"Adam!" Denver shouted, but Adam had started to run. Denver went after him, worried about how upset he was. Trouble was, Adam was fast. Denver could barely keep sight of him for blocks, and when they hit the edge of the pedestrian mall, he lost him completely.

When he made it back to Lights Out, he was out of breath, and Jase stood at the door in his place, looking pissed. "What the fuck is going on?"

Denver waved him away and headed for the back room. He stalked to the back wall, where he slammed a meaty hand into the plaster before collapsing against it, feeling more lost and afraid than he had in a long, long time.

Eventually he righted himself, cupped his hand under the utility sink faucet, and took several handfuls of water into his mouth, then splashed some on his face for good measure. After wiping the drips off with a towel, he headed back to the door, where Jase still looked angry, but curious now too.

Denver fished Adam's papers out of the trash. He scanned them, felt the usual frustration and confusion well up, then thrust them at Jason.

"Do me a favor. Look these over tonight and then tell me what the hell they say."

Jase frowned as he took the crumpled wad, though his face softened a little when he smoothed them out and read the documents. He nodded and tucked them under his arm. "I'll look at them now and report back at your break." With a hearty goodbye grip on Denver's shoulder, he headed to his office.

Denver took up his post again, checking IDs without really looking at them, focusing entirely on getting himself through the rest of the night.

CHAPTER TWENTY-ONE

ADAM WAS fairly sure he would have ended up in an institution after his fight with Denver over the learning disability thing if it weren't for Louisa. Because after months of daily meetings or at least a barrage of texts during his shift at the bar, Denver was now completely silent, and this had Adam on nearly constant panic-attack alert. He was so bad that on the second day he allowed Louisa to come over to his apartment.

He was twitchy with her in his space, but it was better than sitting alone with his thoughts. She sat on the sofa beside him, rubbing his back and telling him he was okay. He appreciated it, but he was acutely aware he had a guest in his house, and his OCD didn't like it. The only boon was that he didn't have a panic attack, simply the usual low-grade sense of unease.

"It's going to be fine," she promised. "He'll respond to your texts eventually, hon, I promise. And if he doesn't, I'll go kick his ass."

The idea of anyone at all being able to kick Denver's ass was ridiculous, but the fact that Louisa said it and that she forgot herself and let her voice pitch low in her fury made Adam feel loved and cared for. He leaned into her shoulder. "I haven't texted him."

"For crying out loud, hon—"

"No." Adam said this with enough force that Louisa stilled. "Look, he's the one who got all pissy on me. Even if he doesn't outright say he's sorry, he needs to be the one to do it. I need that."

"That's fair," Louisa said, and she almost sounded approving. "Though you might have to let him know those are the rules, hon."

"I don't want to tell him. I want him to know. If I chase after him, it's every nightmare with Brad all over again. I don't want that with Denver. I—" His voice broke, and he took a moment to steady himself and wipe away new tears. "I don't want to lose him, but I'd rather lose him than have another fucked-up relationship."

"Oh, honey. That is so good, that you get that. I hope your therapist has praised you for that too."

Adam shifted uncomfortably. "I don't have an appointment until Friday."

"Surely this situation warrants a special appointment."

Adam's sense of unease at having Louisa in his home swelled. "I don't want to talk to her about it. I don't want to go into everything we've been doing. She's not been great about the BDSM thing, and—"

Louisa put a hand on his leg, stilling him. "Sweetheart, do you trust me?"

Adam tensed. "I really don't want to tell her—"

"I know, hon. Do you trust me enough to recommend you a new therapist?"

"Oh God." Adam felt not just uneasy but queasy. "I don't like switching to new therapists."

She moved her hand to his back and massaged again. "I know. But you're with the wrong one, if you want to talk about Denver but can't with her. I get that it's hard, that going to someone new is stressful, worse in concept than staying with the wrong one. If you'll let me, I'll help you find someone who is kink-friendly. In fact, I have someone in mind. He's trans, though, in case that matters."

Adam glared at her. "Louisa, why would I care about that?"

"I know, but I had to check. It's okay, by the way, if it would be hard for you. It's important to be comfortable with your therapist."

It wasn't okay to be a bigot, he wanted to argue back, but he was so tired and strung out, he sagged into the couch. She was right, he needed a new therapist. It hadn't even occurred to him to look for a kink-friendly one. Did they put that on their website?

"If you need to think about it first, that's okay too," she said when his silence went on too long.

He shook his head. "No. You're right. And… yes, I trust you, especially in this."

She squeezed his hand. "Thank you for that. I'll set it up. If you like, I can go with you, either to drive you or to sit in on the initial session. And you can change your mind on that all the way up until the last second too. Okay?"

He leaned into her again, lacing his fingers tighter into hers. It occurred to him, and to his OCD too, that it was very nice, all this touching and hugging they'd been doing, and it seemed like they were both more able to do so in the privacy of a home. So many things were better this way, even if it did jangle all his internal switches. He'd been so looking forward to having Denver over, to building that bridge with him, and that he hadn't been the first one Adam had invited, that he wasn't sure right now if Denver would ever be coming over, made him feel so black and dark he wanted to drug himself into a coma and live in his bed. He was already living on so much Xanax right now he was paranoid he'd become addicted, calling his pharmacy every half an hour as he thought of another variable that might affect his inevitable addiction.

He hated that he was such a mess without Denver, and the more he stewed in that, the more it upset him. Was he using Denver as a crutch after all? Was this going to be the same thing with Brad no matter what? Could he not be with someone and be okay? Was it bad to be doing the sub thing with Denver? Maybe it felt good while it was happening, but maybe it made him sicker in the long run? Should he stop being with anyone altogether and focus on being healthier alone first?

The questions swirled in his head, weighed him down farther on the couch, and he shut his eyes, swimming deeper in his despair.

Louisa kissed his hair. "I'll call Sig and get you in as soon as I can, hon, I promise."

I love you, Louisa, Adam thought, but was too weak to say, so he simply nodded and leaned in harder against her. As his OCD gave way, breaking like a dam with too much behind it, he tried for a moment to decide if that was progress or a sign he was one step away from hospitalization, then decided he was too exhausted even for that and closed his eyes, willing the world, save Louisa, to go away.

DENVER WAS advising someone on how best to modify their free weight routine when the woman stormed up to him.

He'd seen her come in out of the corner of his eye, because he didn't recognize her and because she was in what he thought of as a woman's power suit, the kind that very rarely showed up at Tiny's. People like her tended to go to one of the fancier places by Tuck U, so his first thought had been that she was a lawyer, and he worried that Tiny was in some kind of trouble. When she fixed her angry expression on Denver and headed his way, Denver couldn't help it, he took several steps back, as if this might get him away.

She stormed straight up to him, gave a nod to the man Denver had been speaking to, then pushed a manicured fingernail all but up Denver's nose.

"You," she said, her voice dangerous and low, "are going to talk to me, right now. Are we doing it here, or would you prefer to go somewhere private?"

Jesus H. Denver glanced over at Tiny, who was watching Denver with raised eyebrows. "Uh," he said, trying to buy time. "Do I know you, ma'am?"

Her eyes practically sparked, she was so angry. "No, but we have a mutual friend. Or at least I assume you're still friendly toward Adam. You'd better be, because if you're thinking of fucking him over, I don't care how big you are, I'm going to murder you and drive you to Utah to bury you in the desert."

It was hard to be as big as Denver and shrink into yourself, but he managed it. "Shit." He ran a hand through his hair, wishing he had his hat to pull down over his eyes and hide. "Yeah. Uh, we can go talk in the back."

"Good," she said, though she didn't even remotely back down. In fact, she seemed like she was just getting started.

Frankly, Denver thought as he led her to the storeroom that doubled as Tiny's office, he was willing to let her rake him over whatever coals she liked, metaphorical or literal or both. He knew he'd been a dick for not calling Adam, and if Louisa—this could only be Louisa—was this upset on Adam's behalf, things couldn't be good.

He shut the door behind her and sat down on the edge of a stool, shoulders slumped as he waited for her lecture to begin.

She glared at him for several seconds before she got started. "You do know you're taking all the joy out of this by just sitting there like a lump instead of fighting back. I was kind of hoping I'd get to use some of my self-defense moves on you."

Denver hunkered lower, fixing his gaze on the floor. "Yeah, well, if you want to wale on me a little, that'd be fine. I already feel like crap."

"Then why don't you fucking call him?" Louisa threw her hands in the air. "Jesus, Denver. He's a mess. He's waiting for you to call him."

Denver got off the stool, pacing and rubbing his nape. "I know. Fuck." He slammed a hand into the wall before leaning against it. "I'm trying. I've almost done it about twenty times, but I don't know what to say. I fucked up. I fucked up bad." He pounded the wall again, then sighed. "Jase read through the stuff Adam tried to give me. It scared the piss out of me, because it makes a lot of sense, what he said."

"That you might have a learning disability? Yes, it does. In fact, I'm embarrassed I hadn't thought of it, though Adam hadn't made it clear yet just how hard a time you were having. What I don't get is why this is worth losing Adam over. Are you really that proud?"

"No!" Denver's fingers curled against the wall, and he pushed off it and started to pace again. "It's not that. I mean—fuck, yes, I guess, it's pride a little, but mostly—Jesus, fuck, I don't know what to do with this! It does mean I'm stupid, I don't care what he says, and it's fucking hard to swallow. Ow!"

Louisa had stepped in front of him to stop his pacing, and when he'd tried to duck her, she'd grabbed his arm and dug her nails into his skin. When she spoke, her voice was rough with anger. "I was wrong. This isn't pride. It's ignorance and belligerence. So listen up, bucko. Learning disabilities are not a mark of stupidity, no more than deformations in the eyes are."

"Bullshit. This ain't the same as needing glasses."

God, but she kept getting into his face. "It is, and I'm going to stand here and bully you until you get that." She grimaced and motioned to herself. "Look, babe, I'm living proof that bodies and brains do not come perfect by the hand of some divine being. They fuck up, sometimes because of the way we came, sometimes because of things that happened, and sometimes who the hell knows why. People who don't have that experience are actually quite rare. Some physical and mental misfires come with nice social packaging. Yours doesn't. Big fucking deal. You can find your way to cope, or you can sit and mope off in the corner and use it as the excuse of why you don't live your life. And before you start whining at me about how hard it is, I'm going to warn you that I don't have a ton of empathy. I'm sorry, but I have you beat no matter how you want to stack shit up."

Denver held up his hands. "You're right. And I know, I'm being an ass." He sat down again, but this time he looked up at her. "This is hard for me, okay? I want to be strong for Adam, but I can't. This makes me feel vulnerable, and I hate feeling vulnerable."

"Are you trying to tell me you think he won't want you if you're vulnerable?" When Denver had to look away at that, she snorted. "Okay, I'll grant you that you might be a little stupid, but it doesn't have anything to do with a learning disability."

Denver swallowed hard. "For the record, just because I'm big outside doesn't mean I don't feel small sometimes inside."

"Fair point." Her voice was much softer now, and it soothed him. "But if you really think Adam would reject you, you truly don't know him at all."

"Yeah, well, he don't have exclusive rights on anxiety and irrational fears." He sat up straighter, feeling like he had a little of his shit together again. "So. Since you're so full of opinions, you got any on how I should go about fixing this?"

Her smile made her eyes dance. "As a matter of fact, I do."

CHAPTER TWENTY-TWO

THE NEW therapist, to Adam's relief, was great. To be honest, Adam thought the fact that he was trans only added to his understanding. Sig got some of the challenges of being male that even the best-educated and most well-meaning female therapists never could, and yet he had the same kind of empathy and instinctive compassion that in Adam's vast therapeutic experience came a little easier to women. Maybe that was his own set of stereotypes talking, but whatever it was, he was glad for it, because Sig was well on track to being the best therapist Adam had ever had.

They'd only met once, but already Adam felt anchored, like he had a home base now where he could go and talk about pretty much anything: OCD, anxiety, sex, and how much he wanted to be tied up and fucked and how that need both excited and scared him, how he worried that giving up control to Denver was a cop-out, even though he secretly longed for that release.

They'd barely touched on that last one, because it had taken him the whole session to work up to bringing it up, but Sig had given him some good nuggets to chew on, and Adam had certainly been gnawing on what he'd offered.

"Embracing one's sexuality runs deeper than simple orientation, and when there are kinks involved, practices which fall outside mainstream culture's definitions of acceptability, accepting those parts of oneself can and often does open up whole aspects of one's personality previously muted. Having a yen to be dominated is part of who you are, and just as accepting you're gay made you feel free, so will accepting that you long for your partner to give you this particular experience, to let you surrender control. That longing might extend beyond the bedroom, and there's nothing wrong with that. It's true, you need to moderate yourself and be sure you aren't using Denver to escape your life, and it's good that you're conscious of that danger, but the very fact that you stood up to him when he upset you says to me you aren't in any real danger of subjugating yourself to him to a harmful degree. Neither does he seem to be the type of man who would bully you, though I cannot say the same for your first lover. I suggest you work on soothing that inner voice that longs to lash out at you, the true bully."

The idea that he bullied himself wasn't a revelation to Adam, but he was entirely at a loss as to how to make that situation stop. Sig promised they'd address it.

"You do a good job of accepting that your anxiety is part of you, but I'd like to see you try a different visualization. I know you said you don't have one, but from what I can gather right now you see your disorders as a weight around your neck. I'd like you to see your disorders as a team of horses."

Adam frowned at him. "Horses?"

Sig nodded. "Yes. You can see them as a pair, OCD and anxiety, driving your chariot. Whatever you like. But try horses. Now—can you guess why?"

Adam had to think about it a little. "Because they drive me."

"Yes. Because they can drive you, but with some care, you can also drive them. You're going to have to get around by anxiety horses, there's no changing that. What you can change is how you perceive them. Do you hold on to their manes and scream while they run wild? Do you drive them at a speed that comforts you? Do you take care of your horses and groom them? Do you use a rough bit, or do you give them something soft for their tender mouths?"

"Wow. I had no idea the anxiety-as-horse metaphor was so expansive."

Sig smiled and patted Adam on the leg. "Give it a try and let me know at our next appointment how it works."

Their next session was in a day and a half, and Adam couldn't wait.

In the meantime he had a huge lab project due, which was good because it gave him a distraction. All his focus went into his schoolwork so he didn't have to think too much about how long it had been since he'd heard from Denver. Louisa had told him to hold on, that she had faith that Denver would come around and soon. She sounded so sure of herself Adam thought maybe she'd talked to him. He wanted to ask, but he was too nervous, so he just trusted them both and looked forward to more kink-friendly therapy. He tended his horses, taking them to an imaginary stable and tricking them out in ghetto-fabulous club gear. And, when they were in the mood for it, leather.

Adam also took solace in the memento of his last, amazing night at Denver's place before their fallout: a picture of his bruised and reddened ass. Adam kept this one and a few other of his favorites on a rotation through his phone's home page. He pulled them out when he felt too anxious, reminding himself of how good he'd felt then, telling himself he would get there again.

He didn't like to think about doing anything like that without Denver, but he made himself do it anyway. If he couldn't have Denver, he'd at least let their relationship have been the gateway into discovering this aspect of himself. Sig had promised to help him find safe networks in the BDSM community, and Adam clung to that whenever he felt anxious.

Mostly, though, he looked at the photos, imagining himself still bound and safe. He looked at them several times a day in fact, especially when he lay in bed trying to sleep. He looked at them in the lab too, pulling them up like a kinky security blanket whenever his brain got a little rabid. He was careful to keep them private, and he had his phone on a password as Denver told him to.

Unfortunately, he forgot that Brad still knew all his passwords.

He knew he wasn't supposed to use the same password for everything. He knew he was supposed to change his passwords every so many months or weeks or something. Except he also was terrified he'd forget his password. He had, in fact, a constant internal war with his OCD about it: What was worse, forgetting his passwords, or getting broken into? He'd tried writing them out in a booklet at home, but then he'd lain awake thinking about how someone could break into his house, find his passwords, then attack him and swipe his phone and steal his whole identity. So he had compromised. He had two complicated passwords he alternated between, and as a security measure, he'd asked Brad to memorize them.

It hadn't occurred to him until he came out of the hood to find Brad holding his phone, flipping whey-faced through his gallery, that he should have found someone new to be his backup.

Brad stopped on an image of Adam bound, gagged, glasses dangling, nipples clipped, face twisted up in pain, then looked up at Adam as if he didn't recognize the man standing in front of him.

Panic swamped Adam. There wasn't any getting hold of the horses. The horses were off in a streak, dragging Adam behind. All he knew was panic, because at that point panic was all there was in the world.

Give that back, Adam wanted to demand, but he couldn't speak. He stood with his sterile gloves still on his hands waiting for disposal, frozen, captive, more naked and exposed standing there clothed than he had been at any point during his play with Denver.

Brad kept shaking his head. "What the fuck, Adam? Seriously?" He looked from the phone to Adam, then back to the phone again.

"Give that back," Adam managed in a whisper. "It's mine."

Brad leveled his gaze at Adam. "I kept wondering what you were looking at. I'd have thought this was some kind of threat, like he held it over you so you'd do what he said or something, but you were looking at these like they were your lifeline. You like this, don't you." Brad curled his lip in derision. "Jesus, Adam, you're sicker than I thought."

I'm not sick. Adam couldn't make the words come out, though, because when Brad looked at him with such an ugly face, it was hard to believe them. "Give it back," he whispered again instead.

Of course Brad didn't. He waved the phone in front of Adam, always keeping it just out of his reach. "Sick, Adam. This is sick. You are sick. And that guy you're letting do this to you is a monster."

Adam wasn't sick, and Denver wasn't a monster. He knew that, and even though it was still young, fragile knowledge, he found he could cling to it now. It helped him grab one edge of the horses' reins, tentatively. "No," he said, still whispering, but with heat behind the word.

"Sick." Brad threw the word at Adam, drawing out the sibilant, hissing it, clicking the consonants so hard they slapped. He held up the phone again. "You let him do this to you, and you let him photograph it? Christ, it's probably all over the internet by now."

You're sick, Adam's inner bully tried to parrot. But even it was having a tough time finding a foothold. The rein was only dangling in Adam's hand, but it was there. Adam could see the horses in the distance, and though they were still wild and afraid, he could tell they wished they were under control.

You can be under control. All you have to do is take it.

Being with Denver wasn't a sickness. Maybe they were unconventional, but they weren't wrong, and it wasn't unhealthy.

Adam wasn't sick, period. He wasn't unhealthy. He had some mental illness, but so did a lot of people.

He took his medication and went to his therapy. He managed his health.

I'm not sick. I'm not wrong. I'm my own way, and that way is right.

The revelation should have been a victory. It almost was. Adam crouched inside of himself, for once his bully huddling too, confused and unsure of how to build up a defense, unwilling to pick up the sickness shield Brad offered, the mental image of him giving over to Sig's personification of the horses. It was a victory too in that Adam realized Brad had always been unhealthy for him. Being with Brad was like living in the Laund-O-Rama with drunk frat boys, full of their own problems, bullying harder than Adam's own bully was willing to plug in.

The problem was Adam had found his inner peace, but that was all he had so far, and with his bully mollified, with his horses on rein, with Louisa and Denver absent, he had no one left to defend him because it took everything in him to maintain himself. In the absence of any protection, his brain sent out the last defense, the only shield it knew how to make: a panic attack.

A full-blown, near-seizure-level panic attack.

Brad hadn't stopped monologuing as Adam's world narrowed and went dark, but he'd seen Adam freak out before, so when the shortness of breath began, he smirked and folded his arms over his chest. "Oh, nice. Going to have an attack. Do you see? Sick, Adam. It's not normal to be like this."

Fucking Christ, but Brad was an ass. Of the highest order. *I wish I knew how to deal with him. I want to learn how to deal with him.*

Not today you won't, Adam's anxiety answered. The internal bully burst into tears, the horses reared, and red dots formed in front of Adam's eyes.

He watched as if from a distance as Brad comprehended this was more than the normal weeping and pacing. In a strange way part of Adam enjoyed it, hoping he freaked Brad the fuck out, that he gave the kind of performance he used to offer up at hotels or when his parents had locked him in his room in an attempt to punish him for what they considered excessive carrying on, only to come back and find him drooling on the floor in a near coma. *God, I hope I puke on him*, Adam thought, and then the panic slid over him like a blanket, nothing left to do but take the ride.

Once Adam had watched YouTube videos of people having panic attacks, and he'd been floored at how benign they appeared. They felt like death. The worst part was the pain in the center of the chest, the one that felt like a heart attack. In reality it was adrenaline spiking, a hard jolt meant to fuel anger or spur flight, but in anxiety or panic attacks it only fed the fire. It felt like confirmation to the messages the brain sent out like erratic SOS: *We're going to die. We're dying right now, and you can't stop it, you can only die.*

It's not real, Adam scolded himself. He'd been to this rodeo before, but on a panic-attack scale this was The Big One, and since Adam wanted to stay away from Brad, he couldn't stop it. Maybe if he was a big enough of a mess, Brad would abandon him forever.

We're dying, we're dying! Adam's brain screamed, and any attempt at affirmations or rationalizations ceased. This was death. This truly was death—it was a heart attack. He was dying.

I'll never see Denver again.

Stripping off his gloves with shaking hands, Adam stumbled forward, reaching for his phone. Brad tried to step away, but Adam caught his arm and gripped his wrist until Brad cried out and dropped the device. Adam dove after it, weeping, shuddering, dying, and once he claimed it, he fumbled with the keypad to get to his contacts. Denver answered on the third ring, voice gruff as he said, "Hey."

"I'm dying." Adam's throat clogged with whatever was killing him. Maybe he was dying of adrenaline. It didn't matter. He was dying, and he had to see Denver again. "I'm at the lab. Please I want to see you."

"Adam?" Denver was all business now, a dangerous edge to his tone.

"It's going to kill me." Adam wasn't sure if he'd actually spoken, he was so lost now. There was just panic, fear, the need to escape, all of it swamping his need for Denver, a yearning that kept lifting its head to the surface.

"Adam, I'm on my way." The steel in Denver's tone felt so good. Adam shut his eyes and clung to it. "I'm hanging up and calling 911, and I'm on my way."

"No! Please, don't go!" Adam hoped he wasn't sobbing, but it hardly mattered, since he had to be nearly dead by now anyway.

I don't want to die. I want to be with Denver.

"Jesus," Brad said above him. "Shit, this one is really bad."

Adam met Brad's eyes, pleading. "Call 911 so I don't have to hang up on him."

"Who are you talking to?" Denver demanded.

It hurt to talk, but Adam made himself do it. "Brad."

"Tell that fucker to call 911, or I'll be calling it for him."

Adam tried, but another wave of panic hit him, this one making him curl into a ball, and when it subsided enough that he could fumble for his phone, Brad was gone, and so was Denver.

"No," he cried, trying to dial the number again. He kept trying, his fingers always fumbling, the freight train in his head rushing louder and louder until he couldn't live in the real world anymore, could only curl into the panic, its screaming fury and promise of fatality the only security life had left to provide.

DENVER HAD never moved so fast in his life.

He didn't run any stoplights, but other than that he drove like he was auditioning for a Hollywood chase scene, squealing around corners and weaving through traffic, occasionally across the center line in his desperation to get to East Cent. The dispatcher kept him on the line almost all the way to the university, asking questions about Adam, his health history, and, Denver knew, keeping him occupied and calm as well.

"All I know is that he said he was dying," Denver said again, when the dispatcher kept fishing for health issues beyond OCD and anxiety. "I don't know of what, but he sounded like he believed it."

"Is he alone?"

Denver thought of Brad, his smug, idiot face smirking down at a bleeding Adam in his mind's eye, and then he did run a red light. "I don't know. Someone was with him, but I don't trust him for shit, to be perfectly honest."

"Do you believe this individual harmed Adam in any way? Should we send the police?"

"I don't know." Desperation gripped Denver's chest so tight that he hurt. "I honestly don't know. I wouldn't peg him as the type, but I don't know. All I know is what I already said. Adam said he was dying and that Brad was there with him. If Brad's still there and he's in any way responsible, you might want the police there so I don't kill him."

"I understand you're concerned for your friend, Mr. Rogers," the dispatcher said, moving into her soothing voice.

"My boyfriend," Denver corrected sharply. "And yes, I'm concerned. Can you actually die of an anxiety attack?"

"We're doing everything we can to help your boyfriend, sir. The paramedics are heading up the stairs to the entomology lab now. I'll keep you posted."

"Can he actually be dying?"

The dispatcher sounded like her patience was beginning to fray. "Sir, it's illegal for me to dispense medical advice."

Denver could see the college up ahead but not the emergency vehicle lights. They'd be buried inside the university walkways, which reminded Denver of an important point: he had no fucking idea where he was going to park.

"They're with your boyfriend now, Mr. Rogers."

"Is he okay?" Denver scanned the campus. He was one green space away from the lab, but he'd have to drive two blocks to the parking lot, one he didn't have a permit for.

"He's stable, yes, sir. Please remain calm."

Fuck calm. "I'm almost there. Thanks for your help."

"Sir—" But the rest of her plea was lost, because Denver hung up the phone.

Then he turned onto the green, cranked his truck into four-wheel drive, and aimed himself straight at the entomology building.

CHAPTER TWENTY-THREE

THE PARAMEDICS were bringing Adam down the stairs as Denver swerved onto the road. He parked in a fire lane, leapt out of the truck, and headed straight for the stretcher.

"Is he okay?" Denver demanded, eyes only for Adam. Jesus, he looked pale and sweaty. But no blood. He was weirdly quiet, eyes unfocused as he whimpered. He seemed to calm slightly when he saw Denver.

One of the paramedics motioned to Denver. "Please stay back from the stretcher, sir,"

"I'm the one who called you." Denver took Adam's hand. "Baby. Baby, tell me you're okay."

"I'm sorry," Adam whispered as a tear ran down his cheek. "I don't want to die. I love you."

"You're not dying, Mr. Ellery." A female paramedic addressed Adam in the tone of one who had done as much several times now. "Please remain calm. We'll get something to help you in the ambulance."

Denver gripped Adam's hand as tight as he could without breaking bones. "You're going to be okay. You hear me?" He leaned closer, wanting to kiss him, but it was hard enough keeping up with the paramedics on the stairs. "I love you too, baby. And I'm not going anywhere."

That promise was temporarily in jeopardy as they arrived at the ambulance and the paramedics tried to tell Denver he couldn't ride along.

"I'm getting in that ambulance," Denver declared. He would have been a bit more colorful, but he could see a police car rounding the corner.

The paramedics looked at each other in exasperation, but in the end the female one shrugged. "Let him ride. Look how much calmer the patient is already."

It was true, Adam did seem to have evened out somewhat. He was still breathing way too fast and still looked like shit, but he clung to Denver like a lifeline. He wouldn't let go long enough even for the paramedics to load him into the ambulance; Denver had to climb in as they hefted him up, and since he was there, he gave a boost on the way.

They gave Adam an intravenous drug of some kind as the ambulance rolled on, and he calmed within minutes, though not all the way. He slurred when he spoke, which was mostly to tell Denver over and over that he loved him.

Denver stroked Adam's sweaty forehead, smoothing his hair away. "What happened, babe? What did Brad do?"

"He found the pictures. On my phone." Adam shut his eyes. "He said I was sick."

Brad was a dead man. "Baby, you aren't sick."

"He wouldn't stop. I knew he was wrong, but he wouldn't stop, and I couldn't figure out what to do, and I panicked."

Denver kept petting Adam, but his other hand tightened into a fist at his side. "You're okay now, boy. I won't let anything happen to you."

"I know." Adam turned his face into Denver's wrist, and Denver lowered his hand to touch his cheek.

"I'll stay right here," he promised. "I'm not going anywhere."

He had to break that vow for a minute at the hospital, stuck filling out forms and answering questions he didn't know the answer to while the doctors examined Adam. Several of them had first insisted to Denver there was no imminent danger to his lover, that Adam was to their knowledge only having an attack and nothing more. They'd also had to swear to Adam they'd let Denver back in as soon as they were finished examining him, which made them both feel better.

Denver had Adam's phone, and from it he called Louisa. Then, after some coaching from her, he contacted Adam's parents.

Adam's mother answered the phone, and it was weird, how muted her response was to Denver's news that her son was in the hospital. At first he thought she didn't care, but as her voice began to waver, he realized she was simply holding herself together as best she could.

"They keep telling me he's going to be okay," Denver told her. "They're with him now, but nobody seems to be on any kind of alert. And he calmed down as soon as he saw me, which I'm hoping is a good sign."

"How long have the two of you been dating?" Mrs. Ellery asked him. Politely, as if they were having tea, not discussing her son's hospitalization.

"A while now." Denver cleared his throat. "I just want you to know, Mrs. Ellery, that I care for your son a great deal, and I won't let anything happen to him, as much as I can manage that."

He could hear her smile, soft and sad, when she replied. "I'm glad Adam has a friend like you. It's hard for him, sometimes."

Denver didn't know what to say to that. She might as well have thanked him for taking out the trash. He remembered that Adam had mentioned a distance with his parents, like they didn't get it, didn't get him or his illness. As Denver listened to Mrs. Ellery's strained, emotionally frozen reaction, as he imagined Adam trying to find security in that disconnected reserve—well, things were starting to become much clearer. "I'll keep you posted."

It was then that Louisa arrived.

"I want to see him," she demanded. Her eyes were red, and she kept wiping them with a tissue. Her mascara was running as well.

"They said give them a few more minutes," Denver told her. "But they also keep telling me he's going to be fine."

"I'm going to kill Brad," she whispered, wiping her eyes again.

"Get in line," Denver murmured.

That made her laugh a little. "No fair. If you get to him first, there won't be anything left when I'm through with him."

"We'll take him together."

"Deal."

The doctors called them over then, saying Adam had been asking for Denver. He was in a corner of the ER ward, wearing a hospital gown and behind a curtain, propped up on pillows. He looked doped up but much, much calmer.

"Denver," Adam slurred, reaching for him with a sideways smile. "Oh, and Louisa too. Yay."

"We're only going to keep him a few more hours," the doctor said. "He seems to be significantly better now and is in no real danger. We'd like someone to stay with him tonight, however, just to be safe."

Denver nodded. "I will." He frowned at Adam, realizing this broke one of his rules. "If that's okay with Adam."

Adam nodded and gave another goofy smile. "It's okay with Adam."

He hoped that would be true even when the drugs wore off. Or that they'd give Adam a take-home pack.

Hell, he wondered if he could ask for a hit for himself.

IT WAS dinnertime when the hospital let Adam out, and Louisa volunteered to bring Thai takeout over to Denver's place. That seemed to make the decision about where they were going to spend the night, and since Adam didn't argue, Denver went with it.

"You good?" he asked as he settled Adam onto the couch. He crouched beside him, scanning his lover's face as he looked for signs of increased stress. "Being in my house okay? Not just for the afternoon, either, but overnight?"

Adam nodded. He was still foggy, and he seemed to have a hard time keeping his head up. In fact, by the time Louisa appeared with food, he'd drifted back to sleep.

The two of them sat at Denver's kitchen table, eating silently.

"How are you doing?" Louisa asked eventually. "You holding up?"

Denver nodded. Then shrugged. "I mean, he's fine, right? Maybe it was too much to call the paramedics."

"No, that was smart, especially since you didn't know what was going on." When the silence went on again, she patted his hand. "Go ahead. Ask me questions. Vent. Get it out."

Denver let out a breath he hadn't realized he'd been holding. "I don't know what to say. I feel like I got hit sideways. Nothing really happened, except it sure as hell feels like it did."

"Yes." Louisa leveled her gaze. "This is what it's like, living with anxiety. You don't have it, but you're living with it. There will be other bad days. Other attacks. No matter how strong Adam gets, the world will always be a more difficult challenge for him. And just like you found out today, you can't save him. You can't block it out. More often than not, you'll have to help him pick up the pieces after it falls apart on him. Again."

Denver leaned back in his chair and frowned at his plate. "I'm starting to get that."

"Can you live with that?"

Denver thought about that, made himself consider before answering. Finally he said, "Guess I'll have to, huh?"

Louisa smiled and squeezed his hand. "Good answer."

WHEN ADAM woke up, he wasn't sure where he was at first, and it brought on new panic. Then Denver appeared, hovering over him, and he calmed.

"You're at my place," Denver told him. He held up a plate. "I have Thai. It's a little cold. Want me to heat it up some?"

Adam, starving, shook his head and pushed himself more upright before reaching for the plate. He was woozy and unfocused—they were big-time drugs, the ones they'd given him at the hospital. He felt floaty.

Denver watched him like a hawk. "You still okay? You need anything?"

Just you. Adam smiled and shook his head.

Denver fussed around Adam until he was done eating, then whisked away the plate and came back with a big glass of water. "They gave me pills, if you need them."

"If I take any more pills, I'll be in a coma," Adam replied, slurring a little. He blushed and averted his gaze. "I'm sorry."

"What for?"

What for. "Everything, Denver. I know I overreacted, and I feel ridiculous."

Denver lifted his feet and sat under them on the other end of the couch. "Don't feel ridiculous. You're fine. From the sounds of things, Brad was a real ass."

"Brad's always an ass." Adam stared up at the ceiling. There weren't any tiles to count, so he calculated the angles and shapes of the space, forming imaginary squares and rectangles to fill the silence.

"The doctor wanted you to stay here overnight," Denver said at last. "You okay with that, babe?"

He wasn't, of course. Carving out geometrics in the ceiling was the first sign that his OCD was climbing on top of whatever they'd pumped into his system. He thought of the pills Denver had offered.

Then he lowered his gaze to Denver, and thoughts of taking more drugs faded in the presence of a much more palatable distraction.

Denver caught the look on his face and shook his head. "No way. You just got out of the hospital."

"For a stupid anxiety attack, not a concussion." *I don't want medicine when I could have you.*

Denver stared at him, his face in shadow, his body backlit by the light streaming over from the kitchen. He was big and beautiful, and Adam wanted him. He tried to figure out how he could have him.

Denver averted his eyes and grimaced down at his carpet. "Besides, last I checked I was being an ass too."

Oh. That. Funny how he didn't seem to mind, not anymore, not after watching Denver boss his way around the hospital, bullying doctors, treating Adam like an exotic Russian painted egg. "I don't care. And I think I was an ass as well."

Denver snorted. "You weren't an ass."

"I think I might have been. I didn't think about what telling you about your disability might mean to you." Adam went back to shaping out the ceiling. "I think I was too caught up in the idea of how cool it was that you were like me to think about what—" He sighed. "Well. I guess it's probably not exciting to you to be told your brain is broken." He started counting the shapes he'd made and carving the rectangles into smaller squares, trying to make the space uniform. "I think that's pretty asshole-y, being excited about some-one's learning disability because it makes them a freak like you."

Familiar fingers trapped his chin and lowered his face, forcing him away from his math. Denver's face was still in shadow, but Adam could make out the strong

line of his jaw, the slight curve of his lips, the soft light
in his eye. "You weren't an asshole. And you aren't a
freak." His thumb stroked Adam's jaw. "You just hit
against something I've feared for a long time. Like
that Bugs Bunny short where he's facing some huge
guy, big as me, and nothing can touch him until Bugs
hits this one spot in his jaw. 'His glass jaw!' somebody
says, and the big guy shatters and falls down, defeated.
That's how I felt. Like I'd made myself big and im-
penetrable, but I had this glass jaw, and you found it."
Adam cringed and opened his mouth to apologize, but
Denver gently pressed his lips closed again with the
pad of his thumb. "You could have come at me with the
best, most patient, psychologist-approved explanation
and I'd still have freaked. I been afraid my whole life
that I'm stupid and worthless, just like my daddy told
me. I been waiting for something, anything, to prove
him right, and you found it for me."

Adam felt like shit. Complete, utter dog shit. He
couldn't speak because of Denver's thumb, so he kissed
it mournfully instead.

"Baby, if it hadn't been you, it'd have been somebody else. I been so sure that boogeyman was coming.
I wasn't going to move forward, I don't think, until I
knew where he was. Kind of like your anxiety. I was
afraid of a ghost, but I was sure it wasn't just a ghost,
that it could get me. I let my fear get the better of me,
so when you told me what it was I'd been hiding from,
I couldn't hear or see anything except that it was true, it
was there." Denver smiled a crooked smile. "You aren't
the only one who can have a panic attack, you know."

That made Adam smile, and he shifted away from
the thumb, though he liked that Denver went back to

stroking Adam's cheek with it. "Yes, but you didn't end up in the hospital."

"I'll try harder next time."

Adam looked into Denver's eyes, smile fading into something softer and deeper. He forgot about the ceiling and its geometric possibilities, too caught up in the shape of the man before him. Without his hat, his hair stood on end and his ears stuck out in a way that whispered to Adam this was probably why Denver was so adamant about always wearing headgear. His body was a hulk of muscle in the dark, bent over Adam, so big and powerful. So safe. So strong.

So Denver.

"I love you," Adam whispered.

Denver's face was still in shadow, and then it was right before Adam's, his dark eyes mirrors, his lips parted, his hands on Adam tightening possessively.

"I love you too," Denver whispered back.

"Make love to me." Adam made himself flatter against the couch, sliding his legs so he could wrap his knees around Denver's thighs. "Please, sir."

Denver caught Adam's lower lip, then released it. "It's Denver tonight."

Adam's eyes fell closed in a sweet moment of private bliss. Then he opened that bliss up to his lover and said, "Please make love to me, Denver."

An electric thrill ran down his spine as Denver's mouth covered his own, as big hands pressed him into the cushions. Adam went pliant, moving as Denver directed, going soft for him, giving everything to him not just because it was a relief but because it was right. Not a distraction. Not therapy. Giving himself to Denver, obeying Denver—*being* with Denver wasn't codependency, and it wasn't a crutch.

It was coming home.

When Denver scooped him up, Adam grabbed hold and held on tight, not letting him break the kiss as he carried Adam into the bedroom. Adam's anxiety perked up, putting the OCD on prickle alert, because they'd never done this before, not in Denver's room. Not in a bed, actually. It was new. It was a little scary.

But Denver was still there, strong and safe, asking him to do it, so Adam—and all his internal personalities, horses included—decided it was okay.

It wasn't the raw fucking they usually did. It wasn't playing either, not this time, and it wasn't because they couldn't seem to stop kissing. It was the way Denver undressed Adam, like he was a bridegroom, like he was a present Denver couldn't believe he was getting. It was the way Denver held on to Adam's naked hips and stroked his skin like he was velvet, a precious commodity he'd never thought to possess.

When Denver pressed him onto the bed, still kissing, still stroking, it was Adam who drew his legs up, spreading himself, offering, needing to do it, needing to say not with words but his body, *Yes, this is all for you, Denver, all of me, please take me, because I'm yours*. It made Denver draw back, and in the dim light Adam could see the pleasure on his face, not just at what he saw but at the action, that Adam had done it.

Denver leaned over, fetching a condom and lube from the drawer. He stared at Adam the entire time he suited up, gaze smoldering.

Adam whimpered and opened himself up wider.

Greased fingers slipped inside Adam, once, twice. Then Denver held Adam's ankles and went in fast and deep.

Adam bucked and tossed back his head, crying out both in pain and intensity—good pain, a nasty stretch that burned before it faded into rich pleasure, a rawness that made him feel happy and used and claimed. He clutched at the bed as Denver thrust, and he whimpered and moaned and begged and pleaded for more.

Just when it was building to a frenzy, Denver pulled out with a near growl, flipped Adam over, and yanked him to his knees. One hand gripped Adam's cock and the other wrapped around his torso as Denver lined himself back up and finished the ride, fucking in sharp snaps that he echoed with relentless jacks on Adam's erection until they were both coming hard, convulsing before collapsing together into the sticky mess they'd made of the bed.

"I'm going to take the job with Tiny," Denver said after they'd lain there for several minutes. "I'm going to tell him it'll take me a while, that he can't count on me getting through the classes fast, but that I'll do it. And I'm going to let you help me get that grant or whatever so I can do the test. I wanted to do it on my own, to have the papers filled out when I came to apologize to you, but I kept freaking out, so this time you might have to be the one bolstering me while I do something difficult."

"I will totally do that," Adam promised.

Denver stroked Adam's belly, tracing his finger through the sticky cum. "I want a job where I can be with you more. I want to be able to help you when you need it, to be with you in the evenings when you come home from school or work or whatever you do. I want to be more than a bouncer at a bar. And I want to be able to take the stupid GED, because you're right, I do know all that stuff. I have to figure out how to show them so

I can get the paper and move on." He kissed the back of Adam's neck. "I want to be strong on the inside too. Like you."

Adam's body, already turned liquid, melted all over again. He turned his head to kiss Denver's mouth, lingering for a second before he spoke. "I want you to teach me how to fight back when people bully me. Next time Brad won't shut up and pushes me into a panic attack, I want to know how to knock out his front teeth."

"Boy, you got yourself a deal." Denver chuckled and nuzzled Adam's hair. "Just be sure you do it when I can watch."

CHAPTER TWENTY-FOUR

IT WAS only a little weird to wake up at Denver's.

Okay, it was very weird, and initially when Adam woke up he felt his muscles tightening, his brain gearing up to go back into panic mode. But he shut his eyes and made himself take deep breaths, grabbing the reins and, while not pulling hard, he stood firm. Sometimes he couldn't stop his wild horses from running. But he could wait until they were exhausted instead of getting ramped up with them. He focused on the yummy burn of his ass from where Denver had spanked him, a delicious treat after their lovemaking before they'd gone to sleep. It anchored him as he breathed deeply. While he didn't exactly get himself back to normal, by the time Denver figured out something was wrong, Adam had himself talked down almost entirely from an attack, and he was well on the road to evening out.

Happily, Denver rolled on top of him, played protect-the-fragile-egg for a few minutes until he saw that

Adam was fine, and then he fucked the last of the anxiety right out of him. They showered together after that, which led to more sex, and then they made breakfast together, which also led to more sex. And another light spanking.

It was probably the best aftermath of a serious panic attack Adam had ever known. Hell, it was pretty good aftermath for anything.

"Denver," Adam said, tasting the word as they sat—carefully—down to plates of eggs and toast and fruit. He tilted his head and regarded his lover thoughtfully. "Is that really your name? I've always wondered. I mean, I thought maybe you were from there and it was your nickname, but you said you were from Arkansas."

He could tell there was a good story coming from the way Denver grunted and kept his eyes on his plate, looking like he didn't want to tell it. Adam was just working up to a new angle to coax it out of him when Denver said, "Waldemar."

Adam blinked. "Come again?"

Denver lifted his gaze, looking weary and more than a little embarrassed. "My birth name was Waldemar. It was the name of some great-grandfather from Germany, and my mother loved it. I hated it. They called me Wally at home and Waldo at school, but it always sounded like an accusation. Plus nobody sexy was ever named Waldemar. I had it legally changed when I was eighteen." He didn't eat, only moved things around his plate. "I always wanted to go to Denver. I hated the South, and the East and West Coasts sounded scary. Denver felt like mountains and opportunity, so I named myself after it, and later when I had a chance, I went there." He gave up on his food and took a swig of coffee. "Except Denver was too big and urban, too full of suburbs and stuff that wasn't me. So I headed west and ended up in Tucker Springs. Been here ever since."

Adam didn't say anything for a minute, just stared back at him. Finally he shook his head. "Waldemar. Wow."

Denver rolled his eyes, then leveled Adam with a look that was probably supposed to be threatening but mostly seemed like a plea. "Don't tell anyone. Especially El. He's been dying to know, and I won't say."

Adam's chest swelled with pride at being trusted with such a secret, one Denver kept even from his best friend. He was so overwhelmed he had to lean over and kiss Denver on the cheek. "I won't tell a soul."

Denver brushed a rough kiss back, then nodded at Adam's plate. "Your eggs are going to turn to rubber."

Smiling at the bossy tone, Adam ate.

IT TOOK some arguing to get Denver to allow him to go into school once dishes were put away, and in the end the only way Adam talked him into it was by promising to let Denver come along, at least to escort him to the lab and put the fear of God into Brad.

"You can't hit him," Adam insisted.

"Not with witnesses, no," Denver agreed. Before Adam could protest, Denver glanced at his phone's time display, impatient. "Thing is, we gotta hurry, because I'm starting to worry Louisa's going to get to him first. I texted her I was going in with you, and she's meeting us at the lab."

Jesus, he had bodyguards now? "It's Brad, Denver. Not the Russian mafia."

Denver looked thunderous. "Yeah. It's Brad, the asshole who sent you to the hospital. You ready to roll, boy, or what?"

Adam crossed his arms over his chest, hugging himself as he realized a problem. "I need to go to my apartment. I need to change and get a few things from my desk." He couldn't wear old underwear. Not even for Denver.

Denver rubbed his chin, then nodded. "Okay. We'll swing by on the way. I'll wait in the car, but don't be long. I won't hit Brad in public, but I can't make promises about Louisa."

Adam sat with his anxiety a moment, then said, "Actually, I'd like it if you came in."

Denver stared at him a long time. Adam hugged himself so tight he began to lose nerve sensation at his elbows. Finally Denver nodded. "Let's go, then."

It was hard, admitting Denver into his space. Adam had to focus on his breathing all the way over, and the wild horses were back, ready to go crazy. He kept mentally shushing the beasts, alternately being stern and sweet with them. *It's Denver. He belongs here as much as I do.*

It's not right, the horses told him, and tried to rear.

Adam kept his grip on his mental reins. *We'll find a way to make it right*, he promised them, and for the first time in a long time, he felt victorious in an argument with his mental illness.

He vowed it wouldn't be the last, especially not on this topic.

Inside the apartment itself, he was twitchy. He was hyperaware of where Denver was at all times, though he also had to concede Denver was more respectful of his issue with people-in-his-space, even better than Louisa. He asked permission for everything, even entering a room. As Adam pulled a T-shirt over his head, it dawned on him that Denver was acting the same as he did when they were playing scenes. Always asking permission, always making sure Adam was okay, making sure Adam was safe.

The knowledge so overwhelmed Adam he went back out into the living room in only his shirt and his Green Lantern underwear. He stood in the doorway to the room, stared at Denver in awe and love for a moment, then said, "I want to move in with you."

Though he gave a flicker of approval and longing away, mostly Denver kept up the same facade of control and watchfulness he'd adopted since Adam had said he wanted Denver to come over. "I want that too. But I think we should take it smart and slow so we do it right. To start, would it be your place or mine?"

"Neither." Adam's fingers dug into the wall as he thought of moving again, but he soothed himself with the knowledge that Denver would be there this time. "We should find somewhere new. Somewhere that's ours." His shoulders rolled a little as he added, "I think it has to be a house, not an apartment. It's too hard being in someone else's space. I always worry someone's going to start a fire in a nearby unit."

Denver nodded. "That's another reason to go slow. We'd do well to build something in the development north of town, something we could control the construction on. You could tell them how to set up the outlets and organize the cabinets and anything else you wanted. I'm definitely going to need to have my new job going for that, though Tiny did promise me an advance."

"I have money—"

Denver held up a hand. "We can't only use your money. It has to be *our* money. Understand?"

Adam did, and it made him love Denver all the more. "Yes. I do."

"I think we need to talk about this, a lot. We just got back together after what I guess you could call a fight. I want to make sure we're all ironed out there. Maybe we can have Louisa help talk us through or something."

"I'm seeing a new therapist," Adam offered, beaming. "He's kink-friendly. Louisa found him. I like him and—well, maybe sometime you can come along? For me," he added quickly, worried Denver would think Adam was insinuating he needed therapy.

Denver closed the distance between them—carefully—and didn't touch Adam, but he smiled. "Maybe for me too, okay?"

Adam threw his arms around Denver and hugged him tight.

CHAPTER TWENTY-FIVE

DENVER HAD really been looking forward to taking on that fucker Brad, or at least scaring the living piss out of him, which was why when they showed up at the lab—picking up a steel-jawed Louisa on the way in—and found Brad pale and babbling apologies, it took the wind out of Denver's sails.

He didn't like how easily Adam forgave him, and from what he could tell Louisa was equally displeased. But what could he say? Brad was practically weeping, and the rest of Adam's Bug Boys were hovering and looking like they'd set this all up, making sure Brad arrived for his mea culpa. To Denver it sounded like the usual abusive asshole bullshit: *I was an ass, I won't do it again, I'm such a jerk, you must hate me.* All of it about Brad, none of it about Adam, who was the one who'd ended up in the goddamned hospital. It was Denver's dad and his ex all over again, and it made him want to shove his fist down the guy's throat and show him what the inside of his testicles looked like.

Louisa stayed him with a hand on his arm, though her fingernails dug in a little too, and her jaw was tight.

"I know," she murmured, glaring daggers at Brad. "But I don't think we get to beat him up, and threatening him will only inflate his sense of self-importance. Take some comfort, though, in the fact that Adam doesn't seem plugged into it at all. He wants it to go away."

That, Denver realized, was true. He also noticed how Adam kept himself removed from the rest of his peers, aligning himself closer to Louisa and Denver than the others, even though they were clearly also on his side. He was with a new group of friends, a group of his choosing, not just the set that was convenient— one he preferred. One where he never had to worry about being himself. It was a group with Denver in it, which of course Denver considered the most important variable.

Louisa too. Maybe they didn't get to beat up Brad, but they had each other.

Even so, as soon as everything was over, Denver headed straight over to El at Tucker Pawn and vented his spleen.

Denver told him the whole story of Brad causing Adam's panic attack, of going to confront him and being let down. He told El about the fight that led them there, about what Adam had found out about why he couldn't study. He confessed, too, about the GED thing and how it was why he hadn't accepted Tiny's offer, but that he was going to work on it now.

El sat wide-eyed through it all, and not once did he make a snarky comment. When Denver finally finished, he looked thoughtful. "I had no idea the GED was even an issue. Now I feel like a dick for assuming you had low expectations for yourself, that you liked being nothing more than a bouncer."

Denver shrugged. "I didn't give you any reason to think otherwise."

"Yes, but in hindsight, it never added up." He frowned. "Well, at least Adam had the sense to push. I suppose that's why the two of you ended up together, right?"

Denver's eyes fell to the nicotine patch on El's arm. It hadn't been El's idea to quit, he was sure, but neither was Paul forcing him, only helping him to have a reason to not contract lung cancer at forty. Because that's what the right partner did: they helped you find your better self, especially when you couldn't clear out the cobwebs on your own to find the way.

Denver smiled, feeling easier than he had all day. "Yeah. Guess so."

CHAPTER TWENTY-SIX

Six months later....

IT WAS a warm July Friday afternoon, but the wind was a little too strong for Adam's taste, so he wore a hat and light jacket as he sat on the park bench across from Tiny's Gym, waiting for Denver to get done with his client. He could go inside and sit in Denver's office, but it didn't have any windows, and it didn't feel right, no matter how Denver tried to modify it for him to make Adam feel "at home." It felt like Denver's space in a way nothing else could feel.

Also, it smelled constantly like feet, which had nothing to do with Denver and everything to do with the sweaty locker room next door. Just knowing his high school nightmare sat next to Denver's office was enough to keep Adam away pretty much all the time.

The other reason Adam sat outside instead of going in was that a construction crew was working in the former empty lot beside the gym, and the workmen didn't seem to have the same issue with the wind Adam did. They didn't have their shirts off yet, but Adam lived in hope. They sure looked sweaty. Big and sweaty and wonderful. He sipped at his tea as he watched, smiling behind the rim of his paper mug.

"Hey, faggot!"

The slur made Adam still, and he glanced carefully without turning his head in the direction of the sound. A gang of male undergrads drifted toward him on the sidewalk, and from the way they listed, it appeared they were getting a head start on their weekend partying. The boys came closer, and Adam gripped his cup, his anxiety ramping up like an engine. He let it rev—let the horses paw the ground, he amended, correcting the mental analogy—as he tried to decide what to do.

He knew what he was supposed to do, or rather, what Denver would want. His cell phone lay beside him on the bench. All Adam had to do was send a quick SOS and Denver would come out in a storm of fury and take care of things. It would be hot, and it would definitely be entertaining.

The thing was, Adam wasn't in the mood to be saved, not today. Not by anyone but himself, anyway.

Sig had coached him through just such an exercise, and so had Louisa. Louisa had also dragged him to several self-defense classes, which was empowering but likely wouldn't be pertinent right now, not in broad daylight. This was standard oral bullying, and in fact was more traumatic for Adam. It was something he was working hard on learning to deal with all by himself.

Adam decided now was as good a time as any to put his lessons to the test.

Step one was to remain unengaged while also preparing himself for what was almost guaranteed to be an amplified altercation, given how many of them were heading toward him. No way six young men insecure in their masculinity could handle an effeminate-looking man ignoring their joint attempt to step on him. Their incredibly fragile honor was at stake.

They formed a crescent around Adam, deliberately cutting off escape, trying to make him feel threatened and trapped. Boy, did it work. Adam's anxiety began to whine, and his heart rate kicked up to a healthy pre-panic level. Adam imagined the horses and reins again, and he concentrated on soothing the beasts.

It's just like Sig said, he reminded them. *They're the insecure ones, ten times more anxious than I've ever been. And they don't have a guardian like you to keep them safe.* He mentally stroked the wild beasts, feeling a thrill of power as they responded to the compliment, no longer his enemies but his allies. His wild horses.

Adam lifted his gaze and regarded his bullies as if he'd just noticed they were there. "Oh. Hello. Sorry, I was lost in thought. Can I help you, gentlemen?"

That was Sig's trick, one Adam was still unsure about but was game to try: keep giving the bullies an out. "They don't actually want to fight," Sig said. "They want to win. They want to look big. If you keep giving them opportunities to turn away without being shamed or beaten, eventually they're likely to take it, or at least they're more likely to do so than if you fight." It was a strategy with a hell of a lot of maybe in it, to Adam's eye. But he could understand the logic.

It wasn't quite working yet, but it did seem to throw the bullies off course. They stood staring at

Adam uncertainly. Then one of the larger, drunker ones said, "You're a faggot."

Adam blinked and hesitated, using the pause to calm his anxiety again. *It's just words. They're trying to scare you, and if you let them, it will only feed them. Stick to Sig's plan. But go ahead and keep your finger on that half-composed text to Denver all the same.*

"Is there something you need?" he said again at last, as if they hadn't insulted him, as if he truly still thought they were nice young men who were in need instead of a group of thugs.

"Yeah." One of them stepped forward, eyes bloodshot. He glared at Adam with hate. "This is a faggot-free zone. We need you to clear out."

Panic, panic, panic! The horses reared, and Adam clutched his phone until his knuckles were white. "Ah. Well, if you'll let me pass, I'll go across the street to the gym."

"No faggots at the gym," another one of them said, then giggled at his own joke.

Adam felt a bit ill, and he began to wish he hadn't started this. He was going to have to take a Xanax when this was done, that was for sure. His finger hovered over the Send button, and the horses were ready to bolt and drag him with them.

Just one more try, he promised them. *One more, and then we go.*

"Actually," he said, his voice only wavering a little, "a gay man owns the gym, and my boyfriend works there. So I'm pretty sure I can go there too." He cleared his throat and drew a breath. "How about you step aside, I'll cross the street, and you can congratulate yourself on how it took half a dozen of you to bully a gay man minding his own business in a public park?"

The horses and every other part of Adam froze. *Holy shit, did I just say that?*

Panic, panic, panic!

He went still, and he pushed goddamned Send.

"Wait." This came from a boy who hadn't spoken yet, and he was looking back and forth between Tiny's and Adam as if he were putting two and two together and realizing it truly was four. "Hold on. I had this guy as a TA last semester. If he's dating the same man now as he was then, we want to get the fuck out of here right now."

"Dude, we can handle a couple of—"

"No, you can't," the student said. He was starting to look a little green. "Shit. Here he comes. You guys are on your own. I'm out of here."

He tripped over his own feet as he ran, and in the space he'd vacated, Adam could see Denver crossing the street, sweaty muscles bursting out of his green sleeveless T-shirt, bearing down on them like the god of thunder as he aimed himself at the herd of men around Adam. He didn't say anything, simply walked and glared.

It was more than enough. By the time Denver made it to the sidewalk, the last of the bullies had streaked after his cohorts, swearing and admonishing the others to wait for him.

Denver glared after them a moment, then turned his gaze to Adam, looking only slightly less displeased.

Adam sank back into the bench and closed his eyes, allowing himself to shake in the way he'd been wanting to since the first catcall. He also reached into his pocket for a pill.

"You should have called me sooner," Denver said. He sounded pissed.

"I was trying to be strong." Adam popped the pill into his mouth and washed it down with tea. "Didn't quite work."

"You did pretty well, from what I saw."

Realization dawned. "You were watching. You saw the whole thing."

Denver raised an eyebrow at him. "Of course I was watching. You were sitting out here all by yourself, and Frat Row is two streets over. No way I was doing anything else."

Adam blinked at Denver, surprised—and touched. "Well. Then thanks for letting me try on my own, even though I'm not sure now it was the best idea."

"It was good to try." Denver sat down beside him. His gaze, too, fell on the construction workers.

"I suppose, but I feel rattled. I wanted to call you, but I kept telling myself I could handle it. I fell for magical thinking, like all I had to do was push through and I'd be cured for life."

Denver rubbed the back of Adam's neck. "Sounds like you tested your limits and found the edges. I believe Sig would say, 'Way to grow.'"

Sig would, but Adam still felt queasy. He leaned into Denver. "It was too far too fast. I should have listened to myself, and I didn't."

Denver stroked Adam's neck a few more times before speaking. "Hmm. So what you're telling me is that you've done something bad, and you need to be punished."

Already Adam started to feel relieved, anxiety giving way to Denver's promise to help him out of his bungle. "Yes."

"Then you'll come and sit in my office to start, or in Tiny's if mine still smells like feet, and after I shower, we'll go back to my place and take care of things. But first we're going to swing by the new place, because I got a call half an hour ago, and they have the whole first floor done."

Adam perked up at that. "They do? They fixed it?"

Denver nodded. "The wiring and outlets are all safety ones, and the windows are now the kind you wanted, that lock fast and are easy to clean. And we're not paying for the redo because I scared the piss out of the contractor when I pointed out we'd included all that in the building contract."

"You scared the piss out of him because you looked at him like you were going to pound him into the wall if he didn't do what you wanted him to do."

"That too. Still, the end result is another part of the house is the way you wanted it to be. Let's go see it for ourselves."

"Yes, let's." Adam tried to rise.

Denver held him in place, not letting him. He waited until Adam looked him in the eye, and then he spoke again, this time his voice very gentle. "You're also going to hear me say, before we go, that whether or not you pushed yourself too far or deserve to be punished for it, it was very good of you to try to push yourself, because one of these times your anxiety will be wrong, and you will be ready. Because you are strong and smart, and from what I could see from across the street, you were holding your own. That's good, Adam, and you're not getting out of hearing that."

Adam nodded, but he tried to avert his gaze, and Denver forced him back to his eyes.

"You're a good boy, Adam," he said, no argument in his tone. He nudged Adam. "Now you say it."

"I'm a good boy," Adam whispered, the words almost choking him, but he got them out without looking away.

Denver's gaze softened, and he stroked Adam's cheek. "You're my boy."

That made Adam smile. "I'm your boy, Denver."

Denver smiled back. Then with the construction workers looking on, he bent and kissed Adam firmly, full of ownership, right on the lips.

Adam shut his eyes and opened for him, taking his lover to the place he belonged.

THE DOCTOR'S SECRET

The brilliant but brooding new doctor encounters Copper Point's sunny nurse-next-door... and nothing can stand in the way of this romance.

Dr. Hong-Wei Wu has come to Copper Point, Wisconsin, after the pressures of a high-powered residency burned him out of his career before he started. Ashamed of letting his family down after all they've done for him, he plans to live a quiet life as a simple surgeon in this tiny northern town. His plans, however, don't include his outgoing, kind, and attractive surgical nurse, Simon Lane.

Simon wasn't ready for the new surgeon to be a handsome charmer who keeps asking him for help getting settled and who woos him with amazing Taiwanese dishes. There's no question—Dr. Wu is flirting with him, and Simon is flirting back. The problem is, St. Ann's has a strict no-dating policy between staff, which means their romance is off the table... unless they bend the rules.

But a romance that keeps them—literally—in the closet can't lead to happy ever after. Simon doesn't want to stay a secret, and Hong-Wei doesn't want to keep himself removed from life, not anymore. To secure their happiness, they'll have to change the administration's mind. But what other secrets will they uncover along the way, about Copper Point... and about each other?

www.dreamspinnerpress.com

CHAPTER ONE

DR. HONG-WEI Wu cracked as he boarded the plane to Duluth.

He'd distracted himself on the first leg of the flight from Houston with a few drinks and the medical journal he'd brought in his bag. He nibbled at the in-flight meal, raising his eyebrow at their "Asian noodles" beneath a microwaved chicken breast.

He realized how long it would be until he ate his sister's or his grandmother's cooking again, and his chest tightened, but he pushed his feelings aside and focused on the article about the effects of perioperative gabapentin use on postsurgical pain in patients undergoing head and neck surgery.

When he disembarked at Minneapolis to transfer to his final destination, the reality of what Hong-Wei was about to do bloomed before him, but he faced it with a whiskey neat in an airport bar. Unquestionably he'd require some adjustments, but he'd make it work. If he could succeed at Baylor, he could succeed at a tiny hospital in a remote town in northern Wisconsin.

Except you didn't succeed. You panicked, you let your family down, and you ran away.

The last of the whiskey chased that nagging bit of truth out of his thoughts, and when he stood in line for priority boarding for his last flight, he was sure he had himself properly fortified once again.

Then he stepped onto the plane.

It had fewer than twenty rows, and either he was imagining things, or those were propellers on the wings. Was that legal? It had to be a mistake. This couldn't be a commercial plane. Yet no, there was a flight attendant with the airline's logo on his lapel, and the people behind Hong-Wei held tickets, acting as if this was all entirely normal.

He peered around an elderly couple to speak to the flight attendant. "Sir? Excuse me? Where is first class?"

The attendant gave Hong-Wei an apologetic look that meant nothing but bad news. "They downgraded the plane at the last minute due to low passenger load, so there isn't technically a first-class section. You should have received a refund on your ticket. If you didn't, contact customer service right away when we land."

Hong-Wei hadn't received a refund, as he hadn't been the one to buy the ticket. The hospital had. He fought to keep his jaw from tightening. "So these are the seats?" They were the most uncomfortable-looking things he'd ever seen, and he could tell already his knees were going to be squeezed against the back of the person ahead of him. "Can I at least upgrade to an exit row?"

The attendant gave him an even more apologetic look. "I'm so sorry, those seats are sold out. But I can offer you complimentary drinks and an extra bag of peanuts."

An extra bag of peanuts.

As Hong-Wei stared at his narrow seat on the plane that would take him to the waiting arms of his escorts from St. Ann's Medical Center, the walls of doubt and insecurity he'd held back crushed down upon him.

You shouldn't have left Houston. What were you thinking? It's bad enough you ran, throwing away everything your family sacrificed for. Why did you take this job? Why not any of the other prestigious institutions that offered for you? Why didn't you at least remain close to home?

You're a failure. You're a disgrace to your family. How will you ever face them again?

"Excuse me, but do you mind if I slip past?"

Hong-Wei looked down. A tiny elderly white woman smiled up at him, her crinkled blue eyes clouded by cataracts. She wore a bright yellow pantsuit, clutching a handbag of the same color.

Breaking free of his terror-stricken reverie, Hong-Wei stepped aside. "Pardon me. I was startled, was all. I wasn't expecting such a small plane."

The woman waved a hand airily as she shuffled into her seat. "Oh, they always stuff us into one of these puddle jumpers on the way to Duluth. This is big compared to the last one I was on."

They made commercial planes *smaller* than this? Hong-Wei suppressed a shudder.

With an exhale of release, the woman eased into the window seat in her row.

More people were piling into the plane now, and Hong-Wei had become an obstacle by standing in the aisle. Consigning himself to his fate, he stowed his carry-on and settled into the seat, wincing as he arranged his knees. When he finished, his seatmate was smiling expectantly at him, holding out her hand.

"Grace Albertson. Pleasure to meet you."

The last thing he wanted was conversation, but he didn't want to be rude, especially to someone her age. Forcing himself not to grimace, he accepted her hand. "Jack Wu. A pleasure to meet you as well."

Ms. Albertson's handshake was strong despite some obvious arthritis. "So where are you from, Jack?"

Hong-Wei matched Ms. Albertson's smile. "Houston. And yourself?"

"Oh, I grew up outside of St. Peter, but now I live in Eden Prairie. I fly up to Duluth regular, though, to see my great-granddaughter." She threaded her fingers over her midsection. "Houston, you say. So you were born here? In the United States, I mean."

"I was born in Taiwan. My family moved here when I was ten."

"Is that so? That would make you... well, do they call you first- or second-generation? Bah, I don't know about that stuff." She laughed and dusted wrinkled hands in the air. "My grandmother came here when she was eighteen, a new bride. Didn't speak a word of English. She learned, but if she got cross with you, she started speaking Norwegian. We always wondered if she was swearing at us." Ms. Albertson lifted her eyebrows at Hong-Wei. "You speak English quite nicely. But then I suppose you learned it growing up?"

"I studied in elementary school and with private tutors, but I struggled a bit when I first arrived."

What an understatement that was. It was good Hong-Su wasn't here. Even Ms. Albertson's status as an elder wouldn't have protected her from his sister's lecture on why it wasn't okay to ask Asian Americans where they were from. Though simply thinking of Hong-Su reminded him he wouldn't be going home to her tonight to complain about another white person asking him where he was from.

Have I made a terrible mistake?

Ms. Albertson nodded sagely. "Well, it's a credit to you. I never learned any language but English, though my mother told me I should learn Norwegian and talk to my grandmother properly. I took a year of it in high school, but I'm ashamed to tell you I barely passed the course and can't remember but three or four words of the language now. You must have worked hard to speak as well as you do. I wouldn't know but that you were born here, from the way you talk."

Before Hong-Wei could come up with a polite reply, a bag hit him in the side of his head. A steadier stream of passengers had begun to board the plane, and a middle-aged, overweight businessman's shoulder bag thudded against every seat as the man shuffled an awkward sideways dance down the narrow aisles. Either he didn't realize he'd hit Hong-Wei or didn't care, because he continued single-mindedly on… to the exit row.

Well, for that alone, Hong-Wei resented him.

His seatmate clucked her tongue. "Some people have no manners. Is your head all right? Poor dear. Let me have a look at it."

Definitely a grandmother. Hong-Wei bit back a smile and held up his hands. "I'm fine, but thank you. It's close quarters in here. I think a few bumps are bound to happen." Hong-Wei was glad, however, he was in the aisle and not the frail Ms. Albertson.

"Well, scooch in closer, then, so you don't get hit anymore." She patted his leg. "I'll show you pictures of the grandchildren and great-grandchildren I'm flying north to see."

Not knowing what else to do, Hong-Wei leaned closer and made what he hoped were appropriate noises as Grace Albertson fumbled through her phone's photo album.

He was rescued when the flight attendant announced they were closing the flight door, and a series of loudspeaker announcements meant for the next several minutes conversation was impossible, so outside of Hong-Wei's polite decline of Ms. Albertson's offer of a hard candy, he settled into silence.

The engines were loud as they taxied on the runway, so loud he couldn't have listened to music even if he had headphones. He wished he'd bought some in the Minneapolis airport, or better yet had made sure to pack some in his carry-on. He supposed he could ask for a headset from the flight attendant, but they were always such poor quality, he'd rather do without.

Headphones were just one thing he should have prepared for. He'd rushed into this without thinking, full of the fury and headstrong nonsense Hong-Su always chided him for. It had felt so important to break away when he'd been in Houston, pressed down by everything. Here, now, with the roar of takeoff in his ears, with nothing but this last flight between him and his destiny, he didn't feel that sense of rightness at all. He had none of the confidence that had burned so strongly in him, fueling his wild reach into the beyond.

I can be a doctor anywhere, he'd told himself defiantly as he made the decision to take this job. *I can do surgery in Houston, Texas, Cleveland, Ohio, or Copper*

Point, Wisconsin. The farther away I am from the mess I made, the better.

Trapped, helpless in this plane, his defiance was gone, as was his confidence.

What have I done?

He was so consumed by dissolving into dread he forgot about his seatmate until they were in the air, the engines settling down, the plane leveling out slightly as Ms. Albertson pressed something that crinkled into his palm. He glanced down at the candy, then over at her.

She winked. "It's peppermint. It'll calm you. Or, it'll at least give you something to suck on besides your tongue."

Feeling sheepish, this time Hong-Wei accepted the candy. "Thank you."

She patted his leg. "I don't know what's waiting for you in Duluth that has you in such knots, but take it from someone whose life has knotted and unknotted itself more than a few times: it won't be as bad as you think it is, most likely. It'll either be perfectly fine, or so much worse, and in any event, there's not much you can do at this point, is there, except your best."

The peppermint oil burst against his tongue, seeping into his sinuses. He took deep breaths, rubbing the plastic of the wrapper between his fingers. Any other time he would say nothing. Here on the plane, though, he couldn't walk away, and he had no other means to escape the pressure of the panic inside him.

Talking about it a little couldn't hurt.

"I worry perhaps I didn't make the right choice in coming here."

He braced for her questions, for her to ask what he meant by that, to ask for more details about his situation or who the people saying such things were, but she said only, "When you made the choice, weren't you sure you were right?"

Hong-Wei sucked on the peppermint as he considered how to reply. "I didn't exactly make a reasoned choice about my place of employment. I all but threw a dart at a map."

Ms. Albertson laughed. "Well, that explains why you're so uneasy now. But you still had a reason for doing what you did. Why did you throw a dart at a map instead of making a reasoned decision?"

His panic crested, then to his surprise rolled away under the force of the question, and Hong-Wei chased the last vestiges to the corners of his mind as he rolled the candy around with his tongue. "Because it didn't matter where I went. Everything was going to be the same. Except I thought... I hoped... if I went somewhere far enough away, somewhere as unlike the place where I'd been as I could possibly get, maybe it would be different."

"Ah." She smiled. "You're one of *those*. An idealist. Just like my late husband. But you're proud too, so you don't want anyone to know."

Hong-Wei rubbed at his cheek. "That's what my sister says. That I'm *too* proud, and my idealism holds me down."

"Nothing to be ashamed of. We need idealists in the world. No doubt wherever you're going needs them too. Good for you for taking a leap. Don't worry too much about it. Even if it's a disaster, you'll figure it out, and you'll make it work."

"Except I don't want it to be a disaster. I want to make it right, somehow." He thought of his family, who had regarded him with such concern when he'd said brown hair, bright hazel eyes, a thin strip of beard on his chin, the suggestion of muscles beneath a tight shirt....

The man's eyes met Hong-Wei's, and something crackled in the air.

Hong-Wei threw up walls as quickly as he could. *No.* Good grief, no. He'd said he would consider opening up, but he wasn't interested in romance, or even simple sex, and absolutely not with someone associated with the hospital.

But those eyes. And he'd made a sign. An incorrect, awkward sign. Hong-Wei could tell by the way the man smiled at Hong-Wei—uncertainly, hopefully—that the Chinese had been his idea.

Gripping the strap of his bag tightly, Hong-Wei stepped forward and did his best to meet his disaster head-on.

NO ONE had told Simon the new doctor was beautiful.

He hadn't wanted to drive the hour and a half from Copper Point to Duluth and back again to pick up the new surgeon, especially when he'd been asked at the last minute during an extended shift. He'd worked odd hours seven days in a row, and then they'd wanted him to fetch the doctor everyone had been raving about as if he were some kind of second coming for St. Ann's? It wasn't as if Simon could refuse, though. Erin Andreas, the new human resources director and son of the hospital board president, had asked him personally.

"It's fitting for the surgical nurse to pick up the new surgeon, don't you think?" Andreas had punctuated this remark with a thin, apologetic smile. "I'd originally planned to go myself with a team of physicians, but everyone was summoned for call, and I have an he looked for the welcoming party from Copper Point, ready to see what happened next on his adventure.

No one appeared to be waiting for him.

Hong-Wei paused, confused and concerned. There should be a large group, composed chiefly of the hospital board, poised with smiles and coming forward to greet him. They'd mentioned how eager they were to see him and assured him they'd have a delegation sent to collect him in Duluth. It wouldn't be difficult for them to identify Hong-Wei—they'd seen his photo, and there were at best four Asians in the entire airport. The waiting area was small as well. The entire airport was small. What was going on?

All his apprehension came rushing back, swamping the peace Grace Albertson had given him.

This is going to be a failure before I even begin.

Then he saw it—just as he'd asked for, there was a sign. A literal sign, small and white, and it had his name on it, sort of. It read DOCTOR WU in block letters, but underneath it was the Mandarin word for doctor in hànzi followed by Wu, also written in Chinese character. Except it wasn't quite the right word for doctor, and the character for Wu wasn't the one Hong-Wei's family used. The order was also incorrect, with the character for doctor written before Wu—in Mandarin, the proper address would be *Wu Dr.* instead of *Dr. Wu.*

Still, Hong-Wei *had* asked for a sign, and here it was.

The man who held the sign appeared to be alone. He was young, about Hong-Wei's age, perhaps a bit younger. He looked nervous and haggard. He was also, Hong-Wei couldn't help noticing, attractive. *Cute* was definitely a word that described this individual. Light

Dr. Wu accepted Simon's hand, but he also looked around, searching for something. When Simon realized what it probably was, he lowered his gaze, his cheeks heating.

"I... apologize that it's only me here to greet you. We're a small hospital, as you know, and the team members who planned to greet you were all called away on emergencies. I hope you're not offended."

Wu cleared his throat, not meeting Simon's gaze. "Of course not."

Simon was sure Wu was at least a *little* offended, which made Simon feel bad, but it wasn't as if the man didn't have a right to be upset. It was also pretty much on par for the administration to shove a nurse into the middle of its mess to take the heat for a mistake he had nothing to do with.

This wasn't the time to feel sorry for himself or sigh over the man. Dr. Wu had traveled a long way and deserved some professionalism. Forcing a smile, Simon gestured to the hallway. "Shall we collect your luggage?"

Wu adjusted his shoulder bag and nodded, setting his jaw. "Please."

They walked in silence to the baggage claim area, where the rest of the flight from Minneapolis was already gathered, for the most part. An elderly woman in yellow, surrounded by children and adults, waved at Dr. Wu as he passed, and he waved back. Simon almost asked if it was someone the surgeon knew, decided that was a stupid question, and kept his focus on the matter at hand. *Professional. Be professional.*

"It says your bags will appear at the second claim."

Dr. Wu glanced from side to side, then raised his eyebrows in a look of quiet disdain. "Well, if not, there are only the two."

internal crisis I need to deal with. So, if you would do this for us, please."

He hadn't waited for Simon to agree, only given him directions on when and how to meet Dr. Wu. He'd also sent along another copy of what Owen called That Damned Memo, the one reminding everyone of the strict new penalties for dating between staff members. Simon had no idea if Andreas meant it for him or for the new doctor.

As he clutched his hastily cobbled welcome sign, his pulse quickening with each step the surgeon took closer, Simon decided he'd definitely been the memo's intended target. Dr. Wu could have starred in an Asian drama, he was so beautiful. In fact, he looked a lot like Aaron Yan, one of Simon's top five favorite DramaFever stars. He was also *tall*. Simon wasn't particularly short, but he was compared to Dr. Wu.

Tall. Handsome. Chiseled. Short black hair, not dyed, artfully styled into messy peaks. Dark eyes that scanned the airport terminal with sharp focus, then zeroed in on Simon. A long, defined jaw lightly dotted with travel stubble below the most articulate set of cheekbones Simon had ever seen.

I'm going to work beside this man every single day. Hand him instruments. Follow his every instruction. Except if he smells even a fraction as good as he looks, I'm going to pass out in the OR before the patient arrives.

Mentally slapping sense into himself, Simon straightened and smiled, holding his sign higher as the man approached. "Dr. Wu? Hello, and welcome. I'm Simon Lane, the surgical nurse at St. Ann's Medical Center. It's a pleasure to meet you."

Grace Albertson had called him an idealist with a smile. Hong-Su had always chided him for it. What he needed from Copper Point was some kind of signal that they valued him, idealism and all. That they appreciated the fact that he could have gone anywhere in the country but he'd chosen them. An indication that here might be the place he could find himself, make something of himself. One small sign to show they understood him. It didn't seem too much to ask.

Ms. Albertson woke as the plane landed, and Hong-Wei helped her gather her things, then escorted her down the long walkway to the terminal and out through security.

"You seem to have found some of your confidence while I napped," she observed.

He wasn't sure about that. "I've decided to accept my fate, let's say."

She nodded in approval. "Remember, mistakes are the spice of life. If you arrive and it's a disaster, embrace it. I promise you, whatever you find when you land, if you're lucky enough to get to my age, when you look back at it from your twilight years, you'll think of it fondly, so long as you approach it with the right spirit."

They had come to the end of the walkway leading into the waiting area. Hong-Wei turned and made a polite bow to his companion. "Thank you, Ms. Albertson, for your advice and for your company. I'll do my best to remember what you've said."

She took his hand and held it tight in her grip, smiling. "Best of luck to you, young man."

Hong-Wei watched her go to her family, watched them fold her into their embraces with no small bit of longing in his heart. Turning to the rest of the crowd, he was leaving. *I want to become someone they can be proud of, instead of the failure I am now.*

"Of course you don't. No one wants trouble. Sometimes a little bit of it isn't as bad as we think." Covering her mouth to stifle a yawn, she settled into her seat. "You have to take risks. You'll never win anything big if you don't."

As his seatmate began to doze, Hong-Wei stared at the seat ahead of him, her advice swimming in his head. *Take a risk.* Without meaning to, he'd subliminally internalized this philosophy by accepting this job and moving here. The trouble came with his logical brain trying to catch up.

His whole life, all Hong-Wei had done was study and work. He'd been at the top of his class in high school, as an undergraduate, and through medical school. He'd been praised throughout his residency and fellowship and courted for enviable positions by hospitals from well beyond Baylor's scope before any of his peers had begun to apply. A clear, practical map for his future had presented itself to him.

He still couldn't articulate, even to himself, why he'd leapt from that gilded path into this wild brush, navigable only by dubious commercial jet.

Coming to Copper Point—the town seeking a surgeon the farthest north on the map, a town nowhere near any other hospitals or cities of any kind—felt like an escape that settled his soul. He knew nothing about Wisconsin. Something about cheese, he thought he'd heard. What it *felt* like to Hong-Wei was a clean slate.

Would it truly be different, though? Certainly it wouldn't be Baylor, but would it be different in the right way?

Simon followed his glance. "I guess there are. I never thought about it. I haven't been to any other airport baggage areas. I haven't so much as been on a plane, myself." Realizing he should probably not have said that, he rubbed his cheek. "Sorry, I didn't mean to give away that they'd sent the B-team to escort you. I may not know anything about the rest of the world, but I'm an expert on Copper Point."

For crying out loud, Lane, the man is going to think they sent the village idiot to fetch him. Except even as he thought this, Simon noticed Dr. Wu was smiling a real smile.

It was gorgeous. If the man sent too many of those Simon's way, he was going to need a cardiologist, not a surgeon.

The baggage carousel hadn't started to move yet, so Simon filled the gap with conversation he thought might interest Dr. Wu. "The administrators told me to take you out to eat before we headed to Copper Point, but if you're too tired, we can skip that. I think someone stocked your condo with some starter groceries, but we could also stop somewhere on the way to get anything you might need." He paused, biting his lip and glancing sideways at Dr. Wu. "I should warn you. Our grocery options are seriously limited in Copper Point. I mean, we have food, obviously, but because the population is small and homogenous, anyone who wants to cook beyond the church cookbook greatest hits has to drive to Duluth or order online. A good friend of mine is a bit of a gourmand, and he's always complaining about it. So if you want, we can stop at a store too. But it can also wait."

Crap, now he was babbling. The carousel wasn't moving, though, and the surgeon wasn't talking. A stolen glance revealed he was still smiling, however. *Wider* now, in fact.

Simon swallowed a whimper and clenched his hands at his sides. When he spoke next, his voice cracked. "It's nice to have someone new come to town, and we do need a surgeon at the hospital. An official surgeon on staff, I mean." He could tell his cheeks were blotchy, the stain of his blush leaching onto his neck. "Sorry. I talk too much when I'm nervous."

Wu's voice was like warm velvet falling over him. "I'm sorry I make you nervous."

He *did* make Simon nervous, but Simon didn't want his new superior to know that, and he *especially* didn't want him to know why. "I… you… you don't make me nervous. I mean… I feel bad that you had to be met by me, is all. You deserve a better reception. I'm sure the hospital will make up for it once we arrive in town."

"Your reception is more than adequate. Thank you for coming."

Dr. Wu sounded almost gentle, and Simon couldn't breathe. Also, he was pretty sure his entire face and neck were as red as a strawberry.

The baggage carousel began to move, collecting suitcases spit from the chute, and Dr. Wu stepped away from Simon to retrieve his bags. "Where was it you thought of stopping for dinner?"

Simon fumbled for his phone and called up the list of food options Andreas had given him. "There's an Italian restaurant with good reviews. Oh, but it's in the other direction." Most of the places were, though. He resigned himself to returning home after midnight. Trying not to let his frustration show, he rattled off the other choices on the list. "There's a place called Restaurant 301. 'American classics with a local bent.' I'm not sure what that means, but I could look at the menu. There's another Italian restaurant. Wow. There are, like, five." He scrolled some more. "Tavern on the Hill has Greek wood-fired pizza." He frowned. "What makes pizza Greek? Is that really a thing, or do you think this is a gimmick to punk tourists?"

Dr. Wu had ducked his head, and when he lifted it, he looked as if he were trying not to laugh. Before Simon could apologize for whatever foolish thing he'd said, the surgeon spoke. "I'd prefer a burger and a beer somewhere low-key, to be honest."

Simon was sure *low-key* was nowhere on Andreas's carefully curated list. He opened Yelp, typed in *burger*, and scanned the results. The first hit immediately jogged his memory, and he knew where he wanted to take Dr. Wu. "What about Clyde Iron Works? It's a lot more casual, but the food is good, and they have an extensive list of microbrews. I won't drink, obviously, since I'm driving."

"Sounds perfect."

Once Wu had collected his suitcases from the belt, Simon claimed the handle of the larger one. "Let me take this. You have your carry-on and the other."

Dr. Wu hesitated, then inclined his head. "Thank you."

As Simon had feared, the surgeon's suitcases completely filled his trunk and much of the back seat. "Sorry we're so cramped." Simon's cheeks were hot with shame as he paid the ticket and drove them away from the airport. "I was going to borrow my friend's car, which is bigger, but it ended up in the shop."

"It's not a problem."

At this point Simon couldn't tell if Wu was simply being nice, or if he didn't mind. Uncertainty made him babble again. "You'll meet Owen soon enough. He's one of my best friends from middle school and the anesthesiologist at St. Ann's. He was on the original team that was coming to meet you. Kathryn, another friend of mine and our resident OB-GYN, was going to come too, but too many of her patients had babies."

Wu gazed through the window, taking in the scenery as they passed. "You mentioned you knew Copper Point well. Have you lived there long?"

Simon laughed. "My whole life, and possibly my previous one. I'm one of those people who can trace a great-great-grandparent to the town. When I was four, the town had its one hundred fiftieth anniversary, and they put me on a float in some kind of settler getup with the other kids who were descendants of the founding families." Come to think of it, that meant he'd stood next to Erin Andreas, who would have been just a few years older.

"Tell me about the town. I saw a little online, but of course it's not the same thing as firsthand experience."

"Well, it's on the bay feeding into Lake Superior, and it's one of the first settlement areas in what was the Northwest Territories. Lots of fur trading here before that. The European settlers came for the mining, I think." Simon bit his lip. "Okay, so I don't know the *history* of Copper Point so well. But I can tell you that we have a sandstone mine—I think it was copper the first time, but it's sandstone now—and a college. It's called Bayview University, but it's a small liberal arts college. We have a campus town, which has more places to eat than our downtown and some fun shops. Because we're so far away from everything, our Main Street does okay, even with the big box stores. It's a midsized town, but it's small enough everyone knows everyone. Sometimes more than you want.

"You're moving here from Houston, right? I looked it up while I was waiting. Wow, it's really big. Did you come there from somewhere else in Texas before you went to school? They didn't tell me much about you. I know you were born in Taiwan and did your residency at Baylor, but that's about it." Simon's hand brushed the sign between them, and he decided this was a good time to get his apology over with. "Sorry if the sign was over-the-top. I misunderstood and thought you were more recently from Taiwan than you are."

Dr. Wu glanced at the sign with an affectionate smile. "No, I liked the sign. Thank you. I moved to Houston from Taipei with my family when I was ten. It worked out that the university I wanted to attend was in the same city, and I was fortunate enough to be matched with Baylor for my residency."

"Wow. I would think you'd have more of an accent, if you moved here that late."

"My sister has one, sometimes, but the two of us worked hard to practice our American accents as well as our English. It was important to us both to blend in." He shook his head, rueful. "We watched *so many* movies. She would find the scripts, and we'd read along with them."

Simon hadn't meant to confess, but the road ahead of him was hypnotic, as was Dr. Wu's low, smooth voice, and it tumbled out of him. "I wish I could do that to learn Korean or Chinese. I watch so many Asian shows on DramaFever, but I've only learned how to say *I'm sorry* and *thank you* and *I love you*, and I'm not entirely sure about the last one."

There was a moment's awkward pause where Simon cringed inwardly and Dr. Wu said nothing.

"You… watch Asian television?" Wu said at last.

Simon nodded, refusing to be uncomfortable about his confession. "The romances. They're my favorite. I stumbled on one on Netflix one day and loved it, and of course Netflix kept recommending more, and I was down the rabbit hole. I found out there was an entire network devoted to them, and it was all over. Now I watch the new ones as they're released, but I've also gone back and watched a lot of older ones as well." He resisted the urge to apologize for himself and forged on. "I think it's better than most of the stuff on American television. It makes me wish I could travel."

"Is there some reason you can't?"

Simon shrugged. "I haven't had the opportunity, I guess." Deciding to be honest, he added, "Also, I'm a little scared. I used to want to go everywhere, but the older I get, the more impossible it seems. I still want to do it, but I don't want to go by myself, and…." He forced a smile. "Anyway. You're certainly not scared. I look forward to working with you, Dr. Wu."

Wu made no reply to this, only stared out the window, an unreadable expression on his face. Simon was working up to apologize for whatever it was he'd said wrong when he noticed the surgeon had closed his hand over the edge of Simon's cardboard sign, holding on to it like an anchor.

Maybe he'd messed some things up, but he'd done the sign right. At least he had that going for him.

HEIDI CULLINAN has always enjoyed a good love story, provided it has a happy ending. Proud to be from the first Midwestern state with full marriage equality, Heidi writes positive-outcome romances for LGBT characters struggling against insurmountable odds because she believes there's no such thing as too much happily ever after. Heidi is a two-time RITA® finalist, and her books have been recommended by *Library Journal*, *USA Today*, *RT Magazine*, and *Publisher's Weekly*. When Heidi isn't writing, she enjoys cooking, reading romance and manga, playing with her cats, and watching too much anime.

Visit Heidi's website at www.heidicullinan.com.

You can contact her at heidi@heidicullinan.com.

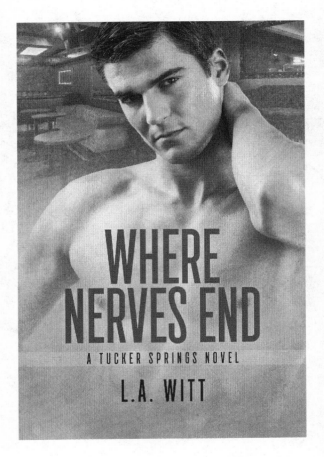

WHERE
NERVES END

A TUCKER SPRINGS NOVEL

L.A. WITT

A Tucker Springs Novel

Welcome to Tucker Springs, Colorado, where you'll enjoy beautiful mountain views and the opportunity to study at one of two prestigious universities—if you can afford to live there.

Jason Davis is in pain. Still smarting from a bad breakup, he struggles to pay both halves of an overwhelming mortgage and balance the books at his floundering business. As if the emotional and financial pain weren't enough, the agony of a years-old shoulder injury keeps him up at night. When he faces a choice between medication and insomnia, he takes a friend's advice and gives acupuncture a try.

Acupuncturist Michael Whitman is a single dad striving to make ends meet, and his landlord just hiked the rent. When new patient Jason, a referral from a mutual friend, suggests a roommate arrangement could benefit them both, Michael seizes the opportunity.

Getting a roommate might be the best idea Jason's ever had—if it weren't for his attraction to Michael, who seems to be allergic to wearing shirts in the house. Still, a little unresolved sexual tension is a small price to pay for pain and financial relief. He'll keep his hands and feelings to himself since Michael is straight… isn't he?

www. dreamspinnerpress.com

SECOND HAND

A TUCKER SPRINGS NOVEL

MARIE SEXTON
HEIDI CULLINAN

A Tucker Springs Novel

Paul Hannon flunked out of vet school. His fiancée left him. He can barely afford his rent, and he hates his house. About the only things he has left are a pantry full of his ex's kitchen gadgets and a lot of emotional baggage. He could really use a win—and that's when he meets El.

Pawnbroker El Rozal is a cynic. His own family's dysfunction has taught him that love and relationships lead to misery. Despite that belief, he keeps making up excuses to see Paul again. Paul, who doesn't seem to realize that he's talented and kind and worthy. Paul, who's not over his ex-fiancée and is probably straight anyway. Paul, who's so blind to El's growing attraction, even asking him out on dates doesn't seem to tip him off.

El may not do relationships, but something has to give. If he wants to keep Paul, he'll have to convince him he's worthy of love—and he'll have to admit that attachment might not be so bad after all.

www. dreamspinnerpress.com